BY ALAN DEAN FOSTER

The Black Hole

Cachalot

Dark Star

The Metrognome and
Other Stories

Midworld

No Crystal Tears

Sentenced to Prism

Star Wars®: Splinter of the
Mind's Eye

Star Trek® Logs One-Ten

Voyage to the City of the Dead

. . . Who Needs Enemies?

With Friends Like These . . .

Mad Amos

The Howling Stones

Parallelites

Star Wars®: The Approaching
Storm

Impossible Places

Exceptions to Reality

THE ICERIGGER TRILOGY

Icerigger

Mission to Moulokin

The Deluge Drivers

THE ADVENTURES OF FLINX OF THE COMMONWEALTH

For Love of Mother-Not

The Tar-Aiyam Krang

Orphan Star

The End of Matter

Bloodhype

Flinx in Flux

Mid-Flinx

Reunion

Flinx's Folly

Sliding Scales

Running from the Deity

Trouble Magnet

Patrimony

Flinx Transcendent

Quofum

THE DAMNED

Book One: A Call to Arms

Book Two: The False Mirror

Book Three: The Spoils of War

THE FOUNDING OF THE COMMONWEALTH

Phylogenesis

Dirge

Diuturnity's Dawn

THE TAKEN TRILOGY

Lost and Found

The Light-Years Beneath My Feet

The Candle of Distant Earth

THE TIPPING POINT TRILOGY

The Human Blend

Body, Inc.

The Sum of Her Parts

THE SUM OF HER PARTS

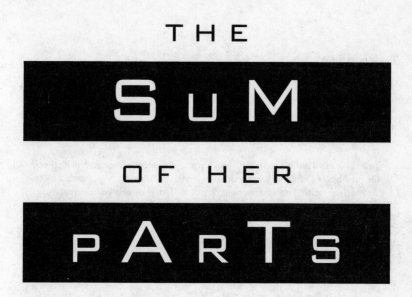

THE SuM OF HER pARTs

VOLUME III OF THE TIPPING POINT TRILOGY

ALAN DEAN FOSTER

BALLANTINE BOOKS DEL REY NEW YORK

A Del Rey Books Trade Paperback Original

Copyright © 2012 by Thranx, Inc.

Published in the United States by Del Rey, an imprint of The Random House Publishing Group, a division of Random House, Inc., New York.

Del Rey is a registered trademark and the Del Rey colophon is a trademark of Random House, Inc.

ISBN 978-0-345-51202-4
eISBN 978-0-345-53563-4

Printed in the United States of America

www.delreybooks.com

9 8 7 6 5 4 3 2 1

Book design by Liz Cosgrove

For Bill Skrzyniarz,

with thanks for proving Shakespeare wrong

THE SUM OF HER PARTS

1

The monster was gruff but polite, with an accent inclining to the French. As she contemplated the hulking sack of bipedal testosterone looming athwart the road, Ingrid could understand why he might prefer to intercept them outside of town and away from staring crowds. Even in a world populated by weird and eccentric Melds, the freewalker's appearance was outlandish.

And make no mistake about it: he had intended to intercept them. Just the way he stared in their direction was proof enough that his presence on the otherwise empty dirt track was no accident.

She and Whispr were almost a full day out from Orangemund on the single road leading north—"road" being far too flattering a description for the ancient 4x4 trail. There was no indication that it had recently been utilized by machine or man. In this forbidding desert terrain a floater, any kind of floater, would be a more sensible way of getting around. So what little track still existed was not maintained. In any event, the linear remains would shortly peter out in the flat gravel plain and they would have to rely solely on the positioning components in their communicators and the secret route that had been given to them by Morgan Ouspel.

Orangemund lay behind them. In every other direction was the emptiness of the Namib; sand and gravel, sun and scrub, and the bluest sky she had ever seen. Except directly ahead, where stood a monster.

A description unbecoming to a physician, she chided herself. The freewalker wasn't really a monster; only one of the more radical Melds she had ever encountered. She could hardly be blamed for her initial reaction. Certainly she had seen nothing so outlandish in Savannah, or even in her med-school studies. Extreme conditions called for extreme manips, she realized, and there were few places on the planet more extreme than the Namib desert.

How she had come to find herself afoot at the southern edge of the Namib in the company of two Melds—one jumpy and unpredictable, the other exotic and intimidating—was a tale of searching and discovery that in retrospect seemed far more dream than reality. Of one thing, however, she could be absolutely certain: it was a long way from her familiar family practice and her comfortable codo back home.

While the freewalker studied them she returned the favor. As near as she could tell he was somewhere in his forties. Either side of that she could not have hazarded a guess. Not considering how his body had been pushed, pulled, bloated, coated, maniped, and remelded. In some ways the melding that had been carried out was more extreme than that required to make a Martian, though less so than what was necessary to produce a viable Titanite. As the integrated autostabilizer adjusted her backpack's position, a glance to the left revealed that Whispr was eyeing the hulk with his usual wariness.

"You a riffler?" His tone was sour, his stance edgy.

The sunscreen-maniped pupils of tiny eyes peered down at Ingrid's companion out of a wide, almost flattened head. The bald pate was composed of multiple folds of melded skin, each one intended to dissipate a little more of the skull's internal heat. Only at the forehead, where the edges of individual layers of skin overlaid one another like exfoliating granite, was the melding evident. The lowest folds combined to create a flexible, almost prehensile brow that further served to protect the vulnerable eyes from blowing dust and a pitiless sun.

"Name's Quaffer. I'm no riffler. I'm a registered guide. Work at it, live by it, made for it. None better between Alexander Bay and Cape Cross. I'd like to guide *you*." A flattened hand the size of a dinner plate gestured casually northward. "You going any distance this way, you going to need a guide."

His voice was deep and booming, though whether the reverberation was due to his height, size, or the mantalike manip on his back Ingrid could not tell. Spread high and wide, the sweeping dorsal area had been radically maniped to permit long-term survival in the desert.

Supported by bone-ladled extensions to his ribs, the fleshy addition was nothing less than a mass of gengineered water-holding cells. The internal plumbing necessary to supply such a growth with water from his throat or stomach had to be more complicated and extensive than the maniped water sac itself. The basic design was simple and practical. As Quaffer's body utilized the water stored in his back meld it would gradually shrink, like the fat stored in a camel's hump. When completely empty the fleshy extension would lie flat and loose against his spine. Though the deeply tanned flesh would also double as a sun shield that was not why the freewalker wore no shirt. To make one would require the skills not of a tailor but of a sail maker.

Below the waist and the bulging storage meld, distant from the flattened skull and tiny eyes protected from the glare, the guide's body was almost normal. Unable to position a pack on his greatly maniped back, Quaffer employed oversized pants' pockets and a lightweight valise to carry his gear. As storage it appeared insufficient. But then, Ingrid reminded herself, he did not need to tote water. She wondered if he made sloshing sounds when he walked.

What she said was, "Thanks, but we don't need a guide."

Expression set, Whispr nodded slowly. "We're fine on our own."

From a greater height, downsized eyes regarded him sharply. "Nobody is fine on their own in the Namib."

"We're only going out a little ways." Ingrid tried a friendly smile. "We're here to look for birds, and other wildlife, and to experience the sights and the sounds of the desert. On our own." Reaching back, she indicated her pack. "We have enough supplies to stay out for a week or more if we want."

"Wildlife?" A thin laugh emerged from the wide mouth. It was nearly lipless, the horizontal fleshy pads having been maniped away. Nonexistent lips could not chap in the heat and wind. "There is some, but without a guide you will not see it. Except for maybe lizards and snakes. You get a cobra in your sleepsheet and you will wish you had hired someone who knows how to keep them away." He shook his head regretfully. "I have guided many visitors. I know people, and I can tell that you are not the kind to spend a week in the desert looking for animals."

Despite the fact that the big freewalker outweighed him in water content alone, Whispr took a challenging step forward. "You don't know what 'kind' of people we are, or what we're looking for."

"Haw! I think maybe I do." The guide nodded past the infinitely slimmer Meld, in the direction of the low-lying buildings of Orangemund. "I live here all year round. Quaffer knows everybody, and everybody knows Quaffer."

Acutely aware of their recent clandestine meeting with the

Nerens refugee Morgan Ouspel, Whispr was immediately on guard. "It must be nice to be popular."

The big Meld's hand shifted slightly to his left. "Anyone in their right mind who comes to this faraway place looking for wildlife looks for it on or beside the river. The only people who search for animals in the desert are scientists. Biologists, zoologists. Herpetologists and entomologists." His gaze narrowed even more. "Are you two scientists?"

"Maybe." Ingrid was startled at the ease with which she responded. Something else she had acquired since partnering up with the street-wise Whispr, she realized. Confidence in her ability to formulate a viable lie. "What business of yours are our professions?"

Quaffer looked more amused than offended. "A guide should know all he can about those for whom he is responsible. I should know if you are like helpless children in the desert, or if you are experienced."

"You don't need to know anything." As he started around the freewalker Whispr pulled his communicator. "We're going. If you try to stop us I'll notify the police." He allowed himself a knowing smirk. "Since you say everybody knows you, I'm willing to bet that the police do too."

"I don't want to hinder your progress," the big Meld rumbled. "I want to assist it. There is no way you are going to get deep into the Sperrgebeit without help."

Whispr gave an exaggerated roll of his eyes. "What makes you think we *want* to get 'deep into the Sperrgebeit'?"

The freewalker's tone changed perceptibly. "Like I said, I know everyone, everyone knows me. Maybe I hear some things—about you."

Ingrid shot her companion a worried look. Though far from intimidated, Whispr was suddenly cautious.

"You don't know anything. You haven't heard anything. You're fishing."

"Perhaps a little," Quaffer confessed. "No harm in that." As he shifted his feet the melded water sac that was part of his back answered Ingrid's earlier unvoiced question by emitting a soft gurgling sound. "I suppose you *could* be scientists. Let's say that you are. In that case you would not have to pay me for my help. I would freely guide you for a share in whatever, um, 'scientific' discoveries you might make."

As she frowned at him Ingrid wished they were having this conversation under cover. Except for the town behind them and mountains off to the east, there was nothing for kilometers in any direction that would qualify as shade.

"I don't understand. How could we share a scientific discovery with you?"

The lipless mouth broke into a knowing grin. "I know that there are all kinds of science and all kinds of scientists. Some I have already mentioned. There are also ornithologists, botanists, paleontologists . . ." He startled Ingrid by leaning forward unexpectedly and winking at her. "Geologists."

A different kind of smile creased Whispr's face. "Ohhh, so *that's* it."

Ingrid blinked at him. "'What' is it?"

Her companion nodded at the desert Meld. "I get it now. Our waterlogged friend here thinks we're after diamonds."

"Diam . . . ?" Shaking her head, she turned back to the freewalker. "We're going camping so we can look for wildlife." For a second time she gestured at her backpack. "If my friend and I dumped everything out of our packs you'd see that we don't have a single geological tool with us."

"Does not mean anything." When Quaffer turned slightly to one side Ingrid got a better look at the remarkable sweep of water-choked flesh that clung to his back like a giant beige coelenterate. "This country is full of diamonds. When the first Germans came here they were filling empty coffee cans with gems by picking them off the ground or sieving them loose out of the sand. You don't always need explosives and heavy machinery. Not if you know where to look." He turned back to her.

"I think maybe you two have a line on a place like that that the Germans—and the British, and the Boers—overlooked. A lot of this land has yet to feel the tread of a human foot. Except for the San, maybe, and they never cared nothing for diamonds. You might have a line on an old alluvial deposit, or maybe an unmined inland sea terrace that has been hidden by shifting dunes." Small eyes burned into her own. "All I know is that nobody leaves Orangemund heading north on foot because they are looking for wildlife."

Whispr started to go around him. "Then this will be a first for you. Come on, Ing . . . my friend."

She moved to follow, having to skirt the bulk of the freewalker to do so. Quaffer tracked her progress but made no move to block her path. As she and Whispr lengthened their strides she could feel his eyes on her back. Calling after them, his warning words seemed to hang in the crystalline desert air.

"You are going into one of the worst places on the Earth! I don't care what kind of communicator or guidance instruments you have with you—the Namib eats people. Without a guide it will eat you!"

Turning so that he was walking backward on the perfectly flat ground, Whispr pulled his communicator and waved it at the freewalker. "If we call for rescue you can be the first to say I told you so."

"I will say that over your bodies!" Quaffer's voice was beginning to fade with distance. "Because if you go more than a day's walk into the Sperrgebeit without a guide, the company security will find you and kill you! Even if you really *are* scientists!"

As Ingrid shouldered her pack a little higher its integrated air cushions inflated proportionately to ease the burden. "Do you think that's true, Whispr? Have we only got a day before SICK, Inc. security finds us?"

Her companion's studied reply was thick with his characteristic fatalism. "If you'll recall, doc, I thought this was a suicide trek from the get-go. On the other hand, I also never thought we'd make it this far. I feel like a rock rolling down a slope that just keeps getting steeper and steeper. Every step makes me have to go a little faster and shrinks any chance of ever going back the way I came." He shrugged. "Can't go back, so gotta go forward."

"At least," she said as she stepped over a purposeful migration of ants, "if anything does happen, you got to see your animals."

"Yeah." As he recalled their time in the wildlife-rich Sanbona Preserve he tucked his thumbs under the straps of his backpack. He was so thin that only the built-in auto-stabilization feature kept it from sliding off his narrow spine. "Yeah, that was something." He glanced over at her. "Thanks for that, doc. Whatever happens from here on out, thanks for that. It sure was different from Savannah."

"You're telling me." She returned her gaze forward. "I wonder what some of my patients would say if they could see me now."

"Probably worry that you're taking a big chance on becoming a patient yourself."

He looked back toward town. There was no sign of movement in their wake. Intensely interested in their goal though he might be, the freewalker was not following them. Already they were utterly alone in the vastness of the southern Namib.

Not utterly alone, he corrected himself. Even though they were now technically intruders in the Forbidden Zone, they were no more than a communicator call away from help. The authorities in Orangemund would not refuse an emergency call from a pair of visiting Namericans. Should a life-threatening situation arise, he and Ingrid could easily request assistance. Doing so would probably mean the end of their quest to learn the secrets of the mysterious metal thread she carried and they might well be prosecuted for trespass, but he doubted they risked incarceration. Especially since his companion was a doctor. He doubted the law worked any differently here than back home, where justice was a mixed salad best dressed with money.

A glance to his right showed Ingrid striding along briskly, her expression determined. With her maniped red hair tucked up under her wide-brimmed thermosensitive hat and her skin biosurge darkened, she ate up meter after meter of the hard ground on legs toughened from days of travel in Florida and South Africa. Her unwavering pace and resolute expression were very different from those of the pale physician whom he had first begged to remove the police traktacs from his back in an office in Savannah. He and this woman, who had acquired more education than he could ever dream of, were rolling down the same steep slope side by side. Of one thing he was by now certain: they would reach the bottom together.

If only she would let him embrace her one time before the final crash.

He sighed. Movement overhead caught his attention and he squinted up at a sky so stunningly sapphire that it hurt his eyes. It was a crow, an ordinary, local black-and-white crow. He smiled to himself. Life in the Namib was not nonexistent—just sparse. Wildlife. Whatever happened now, he had fulfilled that childhood dream and seen his share.

Determining that the two figures moving slowly below it were too big to tackle, the crow moved on, a small winged silhouette set against the bowl of blue heaven. Regrettably for the scavenger, the large two-legged creatures were neither dead nor dying.

Yet.

. . .

THE FIRST NIGHT THEY spent in the Namib would have
been magical had it not been so cold. Thankful they had taken the
time and the care to acquire proper camping gear before setting
out from Orangemund. Ingrid huddled beneath her fold-up but
toasty radiant blanket and gazed up at more stars than existed outside a university astronomy text. Not even perceptible at night in
brightly lit Greater Savannah, the Milky Way was not merely visible, it seemed close enough to touch. She felt she could reach up
with an outstretched hand, grab a handful of stars, and sprinkle
them like grated parmesan on her supper of self-heating pasta concentrate.

Giving the lie to the apparent emptiness, in the distance something distinctly mammalian and unhuman howled. She stifled a
laugh as Whispr looked around nervously.

"What's that? A wolf?"

From another location a second howl echoed across the barren
plain. It continued; dueting tenors in a canine opera. To her surprise Ingrid found the mournful exchange exhilarating instead of
frightening.

"I don't think there are any wolves here. Probably jackals." She
shoveled in another forkful of pasta. "Surely you must have done
some reading about this place too, Whispr. It just looks empty, but
it's not." In the starlight her eyes seemed to shine. "Jackals have to
eat, so that means there are other creatures here besides them."

"I get that," he muttered. "They probably survive on the corpses
of stupid trekkers like us."

She gazed back at him in the darkness, shaking her head.
"Sometimes I think your pessimism will outlive you, Whispr. You'll
die but it'll hang around, like a gray ghost in mourning. Until it can
infect somebody else and make them as miserable as you are."

Having concluded his meager meal and tossed the biodegradable container far enough into the night to ensure that any wandering ants would have easy access to it without having to go over or through him, he settled down beneath his thin blanket.

"I'll remind you one more time, doc: it's that pessimism that's helped keep you alive."

She acknowledged the truth of his observation, rose, and threw her own food container far away. The surrounding silence swallowed up the slight clatter it made as it hit the ground. Whispr tried not to stare as she stretched and, as usual, he failed. While he grew more edgy and anxious the nearer they got to their goal, Dr. Ingrid Seastrom only became more beautiful—and not because of recent minor repair, replace, and regeneration maniping. She turned to look back at him.

"We're going to do this, Whispr. We're going to make it to Nerens, get inside, and find out what the thread is all about."

Tucked beneath the blanket, he mumbled his usual misgiving. "You still believe that if we get to Nerens we can get in."

She regarded his prone, huddled form. "Of course. Precisely because no one is supposed to be able to get to Nerens. Everyone will assume we belong there because only those who belong there are allowed to be there."

"Circular logic, doc. Doesn't hold up."

She blinked. "I didn't think you were familiar with something like circular logic, Whispr."

"Why would you think that?" He rolled over. The ground was hard, but so were the pavements of Savannah, and he had spent plenty of nights thereon. "The street overflows with circular logic. You look like a lawbreaker, so the cops pick you up. If the cops pick you up, you must be a lawbreaker. If you look like a riffler when you walk into a store, the operators assume you are a riffler and you're treated like one." He coughed lightly. "I could go on, but I'm tired."

"Sleep well, then." She settled down and cocooned herself within her own blanket. Serenaded by unseen silver-backed jackals she drifted off to sleep.

For a long time Whispr lay awake, unable to join her. He didn't trust the bitch-burble of the four-legged variety any more than he did that which originated from the two-legged kind.

THEY PAUSED AT LEAST once every thirty minutes to check their position on their communicators. Understandably, Morgan Ouspel's route took them inland and kept them away from the single forbidden north–south road. After several days they lost sight even of scattered 4x4 tracks. That did not mean the rocky, uninhabited terrain was never visited. A floater would leave no mark except where it set down.

They were walking parallel to a dry wash. While Ouspel's course followed the winding arroyo precisely, they saw no reason to navigate every twist and turn. Hiking beside instead of within its five-meter depth allowed them to avoid the rocks and sand at the bottom while cutting off the sharper bends. Staying up top would save time and permit easier trekking.

It also, however, left them exposed.

Fortunately Whispr's enhanced hearing allowed him to pick up the sound before they were spotted.

"Down!" Without waiting to see if she was following he scrambled madly down an eroded slope and into the riverbed. "Don't wait, don't look around—hide!"

As she hurried after him she looked around anyway, and saw nothing. "What—Whispr, I don't see . . . ?"

"Searcher! Get down here!"

By the time she reached the bottom she was moving so fast that she stumbled into him and nearly caused the both of them to fall.

Though she weighed more than his attenuated form, the strength in his wiry arms allowed him to catch and stabilize her. The shock of the close physical contact momentarily unnerved him. He wanted to hold on, not to let go. He finally released her because he did not want both of them to die.

"Here!" He gestured frantically toward a rocky overhang. Without pausing to see if the narrow opening was already occupied by scorpions or snakes he dropped to his belly onto the sand and slithered beneath the opportune cover. Though he left the most room for her, Ingrid still had to struggle to wiggle back far enough so that she would not be visible from overhead. There was no time to remove her backpack. She could feel it scraping against the rock, threatening to trap her.

A minute passed, then several. The sun beat down from above. A couple of jet-black, nearly spherical tok-tok beetles moseyed comically along the canyon floor. The absence of sound, of even a querulous bird, was deafening.

"Whispr, maybe all you saw was another crow." Jammed beneath the overhanging rock, her right leg was beginning to cramp. "We could take a look and . . ."

"Crows don't reflect light. Stay put."

Though she complied with his instruction, frustration increased with each passing minute. Her leg began to throb. Ample experience had shown that her companion was more than a little prone to paranoia. Indeed, he embraced it. In the course of their journey together he had raised previous false alarms; maybe this was another. How long did he expect her to lie here, facedown in gravel and sand?

"Look, Whispr: if there was anything out there then it's gone by now." She started to crawl forward—only to have him grab her arm. Her glare was murderous. "Let go of me right . . . !"

With utter lack of ceremony he slapped his other hand over her mouth. Her eyes widened. Declarations of muffled outrage spent themselves against his splayed and none-too-clean palm.

Then she heard it, and froze.

The searcher drone was of a type she had never seen before. Those employed by the city of Greater Savannah came in several body types depending on the municipal division that operated them. Those utilized by the fire department carried small tanks of highly concentrated fire suppressant, or escape ladders, or other emergency equipment. Medical drones packed first-aid kits and waldos that when operated by doctors seated at hospital control-room monitors could perform emergency triage right at the site of an accident. Police searchers were armed and armored. But this one . . .

Humming softly on its repulsors it headed down the arroyo and glided directly past their hiding place. Whispr pushed his face into the sand but a fascinated Ingrid could not keep from staring. Perhaps the shadows saved them. Or maybe the drone fortuitously happened to be scanning the other side of the canyon when it passed. Coated in heavy-duty flex-black that helped to power it, it traveled in near silence, the only sound being the steady soft hum of its dampened engine. From the top several antennae protruded. From the sides extended—she could not be sure they were gun barrels but she had no intention of finding out. Beneath the power-paint was what she took to be armor. The searcher was not only intended to fight, it was clearly designed to withstand a first attack and offer a devastating response. In the silence she could hear her heart pounding.

Its rate quickened when she felt something moving against her leg.

Looking down the length of her body and seeing the snake slithering across her calves she let out an involuntary gasp. Outside their hiding place the searcher, which had moved on down the gully, suddenly paused. Hovering, it turned slowly from side to side, utilizing fixed-forward scanners to search the terrain directly in front of it. It did not turn around.

The snake was huge, more than four meters in length and a glossy, dark olive-green hue. So dark it was almost black. Staring hard and not moving a muscle Ingrid fought to remember all she had read about this part of the world while crossing the Atlantic on the plane from Miavana. The Namib was home to a number of poisonous serpents and with its distinctive sheen this one was most likely . . .

A black mamba. The second largest venomous snake in the world. Two drops of its venom were enough to kill a person. A snake this size would pack twenty to twenty-five such drops in one bite. They were aggressive and fearless.

She released her bladder. Both her first-aid kit and Whispr's contained doses of adaptive antivenin, but if she was bit out here by a mamba this big it was doubtful she would survive.

At least, she thought as total and complete terror threatened to overwhelm her, as a physician she would be fully aware of the symptoms and effects as the poison consumed her.

Turning to follow the warm curves of her body, the snake came toward her face.

It had a deceptively small head, she thought. Smooth of side, wicked in outline, with bright dark eyes. As its heavy, muscular body climbed up her torso and advanced onto her left shoulder it felt as if someone were pulling a steel cable across her back. While it advanced its tongue flicked in and out just like in the nature vits she had seen while relaxing in her codo. Her wonderful, climate-controlled, view-enhanced, utterly civilized, snake-free codo back in Savannah. She tried to will herself to that remembered distant domestic paradise, away from the lethal serpent, away from the hard, cool, pebbly ground on which she lay confronting one kind of death inside the shallow cave and an entirely different one drifting on the air of the dry ravine outside. She closed her eyes.

The weight stayed a little longer, and then it was gone. She was still alive. Opening her eyes she saw the snake moving away from her. It was making a leisurely slither for the other side of the canyon.

She was not the only one who noted its passing. Beside her Whispr had raised his head. He was gaping wide-eyed not at the retreating reptile but at her. It took her a moment to interpret his expression.

Admiration.

Then they were both pushing their faces into the hard ground as the earth outside their hiding place vomited skyward.

At first Ingrid thought she had been shot, only to realize that the sharp stings assailing her head and shoulders were a consequence of being struck by shattered rock and not bullets. Looking up she saw more chunks of rock falling to the ground. These were interspersed with dust, sand, and bloody fragments of the unlucky mamba. Having detected unauthorized movement behind it, the finely tuned searcher had pivoted in the air and fired its primary weapon. Analyzing the organic debris that resulted and determining that the original form was no longer a possible threat, the machine recorded the relevant information on its internal drive and broadcast it to its home docking station.

Deep within the SICK, Inc. complex at Nerens, a bored security technician perfunctorily made note of the fact that Searcher Eighteen had killed a snake. All the facility's armed searcher drones were supposed to be programmed to recognize and spare a long list of Namib wildlife, but the admonition was one that was enforced by the division only indifferently if at all. Among Chief of Security Het Kruger's minions the possibility of a sudden raid by infuriated representatives of the World Wildlife Fund was not foremost among their daily concerns.

As soon as the searcher had moved out of sight down the ravine Ingrid started to scramble out from beneath the stone overhang. Given the adrenaline surging through her veins the stronger but lighter Whispr was hard put to restrain her.

"Not yet!" he hissed. "It's too soon." He nodded toward the curve of the arroyo where the searcher had vanished. "It might be lingering just around the first corner, or it might decide to come back and do a double check."

"Double check, hell!" she said. Her full attention was focused on the darkness that lay at the back of the cave. "What if there are more snakes in here?" A sour gorge rose in her throat and she fought it down. "What if—what if this is a *den*?"

He worked to calm her. "Listen to me, doc. I've spent time in the coast swamps. Not long ago, in fact. They're bolo with bad snakes. Copperheads, water moccasins, anacondas, other bad migrants from S.A. I've never been bit. You leave them alone, snakes will leave you alone. They don't like to waste their venom." He smiled crookedly. "Kind of like cops don't like to waste bullets."

Her heart rate was starting to slow to something resembling normal. "How long do you think we have to hide here?"

His speculative gaze studied the expanse of sunlit ravine. "As long as you have to hide anyplace from anything, which means longer than you think. Let's give it half an hour to be sure."

Her eyes widened. "Half an hour!" The urine-soaked right leg of her pants was beginning to itch.

He looked over at her. "I'll keep watch. Take a nap."

She envisioned a second mamba crawling over her while she dozed. Or maybe a cobra this time. Investigating the strange, warm intruder. Her pants legs were securely tucked into her hiking boots, but still . . .

"You watch the canyon," she told him. "I'll watch my toes."

2

If they stuck to Morgan Ouspel's route (and didn't run into any more patrolling searcher drones), Whispr estimated it would take them roughly two weeks to walk unhindered to the SICK facility at Nerens. The map and coordinates the renegade company employee had transferred to their communicators showed the location of small water holes where they could refill their compact water bottles. In an emergency the tightly folded collection fabrics contained in these compact devices could be unfurled and raised to extract a limited amount of moisture even from air as dry as that to be found in the interior of the Namib. As for sustenance, they had plenty of concentrates and he had departed Orangemund well equipped with the necessary supplements to ensure that his internally grafted NEM would function properly. Once they successfully infiltrated Nerens, Ingrid insisted they would find a way to access food and drink.

All of this was predicated, of course, on her managing to pass herself off as an employee and him as her assistant. A long reach, he told himself as he easily kept pace with the doctor. But then this entire journey had been a long reach from the day they had left Savannah. He soothed himself with the knowledge that great rewards come from taking great risks.

He continued to tell himself that as the vast treeless expanse of the Sperrgebeit stretched out before them.

INGRID WAS SURE IT was all over and that they were done for when they fell on the sleeping stranger.

Though Whispr was slightly in front of her he was not to blame. The fabric that collapsed beneath him boasted the exact color and texture of the last kilometer or so of ground they had crossed. The fact that it gave way under his very modest weight indicated how fragile were the supports that had been holding it up. The yelp her companion let out when he fell was followed by her own short, sharp scream as she scrambled to avoid tumbling in his wake and failed.

The hoarse bark of surprise that accompanied their descent did not come from either of them.

As she struggled to regain some semblance of stability, the camouflaging material in which she had become entangled was yanked away from her. Rolling to a stop, she found herself staring at the business end of a sharp-nosed shovel. Beside her Whispr confronted the point of a pick. Looking up, she saw that their captor also wielded a thick, short-barreled weapon that was trained in their direction. With his fourth arm he was shielding his eyes against the sudden influx of desert sun into his formerly concealed encampment.

She found herself staring. Like the spines of a dinosaur, the pickarm and shovelarm protruded from the Meld's shoulders. Additional muscle together with a supportive titanium weave had been grafted on to support the extra limbs. As for the pick and shovel themselves, they were not being held by additional hands.

They *were* his additional hands. Instead of fingers, the ladled bone at the end of each melded limb had been fused and sculpted to form the two disparate excavating utensils. Each was covered with a sheath of organic Kevlar that formed a protective glove over the solid bone. Despite having seen her share of exotic melds, she had never encountered anything quite like the figure who now stood guard over them. This was, she was soon to find out, because there were no independent prospectors operating within the city limits of Greater Savannah. She grew aware that Whispr was muttering at her.

"Well, that shreds it. We're discovered, diced, and done. It's all over."

"I'll say it's all over." The quadridexterous speaker shifted the muzzle of his weapon so that it was aimed directly at Whispr's face. Meanwhile the four-armed Meld kept glancing anxiously at the sky. "Where's your floater? On its way already? Won't do you any good. There'll be nothing left of you but mucus after I put your bodies through the sifter!"

Ingrid had just enough presence of mind to stammer, "Floater? We don't have a floater. What are you talking about?"

"You gonna try an' tell me the company put you out here on foot?" As he tilted his head to one side Ingrid saw that his right eye had been replaced with a magnifier meld. The way the embedded lens complex caught the sun was unmistakable.

"The company?" She exchanged a glance with Whispr before turning back to their captor. "We don't have anything to do with the company. We're independent. Scientists. We're out here on our own, studying wildlife."

Straight and white as salt, the Meld's long hair fell to his shoulders. In the other direction, it halted long before it got anywhere near the top of his head. "Then you know you're here illegally. SICK doesn't allow scientists into the Sperrgebeit unless they're company supervised." The muzzle of the short-barreled weapon came up and the shovelarm and pickarm withdrew. Both double-jointed utensilized arms folded up behind their captor's back as the maniped muscles supporting them relaxed.

Then their owner began to laugh.

Whispr let the wheezing guffaws flow unchallenged for a while before deigning it permissible to interrupt. "So—you're not gonna turn us in?"

Sniffling, the old Meld rubbed a filthy forefinger across his nose and flicked away something better left undescribed. "Me? Turn *you* in? Bug's breath, I thought you were going to turn *me* in." Extending the hand he had just employed for suspect hygienic purposes he smiled at Whispr. "Pul Barnato's my name, giving the company a finger up the ass is my game. Has been for more than thirty years." The pride in his voice was unmistakable.

From the time she had first made Whispr's acquaintance Ingrid had never admired her companion more than the moment when he took that hygienically dubious hand and shook it firmly.

"Pleased to meet anyone who's giving a major international corporation the finger." Whispr did not provide the oldster with his name. Nor did Ingrid when, setting aside professional and personal thoughts of germs rampant on a field of bacteria, she took and shook the hand in turn. Thankfully, Barnato did not press them for further identification. As they were later to learn, it was enough for him that they were not minions of the hated company.

"Give me a hand." He was busy gathering up and stretching out the crumpled fabric that had failed to support his unexpected visitors. "We got to get this back up before a searcher comes over."

Whispr and Ingrid helped to wrestle the material back into place over their heads. Once it had been repositioned, Barnato scrambled out of the depression and fixed it back in place at the corners and along the edges. He used no metal or composite stakes or weights, she noticed. Only carefully placed rocks that would draw no attention and set off no alarms.

Slipping back down into the excavation, he rejoined them. No longer fearful of being shot, picked, or shoveled, Ingrid found herself with time to examine their surroundings. Niches quarried into the walls of the depression held basic gear and simple stores. Except for a solar still whose automated tracking funnel was exposed to the sun, everything was concealed under cover. Most surprisingly, she could not see a single electronic device. The Meld had been careful to construct a subterranean dwelling that was electronically dead. In this day and age that was by itself enough to render him invisible to the senses and sensors of the outside world.

"You live here?" She did not try to mute her disbelief.

"It's more a base of operations than a home. I move around a lot. Because I want to, because I need to, and because it helps me to avoid attention." He smiled again, exhibiting orthodontics that in lieu of missing or melded teeth had been replaced by two bars of solid white composite. "It's worked for thirty years. I expect it'll work for another thirty."

"But what do you do?" When it came to matters of personal curiosity Whispr was a virtual stranger.

Barnato gazed innocently back out of his one natural eye. "I'm a scientist. I'm here to study wildlife."

There was a pause while his guests digested this. It lasted longer than it otherwise would have because their host had delivered the reply with an absolutely straight face. Then both Namericans burst out laughing.

"Okay." Whispr wiped at his eyes. "We get it. No more intrusive questions." He raised a hand. "Promise."

"It's amazing to me that you've been able to live out here, in this wilderness." Ingrid was inspecting the surrounding wall niches for anything resembling modern survival gear. So far she'd found nothing. She indicated the fabric that had been pulled out and stretched back above their heads. "Is this all it takes?"

Barnato cast a squint upward. "The material has the same absorption number as the ground. Searchers and satellites don't see me. When I move around it's mostly at night. They use infrared, but I'm careful and I know how to mask my heat signature. You can live off the land here if you know what to eat and where the water is. The San people have been doing it for thousands of years."

Whispr frowned. "San people?"

"Might as well be. I try to avoid them as much as possible. Which suits them just fine, since they try to avoid everybody. It's a habit they picked up a long time ago when one of the then-regional governments kept kicking them out of their homelands and trying to make them into farmers and tradesfolk. Not everybody wants to live in city or on a mechanized farm. Some folks, they like the old ways."

"I understand." Whispr spoke emphatically. "For example, right now I wish I were enjoying the old ways back in Savannah. Sitting on the riverfront sipping an iced coffee and eating a beignet." His voice faded, growing dreamy.

"Actually," Ingrid told their singular host, "if there's anything we can do for you in return for your—hospitality—you just have to ask." Ignoring Whispr's increasing disquiet she added boldly, "I'm a doctor. I could check you for problems, maybe prescribe some remedies."

"A doctor." Barnato did not try to hide his incredulity. "Sure you are, pretty missy." As she bridled he added, "Anyway, it doesn't matter. I don't have any problems." He stretched, extending all four arms before retracting the two that were tipped with digging tools. "By Society's lights I shouldn't be alive. Yet the lifestyle I've chosen has kept me healthier than any thousand men my age you might stop at random in Lela or the canals of London. I'm happy here. It's peaceful, I pay no attention to the conflicts of an overpopulated, confused world, and if I wish I can dig for pretty rocks all night long."

"I don't think the company would respond real well if they were aware of *that*," Whispr remarked.

Barnato shrugged. "Doesn't matter what I do. Just living here puts me in defiance of every regulation that's governed travel in the Sperrgebiet for the last two hundred years. If they find me they'll shoot me for shitting sand as soon as they would for prospecting."

"Have you?" Whispr could not keep himself from asking. "Ever found anything, I mean."

"Rocks." Barnato smiled. "Lots of rocks. I like rocks."

"Okay, okay." Whispr was disappointed despite himself. "I should've guessed."

"You never go down to Orangemund or Alexander Bay?" Ingrid prompted their host.

Barnato shook his head dolefully. "Too many people. Shouting and yelling, arguing over nothing. Trying to sell stupid electronic gadgets, qwikmelds, outdated food, religion. I prefer the desert. Snakes, scorpions, lizards, insects. We understand each other. It's not all about predation out here, the way it is in town. Though sometimes I see leopards or cheetahs. Sometimes I encounter a herd of gemsbok." He licked his lips. "Good eating, gemsbok. So are a lot of the local grubs."

Whispr licked his lips. "You'll excuse us if we don't stay for dinner, but we're on kind of a schedule."

Barnato turned serious. "Which way you two—scientists— going?"

"North." Despite their strange host's apparent affability Ingrid saw no need to be more specific. She wasn't as naïve as Whispr often seemed to think.

Barnato's expression grew dour. "You keep on north and company security will catch you for sure. You'll end up food for crows and vultures. Better you should turn back now and return to Orangemund. With caution and luck you'll make it without being spotted or picked up."

"Can't do that," Whispr told him. "As dedicated scientists we have no choice but to keep on until we achieve our designated objectives." Ingrid's jaw dropped as she stared at him. Flush with unexpected confidence, he paid no attention to her. "We've come too far to give up on our research objectives now."

"Um, yes," she added quickly, "we've come too far to turn back."

"It's never too far to turn back," Barnato told her solemnly. "Return to where you came from, red missy. I have lived here for so long and yet I can barely call this place my home. It'll never be yours."

Not wishing to argue, Whispr sought to change the subject. "I was wondering, Meld brother, why if you decided to dwell in a place like this you didn't just go full inside-out and opt for a Martian meld? Without the respiratory rework, of course."

Barnato cackled softly. "Couldn't afford it, for one thing. And I've never been one to do anything half-assed, which is what you're describing." His shoulders flexed and the pick and shovel boneworks rose until they dented the fabric ceiling. "All I wanted was to be able to dig. To prospect in the old way. Don't need any electricity to run my gear, don't need to worry about motors failing or circuits frying. Just have to get enough protein and carbs." He peered amusedly at Ingrid. "Grubs are chockful of protein and carbs."

If he was looking to gross her out he was picking on the wrong woman. But then, she reflected, he didn't believe that she was a doctor. The only thing that could gross out a practicing physician of her experience and skills was insufficient repayment from the government for services rendered.

"Why don't you spend the night?" he suggested. "I guarantee you'll be warmer and more comfortable than up top, and you can catch me up on this and that bit of *real* news. I'm not a hermit, you know. I just prefer living by myself."

"Isn't that pretty much the same thing?" she pointed out.

"Nope. Reflections of my feelings toward today's sociocultural trends."

She looked toward Whispr, who shrugged. If this Barnato meant them ill he had already had ample opportunity to demonstrate it. Unless, she thought, his intention was to get them to sleep so he could notify Nerens security and turn them in. There was probably a company reward structure in place for ratting out intruders. She shunted the thought aside. As much time as she was spending in Whispr's company it was only natural that she should pick up some of his paranoia. Barnato's dislike of the Company seemed as genuine as his disinterest in worldly goods.

As the sun disappeared somewhere over the South Atlantic their host brought forth a convective containment cooker. At last, she thought: a modern accoutrement. But not one that required potentially revealing electricity. Powered by solar energy acquired during the day, it would turn all of it into heat without releasing any as radiant waste for a wandering nocturnal searcher drone to detect. Using only local ingredients including spices obtained from native plants, Barnato put together the first nonconcentrate meal the two Namericans had enjoyed since leaving Orangemund. Hewing to a pact of mutual silence, neither Ingrid nor Whispr asked what was in the bowls Barnato handed them.

When they had finished, Ingrid complimented him as she handed back her dish. "Not bad. In fact, very tasty. Thank you."

"I've had worse," the ever diplomatic Whispr conceded. "What do you use to clean your utensils? Surely not water?"

"Actually, there's a small spring not far from here. When I want to, I can even do washing. And not just my clothes and gear. It's big enough so that I can bathe."

"I was wondering about that," Ingrid commented with a smile.

Barnato laughed appreciatively. She had already noted that his pickhand meld had been fashioned so that the flat side lay against his back when his work arms were folded back over his shoulders. Otherwise a hearty belly laugh could have resulted in a self-inflicted injury. Checking to ensure that the camouflage fabric that formed the roof over their heads was secure at the edges so that no light would leak out, he brought out a small coldcandle and rubbed it to life. Settling himself in a low-slung folding chair, his gaze roved from one guest to the other.

"Now then," he began firmly, "I want to know all about current local politics. By local I mean the SAEC, points north, and relevant international relations. This is my home and it's useful to occasionally know how it's being treated."

Whispr looked helplessly at Ingrid. With a sigh, she began relating what she could recall from the last news she could remember reading. Fortunately the soft-voiced give and take between her and their host did not last long, and the three of them were soon fast asleep in a landscape of such complete silence that it was almost painful.

CLIMATE-WISE, MORNING SAW AN exact repetition of the day before, and the day before that.

"There *are* seasonal changes here." Barnato was finishing the breakfast he had prepared. "Mostly when the fogs make it this far inland. Then, desert or not, you can have some really cold mornings. But it sure is good for water extraction."

Ingrid nodded and rose. "Thank you for your hospitality, for the food, for the conversation: for everything. But we really need to be on our way."

"That's all right." Putting his eating utensils aside he turned and scuttled to the far end of the excavation that was his home. When he returned it was with one fist clenched.

"You've both been very kind to a solitary old fool. So I'd like to give you something." Though he was speaking only to Ingrid, Whispr was not offended. Had their situations been reversed he would have done exactly the same.

"You're the prettiest woman I've seen in some time. Hell," he said, chuckling, "you're the only woman I've seen in some time. I told you I like pretty rocks. Maybe you do too." Opening his palm he passed her a rough, shiny stone about the size of her eye and the color of cranberry lipstick. "I'd like you to have it. Because I like giving stones away and because I'd like you to remember me." His gaze rose slightly. "It's a little too dark to match your hair."

Taking it from him she held it up to the light and made a show of studying the badly scratched present. The least she could do was humor him. She could toss it away later, somewhere safely distant along their route.

"It's very pretty. Thank you, Pul." She made a small ceremony out of putting it in her backpack.

Later, looking rearward as they resumed their march to the north, she could see the old prospector standing atop the edge of his simple underground dwelling. He was waving to them with all four of his arms: two sporting hands and two maniped digging melds. She returned his wave.

"What a way to waste a life." Whispr was not looking back and not waving. "Living in a hole in the ground, surviving on scraps and bugs, slaving away at manual labor for nothing." He nodded curtly toward her pack. "I was hoping he might give you something worthwhile, but clearly in all his years of wasting away out here he hasn't found anything."

"Yes he has, Whispr," she countered. "He's found happiness. Most people dig for that their whole lives and never strike pay dirt."

Her companion shook his head sadly. "You and I have always had different definitions of both happiness and pay dirt, doc. Me, I would've liked to have gotten something salable. Not a worthless pebble. You gonna keep it? I shouldn't have to tell you by now that the farther you walk the heavier every gram gets."

She returned her gaze forward. "I don't know if I'll keep it or not. Maybe it's not worth anything, but I like the color. As far as weight goes, the more of our food we eat, the lighter our packs get." She indicated the programmed line they were following. "What's more interesting to me is that the location of the spring Barnato mentioned matches the coordinates for one of the water holes on our maps. That's the first solid indication that Morgan Ouspel didn't sell us a bill of goods."

"Or set us on a wandering path to a slow death. So long as there's water and I have my NEM supplements . . ." He picked up the pace. Several weeks ago the now travel-hardened Ingrid would have been unable to match his gangling stride.

Pul Barnato watched them until they disappeared. Given the supernal clarity of the air in the Namib that took quite a while. Then he turned and dropped back down into his home. The excavation was also the entrance to his diggings, though as much as he had enjoyed the previous night's company he had seen no reason to inform his guests of that fact.

Pulling aside an unprepossessing piece of camo cloth he bent low and started walking. A modest distance later he entered an old volcanic tube. One side of it had been broken down by heavy manual labor. Removing his ragged vest he stretched, took a deep breath, and brought his melded arms forward. Armored osseomelds alternately slammed into and shoveled aside rock and rubble. Once he had accumulated a decent pile of the latter he sat down and picked up a sifting pan. Like all the rest of his equipment it used no power, required no batteries, and gave off no emissions for a patrolling searcher to lock on to.

An hour or so of careful sifting produced three glassy pebbles and a number of much smaller stones. These he dumped into an ancient five-gallon jerry can that he had salvaged from a rusting wreck farther to the south and west. The can was about half full of similar pretty rocks. Among them were one or two that were identical in color to the much larger stone he had bequeathed to his courteous red-haired guest.

Idly, he wondered if either she or her acerbic companion had ever seen a natural red diamond before.

3

The last thing they expected to have to deal with was rain.

They had set off from Orangemund equipped with food, water and water extractors, communicators, lightweight sleeping gear, appropriate footwear and outer attire, and everything else they could think of that would enable two travelers on foot to survive in the unfamiliar Namib. They had not considered the possibility of rain. Not with the region they were traversing typically receiving a couple of centimeters of precipitation in a good year.

It seemed as if all of it was falling on them now.

Designed to keep off the sun, their wide-brimmed hats soaked up the pelting moisture instead of repelling it. While there was nothing in their packs that could be seriously harmed by getting rained on, including their sealed concentrates and waterproof communicators, Ingrid had no desire to see everything soaked.

"This is ridiculous!" she declared as she trudged up the dry riverbed alongside Whispr. Contrary to the hoary jokes he had been forced to deal with ever since he had gone through his extensive slimming meld, he was not so thin that he was able to step between the falling drops. Five minutes into the unexpected downpour he was thoroughly drenched and more depressed than usual. If the day had begun hot, the shower would have been welcome. Instead, it simply rendered both of them miserable and clammy. While she couldn't vouch for her companion's personal supplies, Ingrid had the foresight to bring along spare underwear. Her single outer set of safari attire would just have to dry out in its own good time.

"Ridiculous and uncomfortable," he agreed. Unlike the gully where days earlier they had taken refuge from the patrolling searcher, the current winding channel was smooth-sided and offered no shelflike overhangs capable of sheltering them from the momentary deluge. They had no choice but to tolerate the rain until it ceased. From everything he had read about the Namib prior to leaving Orangemund, that was likely to be soon.

Sure enough, the entire storm lasted less than fifteen minutes from the time it unloaded its first drops until the sky cleared and the sun reappeared. Making a face, he swung his pack around in front of him and jiggled it firmly, shaking off as much of the clinging liquid as possible. Ingrid did her best to put a good face on their situation.

"Look at us, wasting water in the Namib. I can think of at least half a dozen public and private environmental organizations back home that would condemn us out of hand."

Her efforts failed to amuse her companion. "I don't care if we are in a desert—I don't like being *wet*. Ever since I locked up with you on this madman's outing it seems like I've spent half the time being wet. In Savannah, in Miavana, in Sanbona, and now even in the middle of the world's oldest farking desert!" He glared across at her as he slipped the self-cushioning pack around onto his back. "Despite the chance to make some serious subsist out of all this there are times since I wish I'd just given you the damn thread and walked out of your neat and tidy little office." He turned wistful. "I could be back in Savannah sharing stim with my friends instead of out here hiking from nowhere to Nowhere."

So much for trying to lighten the atmosphere, she thought. Her tone hardened. "I got the impression you didn't have many friends."

He looked at her sharply. "Hey, I knew plenty of people! Lots of people."

"There's a world of difference between acquaintances and friends."

"That so? I thought you were a doctor of medicine, not philosophy." His voice turned challenging. "How many 'friends' you got, doc? Not professional colleagues. Not grateful patients. Real friends."

She bridled. "I've got plenty! There's Suzanne, and Leora. . . ."

Whispr's angular face screwed up in a rictus of dismay as he interrupted. "What the hell kind of name is Leora?"

"It's a perfectly good name!" she snapped back at him. "She's a probe specialist who works in my tower, a fine technician and a true friend and . . . why are you nodding and smiling like that? Are *you* patronizing *me*?"

He looked away. "How could I do that, Ingrid? I'm just a lowly subsist-scrabbling street Meld and you're a respectable uptown doctor. Why, just look at how respectable you are! Entering another country under a false name, maniping your body and face to conceal your identity, flaunting your beauty to distract attention and questions from what you're doing here. . . ."

"That has nothing to do with the number and quality of friends that I . . . !" She paused and her tone changed abruptly. "Flaunting my what?"

"Your beauty." He continued without hesitating but with his gaze fixed firmly on the next bend in the ravine that was leading them northward. "It dazzles men, and probably some women. Naturals and Melds alike. I know: I can bear witness to its effects. And that was *before* the hair and boob manip. Maybe you're unaware of it, but you stun people quietly."

She gaped at him. Then she shook her head and irritably kicked aside a small rock in her path. "You have the most peculiar way of pissing people off, Whispr."

Now he did turn to look at her, his reply floating on his characteristic sardonicism. "Riffling isn't my only talent."

She drew herself up. "You're just trying to flatter me, to win the argument."

He scowled. "Whenever a woman says to a man 'you're just trying to flatter' me, what she's really saying is 'flatter me some more.'"

They strode onward in silence for several minutes. Off to his left a lizard vanished into a crack in the ravine wall, its black-and-gray striped tail a swift shrinking, highly agitated punctuation mark.

When she finally spoke again it was to say something that shook him to the core, affecting him even more powerfully than had Napun Molé's attempt on their lives in Florida or the recent pursuit of their vehicle in the Sanbona Preserve.

"As long as we're arguing about friends—have you ever been in love, Whispr?"

He dared not look at her. What could he say that would not give him away? That at first he'd been able to muster only adoration for one so exquisite and so far above his social station? That when they had decided to work together to try to unravel the mystery of the thread and she had become suddenly approachable his adoration had advanced (or more appropriately devolved) into lust? That what had developed subsequently was a jumble of feelings to which try as he might he could not put a suitable label? Was that love? Was it shallow because he was shallow, or might he dare to believe that despite his generally miserable life that he was capable of something deeper and more meaningful?

He was confused. Confused, uncertain, fearful, ashamed, and

most of all in pain. The pain blasted through him every time he looked at her. When she walked, when she ate, when she slept and he could gaze upon her openly and without having to worry that she would notice and take offense at his stare.

You're a riffler, he told himself. A riffler, a murderer (however unintentionally), a haunter of the fringes of respectable society, a disposable blowaway Meld. You're only hurting yourself if you think anything more than a short-term business relationship could ever eventuate between you and this woman.

Except for the pain, of course. Unlike her, that would always stay with him. On such pain he skated across an emotional land-scape as frozen as any arctic lake. Each casual word hurt anew, each criticism only brought more agony. He wanted it to go away, to leave him, to evaporate like the water from the recent atypical downpour. But it would not. It stayed strong and throbbing and was eating him up from the inside out.

Yeah, he concluded. It felt like love, all right.

"Whispr?" She was pointing in front of them.

A snake was crossing from one side of the arroyo to the other. It was brown and much smaller than the ferocious mamba that had indifferently slithered across Ingrid in the cave where they had hidden from the searcher drone. He didn't know if this one was poisonous or not. He found that he didn't care.

"Easy to go around it," he told her. "As for—what were we talking about? Oh, yeah, love. Sure I've been in love," he told her. "There was one particular woman . . ." He did not complete the thought. He could not.

Her interest was genuine—and its innocence only added to the pain. "I take it that it didn't work out?"

"No." He struggled to articulate. "It didn't work out."

"What was she like? Natural or Meld?"

"She started as a Natural. But everyone starts out as a Natural," he added hastily. "Beautiful. Smart—much smarter than me. A professional, not a street Meld. We fought a lot, but we managed to get along. As a matter of fact, I think we were both surprised at how well we managed to get along even though we didn't really have a lot in common. Even though she was pretty she was a tough little bugger. Resilient. I liked that about her."

Ingrid was smiling now. This was much better than arguing. "And what did she like about you?" she teased him.

He spat to one side. "Damned if I know." A pause. "Maybe she liked me because I let her be herself, and do what she wanted to do, and I didn't demand too much of her."

She nodded enthusiastically. "Yes, a woman likes that. Of course, so does a guy. Anyone would, I suppose."

"You would too, of course," he said flatly.

"Of course. If—when—I find myself in a permanent relationship it'll have to be with someone who espouses all those things."

A familiar, frustrating wall thrust up between them, the portcullis slammed down, and his expression twisted. "What does 'espouse' mean? Is it like 'expose'?"

"Not really. It means . . ." She stopped, frowning. "Do you hear something?"

Besides the warm liquid honey that is your voice, you mean? He forced himself to concentrate on the surrounding reality—and then he also frowned.

"Yeah, I hear it." He was suddenly alarmed. "Sounds like a truck, or at least a 4x4. Not a floater, and too loud to be a drone."

The noise grew louder, a steadily rising roar. "Awfully big truck, if that's what it is," she commented uneasily. "Especially for a place where there's no road."

"Could be a freight transporter. Big one." He began searching the flanking, winding walls of the ravine for another hiding place.

"Anything like that out here, it would have to belong to the company."

Another long moment passed while they stood standing motionless and listening. The growl continued to grow in volume.

"That's no truck," he muttered. "Too consistent, too loud, too . . ."

He never finished the thought, as it was interrupted by the raging wall of brown and white water that came thundering around the nearest bend in the canyon.

Flash flood.

The atypical downpour that had temporarily soaked them had been far more intense off to the east. There, on the westernmost slopes of the Jakkalsberge, the deluge had filled rivulets and streams, arroyos and canyons, gathering volume and strength as it made a doomed rush toward a shore it would never reach. Instead the water spread out over the vast gravel plains, soaked into thirsty spongelike sands, and briefly filled to overflowing every dry gulch and desiccated gorge that striped the mountain slopes.

Including the one up which they were presently hiking.

"RUN!"

She followed his lead as he turned and bolted back the way they had come. As they ran they frantically scanned the passing stone walls for signs of a way out, a way up, or even simple handholds. There was nothing; only the slick curving rock walls like waves frozen in time, whose sides had been scoured smooth by thousands of years of churning, rushing, polishing water. Predecessors of the thundering flood that was closing rapidly on them right now.

"Here, doc, over here!"

The several fissures in the rock wall that Whispr had found were too narrow to admit human fingers. Natural human fingers. The desperate street Meld jammed the bony pitons that were his attenuated digits into the barely visible cracks and started to pull himself upward. With his slender body flattened against the cool stone he looked like some skeletal desert arachnid.

Hurrying to follow him, Ingrid stumbled in the sand and gravel, regained her footing, and tried to start up in his wake. Even with heavily trimmed nails her fingers were unable to gain a purchase on the rock. She screamed, but the apocalyptic bellow of the oncoming water drowned her out. Keeping the fingers of one hand firmly jammed in the deepest fracture he could find, Whispr reached down and grabbed her fluttering right hand.

"Climb! Use your feet, doc! *Move!*"

The water slammed into her, bursting upward over her shoulders as she turned her head away from the brutalizing current. The thin cablelike muscles in his arms strained as he strove to maintain his grip. Water surged all around them, tugging at her and stretching her out like a beige-colored flag with her legs like tatters pointed downstream. She was too heavy, he was too weak, the flood was too strong. Her fingers slipped from his.

"Whispr!"

All the high-tech trekking equipment in his pack could do nothing to strengthen his grip. He could only watch as the powerful current swept her away from him and carried her downstream. He saw her go under, come up with her head tilted back, and, spitting water, go under again. She reemerged at the first bend, trying desperately to get a purchase on the indifferent stone. Her hands flailed at the smooth rock. If she could hold on until the initial rush started to subside it would be okay, he told himself. His heart was pounding.

For a moment he thought she had succeeded. Then she lost her newfound grip, wailed again, and slipped from view. The last thing he heard was his name, rising just above the roiling waters.

Well, crap, he thought as he pulled his fingers out of the anchoring fissure and resignedly let go.

He was a decent swimmer. Not trained, but living in a city threaded by canals and bulwarked by swamps it was a skill every child picked up at an early age. Trying to stay in the middle of the rush where the current was swiftest he made up the distance between them at an impressive pace. He would have gone much faster without his pack, but abandoning it would only see him trade drowning for a slower death. Without his special supplements he would leisurely starve. In the water his whiplike melded body offered almost no drag.

He could see her now, not far in front of him. She was no longer making any effort to swim, either toward him, the canyon walls, or anywhere else. It was all she could do to keep her head above water. Though her eyes were half shut she continued to strike at the water with wild splashing, slapping waves of her arms, as if she could somehow subdue it physically. Her flailings were growing increasingly feeble. He noted that her own pack was still on her back. It would take more than the force of a flash flood to break the magfab straps. But it was weighing her down and making it difficult for her to stay afloat. Whispr had never seen such an awkward swimmer.

Probably she'd initially panicked when she had been swept away from him and had never regained control of herself. Go figure. Street bum keeps his cool and doctor panics. He'd have something to say about that.

Then she went under again, did not resurface, and he feared he might not have someone to listen to the chidings he intended to deliver.

Only the fact that some air had become trapped in her pack saved her. As he was giving up hope this added buoyancy bounced her back to the surface, facedown in the water. Having outdistanced its burden of plant matter, drowned small creatures, sand, soil, and sodden humans, the front of the flood and its throaty roar began to recede southward. Ramrod current had given way to irritated swirls by the time he got a hand on the upper straps of her pack, rolled her over, and started swimming to his right. Though equally flush with flood, the water in the tributary ravine he had spotted offered no resistance to his methodical strokes as he towed her out of the main flow. Narrowing while its floor rose rapidly, the bottom of the side canyon soon provided slippery but welcome purchase for his feet.

Without knowing quite how he did it, his boots slipping on loose gravel and slick rocks and his slenderized muscles on fire, he hauled her body, backpack, and all up out of the side stream and onto dry land. There he laid her out on her back and collapsed beside her, his chest heaving. The empty blue overhead offered not even a solitary cloud by way of consolation.

"Didn't think . . . didn't think we'd make it, doc." He wiped at his mouth, coughed, and spat onto the moisture-welcoming surface. The droplets vanished instantly as they struck, sucked down into the ever-thirsty ground. "I couldn't hold you . . . I'm sorry. Why—why didn't you try to swim back to me? I didn't think I was going to be able to catch up to . . ."

She wasn't responding. Her eyes remained shut. Around her head her maniped red hair spread out in a saturated flaming corona. She was not moving. A coldness born of something much deeper and more malign than his recent swim crept over him.

"Doc? Ingrid?"

Oh hell, oh damn, oh shit. She was dead. She was dead and he was alone. Alone in the desert. Alone in the Namib. Alone inside. Or—maybe not. Could the patient save the doctor? Try, try, he had to try—but what to do?

Bad water, good air. A prescription that was as straightforward as it was simple. Slipping frantically out of his pack, he rose to his knees and dumped it quickly to one side as he bent over her. Pressing both hands against her stomach, he pushed, not knowing if he was pressing too hard, not knowing if he was doing it right. He repeated the thrust once, twice. On the third time her body reacted: arching sharply upward, she retched from the bottom of her toes, spewing foul water and other stomach contents all over him. Turning his face away he ignored the warm dousing and prepared to push some more.

He couldn't. Her stomach was out of his reach. Having rolled onto her left side she was jerking and spasming violently while clutching her midsection with both hands. More water gushed from her mouth to disappear in seconds into the desiccated earth. When the last foul drops had dribbled from her lips, her hands relaxed and all the air seemed to sigh out of her body. Her eyes remained closed. She was motionless once more.

"Ingrid? Hey, doc, you okay?" Reaching over, he put a hand on her side and shoved. Gently at first, then when no reaction was forthcoming, more forcefully. Her right arm bobbed loosely.

He didn't want to roll her over onto her back again in case there was still any water in her stomach or lungs, but he felt he had no choice. As he bent over her he startled himself by realizing that despite the desperate circumstances he was still able to recognize the irony of the situation. Here he was, targeting the lips and mouth with whose contact he had longed for since that day in her office, and he felt no stirring beyond a distinct touch of nausea that threatened to make him empty his own guts.

Mouth-to-mouth. He wasn't trained in that ancient revival technique either, but he would do his best to improvise. Inclining his head forward and down he bent nearer, his open palms bracing themselves against the warm ground on either side of her shoulders. He was very close to her when she coughed in his face and her eyelids fluttered.

He drew back hurriedly.

Her eyelids snapped open and she took a moment to focus. "I think I'm not dead."

A tight smile creased his narrow visage. "I'll take that as an official medical pronouncement."

She started to reply and instead found herself trying to throw up again. The resulting muscular confusion generated one of the more remarkable facial expressions he'd ever seen on a Natural. Once her body relaxed, she swallowed and tried again.

"I feel like I did though. Die, that is. What happened?" Raising her head slightly she looked around. "Where's the water?"

"Where it belongs, in the canyon. The level's going down almost as fast as it came up. Speaking of coming up, I doubt there's much of anything left in your stomach, so you should be all right now." He smiled. "Just my street medical opinion."

Looking down at herself she pressed the fingertips of both hands lightly against her torso in the vicinity of her navel. Her expression turned queasy but she did not heave. "Doesn't feel all right. I really thought I was dead." Sudden realization made her look at him sharply as she sat all the way up. "How did I get out?"

"I came after you. Swam, pulled you out. Saved your life. Sorry, but I don't believe in false modesty. If I hadn't risked mine you wouldn't now have yours."

She pondered this for a long moment. "Why did you do it, Whispr?"

He looked away from her and toward the ravine. Moments ago it had been filled to the brim with a roaring torrent. Now it gurgled merrily, like a retired professional athlete toying with outmatched neighborhood opponents.

"I dunno. Congenital stupidity, maybe." When she started to say something he jumped in ahead of her. "Speaking of congenital stupidity why the hell didn't you swim toward me when you saw me coming after you? I know you saw me—our eyes met. It would've made things a lot easier. You wouldn't have sunk so close to the edge." His anger helped to shove thoughts of the near mouth-to-mouth experience out of his mind.

She looked away. "Whispr—I can't swim."

That was not one of the responses he had been expecting. "What the fark do you mean you can't swim? Everyone in the Greater Savannah region can swim. They have to learn. Too much of the place is underwater. What idiots never taught you to swim?"

Her voice strengthened a little. "My idiot parents, who raised me in Topeka, overlooked passing along that particular skill. Not a critical need for it in Topeka."

"I suppose not," he acknowledged. "Uh, where's Topeka?"

She told him. "Dry country. High country. Safe country. I learned a lot, but not how to swim. I was always too busy with academics. Didn't even get to the local soche very often to mix with the other kids." Noting his expression she added, "I know it doesn't make any sense. There are several exercise pools in my tower, salt water as well as fresh, and I've never done more than wade in any of them. I love the beach, I even love the water. I just can't swim." She swallowed hard and her voice dropped. "If you hadn't come after me, Whispr, I'd have drowned."

Before he realized it, he spoke more harshly than he intended. "Tell me something I don't know." He was stunned and confused by what happened next.

Dr. Ingrid Seastrom started to cry.

Despite everything they had been through, despite all they had endured since leaving Savannah, she had always maintained her composure throughout. She had not cried when Napun Molé had held them at gunpoint in the Everglades, nor when their fleeing 4x4 had crashed into the river in Sanbona. She had not cried when Josini Jay-Joh Umfolozi had stuck a gun in her face in the cab of his nephew's commercial transporter and threatened to blow her brains out.

Whispr knew how to deal with an attack on the street. He knew how to disarm aggravated police with flattering words and outmaneuver muscle-bound lods with practiced side steps. He knew the best way to wrangle "donations" from kindhearted tourists and riffle unaware business folk. But he did not have the slightest notion what to do now. So he fell back on his tried and true method for minimizing mistakes: he did nothing.

"I can't . . . I don't know, Whispr," she coughed between sobs. "I'm not . . . I wasn't made for this. I should be in my office back home treating the sick and injured, not *being* the sick and injured. 'Physician, heal thyself.'" She started to laugh but was too weak to do more than gasp a few desultory chuckles. "This is all a bad dream. You, assassins, SICK, the thread; all of it. We're going to die here and it's my fault. My stubborn, stupid, single-minded fault! A bad dream. Bad karma."

He'd had enough. "Bad drama, you mean." Reaching down, he slipped his arms under hers and lifted her to her feet. In her expression, confusion and despair made room for shock. "Get a *hold* of yourself, doc! First of all, the 'we're all gonna die' mantra is mine. I claim it by right of origination. So you can forget about blubbering that one again. You want to bawl? Fine, go ahead and tearwork your lady ducts until they're as dry as the ground where we're standing. But we *are* here and we *are* going to go on and we are going to get into the facility at Nerens and learn what that thread is all about. Then maybe we'll end up dead, but not before. Because I'm damned if I've wasted all this time and trouble and energy and effort just to indulge some spoiled bitchwitch of a doctor who thinks she's on some tiptoliday and can just up and quit and call a cab to go home because she's decided to go all boredass on me!"

She stood gaping at him wide-eyed until he finally ran down. At first he thought she was going to break out crying again. Then what he hoped would happen began to take place before his eyes. She started to get mad. Serious mad. When she swung at him he dodged. When she aimed a furious frustrated kick at his crotch he slipped easily to one side. The fact that he was smiling at her all the while only squared her fury.

"You bastard! You miserable bumscum, you filthy . . . !"

"That's it, doc." As he avoided her futile, untutored blows and kicks he did his best to egg her on. "Get it all out. All the aggravation, all the anger; leave it here on the sand and rock. Mix it with your vomit. Whoa!" Her next blow nearly connected with his face. "I can't argue about one thing, though," he concluded as he continued to dance around her. "You got me all wet again."

Still livid but too exhausted by her near death swim to keep swinging, she paused and blinked at him. Then she started to laugh again, only this time it was more than a couple of transitory chuckles. She laughed until she cried, and then she was crying again, and then laughing. Holding at a safe distance and watching her he was reminded of why, as a friend had once told him while sharing a particularly potent stim in Eastwood Park in the north of the city, women were not just another gender but another species.

He let her face flood until he feared she might sprain something. "Okay, doc. That's enough. I think you got everything out now. Food, flood water, emotions. You *look* drained, anyway." Approaching warily, he gripped her right shoulder and squeezed reassuringly.

Her eyes tilted up to meet his own and for a moment, for an instant, there was something in her expression that . . .

He imagined she was going to embrace him. He welcomed it and he feared it. As it turned out, the emotional energy he devoted to both possibilities was wasted because she held off, held back, and instead of moving toward him, knelt to fumble with her pack. Within his shriveled soul a small spark winked out as swiftly as it had unexpectedly sprung to life. Wordlessly, he bent to help her.

Her communicator was gone, swept away by the force of the flood that had ripped open the pockets of her pants. That left them with only his own device and, in a dire emergency, a simple mechanical compass. Using only those instruments they would have to make it the rest of the way to Nerens. The antique compass with its magnetic needle and flat unilluminated face had been an afterthought, pressed on them by the shopkeeper in Orangemund who had outfitted them with their trekking supplies. It was one piece of gear that did not need batteries.

Leaving her to finish going through her battered pack he left to make an inventory of his own supplies. Thanks to the unbreakable pack straps both of them still had their sleeping blankets, waterpaks, and most of their food concentrates. For one terrible moment he thought that the tubes containing his vital nutrient supplements had been swept away. He finally found the package, still dry and intact, where it had become wrapped up in a shirt. All they had surrendered to the rampaging flash flood was some food, some time, and some unreasonable assumptions.

"You can do this, doc." He stood nearby as she finished repacking her gear. "We can do this. Sure we'll end up dead eventually, but we can do this."

She had tied the bottom of her shirt up in a knot beneath her breasts, exposing her belly. Not that the sight of the few creamy centimeters of exposed flesh were all that he could have wished for, but he would take what he could get. They constituted a wondrous diversion from the desiccated terrain around them.

"Once again, Whispr," she observed dryly, "I find myself having to rely on your unreserved enthusiasm to motivate me." She took a deep breath, which did wonders for his own motivation. "I promise you this: if we make it to Nerens and I can get us inside, you won't be killed."

"How can you make a promise like that?" He hastened to parallel her as she struck off northward, following the edge of the ravine that had tried to kill them.

"In the full knowledge that if I'm wrong I won't have to listen to you harangue me about it."

He snorted. "Ah, see—now *you're* the one who's smiling."

Periodically pausing to check their progress against the maps contained in his communicator, they followed the ravine northward until it turned east toward the mountains that had spawned the flash flood. There followed another broad stretch of hard ground that save for scattered gravel was as smooth and flat and lifeless as the paved floor of a building supply warehouse. As they advanced, Whispr kept glancing nervously at the sky. Out on such open terrain they would be as visible to a searcher drone or passing hi-rez satellite as the Eiffel Tower in a cornfield.

But nothing materialized to question their progress. Even the ubiquitous black and white crows had temporarily foresworn the travelers' company, there being nothing for them to scavenge in such a dead, barren place. Occasionally they would stop at pools of fresh rainwater to slake their thirst, grateful for these smaller and less violent echoes of the recent atypical downpour and the chance to hydrate without having to dig into their supplies.

Both were relieved when the flat pan gave way to low hills cut by smaller gullies than the one from which they had recently escaped. True to form, Ouspel's course followed one of these northward. Whispr especially was thankful for the opportunity to once again advance under cover. It took some urging on his part to persuade Ingrid to descend once more into a winding fissure in the rocks. The memory of having nearly drowned in another was still far too fresh for comfort.

"We *have* to stay in the ravines," he reminded her firmly. "They're the only cover we have from Sperrgebeit patrols. Also, in the sun it makes for cooler walking."

"I know, I know. It's only . . . I know it isn't reasonable, Whispr. But most psychological blocks aren't. It's not that I've turned suddenly hydrophobic. It's just that the close call I had, that we had, is so recent." She nodded toward the gully's shadowy depths. "Why can't we follow it by walking along the edge?"

"I just told you why. Because a searcher drone would be able to spot us from a distance. That's why Ouspel's instructions insist we go down into them. This is the kind of terrain that let him get away clean from the facility." He marshaled more of his argument. "It would be hell to have made it all this way only to get picked up by SICK security because you can't handle walking in a gulch that's four meters deep."

She stood contemplating the silent fissure in the earth for another few minutes. He said nothing more, waiting patiently. Finally she nodded and started down the slope before them, sliding and slipping her way to the sandy bottom. That it was covered with a centimeter or so of pooled rainfall did nothing to improve her mood. Feeling as though she were standing with her feet sunk halfway into a mirror and that if she took one wrong step she would sink out of sight into it forever, she looked over at him.

"If we're caught in another flash flood you'll save me again, won't you?"

He smiled. "Sure. Why not? If I drown out here chances are it'll be quicker than what's waiting for us in Nerens."

She made a face and allowed her pack to reposition itself against her shoulders and spine. The integrated pressure pads expanded downward to compensate for the shift.

"I'll try my best not to inhibit your demise, since the speed with which it will occur seems to be of paramount importance to you."

"You bet your ass it is, doc." As he walked beside her his narrow feet kicked up rainwater. The drops hung briefly in the desert air like glass marbles. "Maybe if I die first you can time it."

4

The House of Nasty. An admirably straightforward description, Molé mused. Also an in-your-face acknowledgment of what lay within.

As he stood contemplating the floating glowing sign that hovered above and just in front of the dubious establishment, the pedestrians shuffling and hurrying around him ignored the unremarkable old man in their midst. It was no different here than in Tokyo, or Newnew York, or London or Hio Janeiro or Sagramanda. He was a nonentity. Even more, he was an elderly nonentity. Clearly no threat to anyone, too plainly dressed to be worth riffling, a cipherous bit of perambulating protoplasm that posed no evident threat to man, Meld, beast, or any combination thereof.

That was just how he liked it.

Should anyone happened to have glanced in the direction of the innocuous figure who was staring at the sign over the basement entrance they would never have guessed that beneath the elderly exterior surged an occasional and sometimes lethal volcanic eruption of aggravation. It was just as well that no one did. Molé was in no mood to suffer the inquisitive. Curiosity was intrusive, intrusion was invasion, and invaders were as likely to have their throats cut as their cheeks patted, depending on his frame of mind. At the moment the latter was as dark as the hour of night. The heavy cloud cover that had settled in over Cape Town like a thick wool blanket matched his mood.

He had lost the trail. Lost track of his quarry. The mildly deranged doctor and her nonentity stick-man Meld of a companion had vanished from the hunter's ken, plucked literally from under his gaze by the operator of a counterfeit elephant. While Molé had looked on helplessly from atop a hill in the backcountry of the Sanbona Preserve, the quadrupedal mechanical transport had picked up his targets, turned, and strode off to the north. That did not mean its final destination lay to the north. Once out of his sight it could have gone in any direction, further complicating his interrupted pursuit of the two Namericans.

The machine itself was the only clue he had left. He still had no idea where the two mismatched thieves were going or what they intended to do with the thread. The fact that they had come here, to the heartland of his present employers, had been a sufficiently startling development in itself. Subsequent to their arrival everything they had done had been characteristic of the classic African tourist. They had done nothing to suggest that they were travelers in possession of extremely valuable stolen property.

Did they know that it was him who had nearly run them down in Sanbona? Not that it mattered. Having been alerted to the fact that their presence in southern Africa had been discovered they would be even more on their guard than ever. Which would make his job of locating them all over again harder than ever.

Despite his frustration he did not despair. Failure was not in his vocabulary. It was one reason why he was repeatedly hired for such

difficult tasks. He had never failed to complete whatever assignment he had accepted. Nor would this be the first time. He certainly
would not be bested by a pair of bumbling amateur know-nothings
from Namerica who did not even understand the significance of
what they had taken.

If the trail ahead disappears a good tracker knows to retrace his
steps and search for overlooked clues on ground already trodden.
Careful probing and questioning had led him here, tonight, to the
least reputable section of Cape Town; a district so despised that the
honorable citizens of the city could not wait for the planet's slowly
rising waters to overtake and consume it.

The House of Nasty, in fact, lay below sea level. The original
brick walls of the basement in the old harbor warehouse had been
reinforced and rendered watertight by being infused with a penetrating liquid epoxy. The result was the modern but far sturdier
chemical equivalent of the Delft tiles the Dutch had once used to
waterproof the lower floors of their own buildings. While not as attractive as the hand-painted seventeenth-century Dutch materials,
the newer composites were considerably more hydrophilic.

Within the shimmering sign above the entrance a continuously
scanning optical pickup concluded that the eyes of the small man
standing in the street had been focused on the front of the building
for the requisite predetermined length of time. Responding to its
programming, the sign dispatched a targeted mobiad. Descending
onto the street, this slowed to a halt at the psychologically predetermined optimum distance from the potential customer's eyes. The
glowing motile advertisement then proceeded to flash fire a series
of three-dimensional vit images calculated to stimulate the more
degenerate crevices and recesses of the singled-out viewer's brain.
For a modest fee, any and all of these advertised depravities could
be had by simply strolling to the entrance of the named establish-

ment, suitably identifying oneself at the door as an adult, and requesting admittance.

Molé irritably waved the mobiad aside, his hand brushing through the images. Casual obscenities were obliterated, outrageous smut interrupted. If the information he had accumulated over the previous several days was accurate, he would find the individual he sought partaking of the soiled delights within. The fiercely touted attractions did not inveigle him. He was quite capable of amusing himself without having to pay an unimaginative supplier.

It was noisy inside the House of Nasty, but not oppressively so. The intense goolmech that directly tickled one's tympanum was comparatively subdued. So was the lighting. The latter condition was a given. Although perfectly willing to pay whatever was asked in order to indulge their preferential perversions, that did not mean the participants were prepared to have them highlighted for the delectation of potential tattletales. It was all well and good to delve into the depths of depravity and splash around in the muck, but not so if the details were allowed to find their way back to a spouse or relative or fiancée.

As he threaded his way through the prattling, giggling, sucking crowd, the ambient illumination in the club's main chamber shifted from red to purple and back again as artfully as in a properly mixed drink. Though the music being hammered out was not to his taste, he was grateful for the strings and percussion that drowned out most of the dim-witted palaver passing for conversation around him.

Two bar counters separated by a dance floor and scattered tables faced each other across the basement. If they ran true to form they would offer more than alcohol. It was a truism of humanity that once a new stimulant or narcotic became available, a thousand people would line up to try it without a care as to whether it was effective, indifferent, or fatal. When it came to stimulants, reputation always trumped well-being. A place like this, he reflected, would stock the latest of everything. Better living through chemistry. Or better dying.

Someone stepped in front of him to block his path. In her late thirties, the Meld was still attractive, with a voluptuous body whose gym and pill-toned attributes included three breasts that threatened to erupt from her single-piece cerulean dress like toothpaste from a broken old-fashioned tube. He eyed the various regions of bulging tanned flesh distastefully while drifting spheres of lime-green light ambled across them. Having no time for such diversions he impatiently tried to step around her. She sidled sideways to intercept him once again.

Already bent slightly forward at the waist to emphasize his fragility, he twisted his torso into an even more damaged posture. "Please excuse me, madam. I am here only to quietly imbibe and perhaps have something to eat."

Putting hands on hips she struck a pose that was at least five thousand years old and threw him a lecherous smirk. "What, all supping and no tupping? Don't you find me attractive?"

"Even at my age and with my poor vision I can still say yes to that, my dear. Surely you do not think the same of me?" Before she could respond he raised a trembling hand to forestall the rote response that he knew would be forthcoming. Anything to get rid of her. "Please, no falsified flattery. I am not ashamed of my natural condition. Find yourself someone who can muster at least a minimum of endurance to match your intentions and leave me to drown my musings in peace."

The leer she wore like a carnivale mask widened. "So drinking's your thing? Want to know what mine is?" Before he could demur she leaned toward him, multiple cleavage on ample display. "I like old guys," she whispered and then straightened. "Want to know why?"

He did not, but neither did he want to cause a scene and possibly scare off the person he was really looking for. "Why, my dear?"

"Because I get off on their gratitude. It gives me a chill thrill. That's a fair swap, isn't it?" Reaching out she rested a hand on his left shoulder and squeezed, the nails that had been permanently bonded to the finger bones digging slightly into his flesh. "I know I'll get mine. I guarantee you'll get yours."

The vast variety of decadent tastes exhibited by humankind never failed to sadden him. "I know I could give you a surprise, madam, but I have neither the inclination nor the time nor the strength." He took a step forward. A pale yellow orb drifted past his face and for the barest instant was reflected in his eyes. Had the trolling slummer blocking his way seen it she might have fled. Instead she stood her ground.

"A surprise? *You?* That would be a first, but I like firsts. Maybe you're not up to much, but you strike me as someone who's been around. I'm willing to take my chances." She gestured to her right. "We could rent a gas tube. I'd split it with you." She grinned. "Then you can split me, old man."

Her leering persistence had become intolerable. Mustering a smile, he caught her gaze with his. Peering into his eyes she sensed rather than saw his right hand slide up the front of her body. Convinced she had made a sale she relaxed, expecting the hand to go higher. Instead it halted below her breasts in the vicinity of her solar plexus. Unexpectedly powerful melded fingers moved and thrust. Her eyes bulged. Her mouth opened in a wide "O" and she inhaled sharply, only to find that her lungs wouldn't work.

"Will this do for a surprise?" he murmured softly.

Eyes still wide she continued to stare at him. Then they fluttered shut and she crumpled to the floor like a pile of overcooked yams. Two nearby couples interrupted their simulated coitus to look over in surprise. Molé smiled at them.

"I think she took too strong a stimcomb. She'll be fine." He stepped over the motionless body that had contracted into a fetal position. "Let the staff handle it. They are paid to do so."

The two couples eyed the speaker, who was patently too old and feeble to have done anything untoward, and returned to their loveless playacting. Having dealt with the brief nuisance, Molé worked his way through the gyrating crowd to the nearer of the opposing bars.

It was crewed by two mixologists, one Natural and one Meld. The latter flaunted a pair of double-length arms, the better to reach the high shelves and distant reaches of the container-laden jet-black back bar. Each of his hands featured eight nimble fingers capable of handling the most complex components of the bartender's art. For several minutes Molé watched both men at work before sidling over to sit across from the Natural. Being less busy than his counterpart he would have more time to observe, and more time to talk.

"'Evening, *ou man*." Despite his youth the much younger man spoke with the practiced control and timbre of experience, as if his voice had been tuned like a piano. "I wish you a short day and a long night. What will you have?"

"Water." Molé was scanning the crowd that had washed up at the back of the room, human flotsam that had been left behind as the tide of daily life had receded. Away from the gyration floor there were tables and booths and time for moneyed wastrels to contemplate a multitude of whispered inanities.

The bartender turned to feign a serious inspection of the rows of bottles and other containers behind him. "Sorry. We're fresh out of that. Try again. Or you could go back outside." He nodded in the direction of the entrance that led to the street above. "Harbor's full of water."

"Ah. Humor. I appreciate humor." Molé's voice was perfectly devoid of inflection. "Since you insist, I will have a single shot of raki flavored with synchoc. Light on the phenylethylamine content, please."

The Natural smiled professionally. "Interesting call. You from around Istanbul?"

Having turned again on his seat to resume studying the crowd, Molé did not answer. The bartender shrugged, prepared the drink, and served it in a small glass at room temperature. Reaching behind him, Molé picked it up and sipped delicately; staring, watching, searching. . . .

There. Setting the half-full glass back on the bar he passed his credit card across the sensor set flush into its side, not bothering to see if the transaction took. He was not running a tab and the bartender, busy with other customers, did not check to see if the old man's cred had been accepted. His attention was not necessary. Had payment been refused the alarm in the glass would have reacted by alerting club security.

His informant had earned his subsist, Molé mused as he made his way toward a table located close to the back wall. Of course the woman sitting there by herself might be a completely different good-looking tentacular Meld than the one he was looking for, but the bright red stripes that adorned her fingerless grasping limbs suggested otherwise. Mindful of her professional reputation, local though it might be, he halted on the other side of the table.

It took a moment before she noticed him staring at her. Deliberately she reached out and wrapped the attenuated sucker-lined end of one limb around the four-sided quarter-meter-tall metal drink holder in front of her.

"I don't like men who stare. And old men revolt me. So you

disgust me doubly. Find someone else to feel up with your eyes before I wash them out with alcohol."

Molé was not in the least disturbed by the affront. Instead of complying he quietly took a chair across the table from her. Her right tentacle tensed around the drink container. He began patiently, speaking as one would to a child.

"Your name is Lindiwe. Together with an unfortunate companion named Terror and a self-evidently incompetent European team leader named Chelowich you broke into the house-business of a local witch doctor named Thembekile. You were seeking information on a pair of visiting Namericans whom I have found out paid her an earlier visit: a doctor named Ingrid Seastrom and a vapid male Meld companion who calls himself Whispr. I have attempted to get in touch with the witch doctor herself. This is at present not possible because the thoroughly botched intrusion by you and your friends has apparently unnerved her and sent her into deep hide somewhere else in the country.

"I am sure that I can eventually locate her but it will take time and much effort since she appears to have many friends and colleagues. Since you do not, it was far easier to find you. Being conservative by nature and in this particular instance more than customarily impatient, I naturally decided to begin by seeking the information I require from one who may already have obtained it."

Molé essayed a trustworthy smile, an expression at which over the years he'd had occasion to have considerable practice. Taken together with his age and general appearance this rendered his aspect positively avuncular.

It certainly struck the tentacled woman as such, though not exactly in the way Molé would have preferred. Hard-staring back at him she admitted nothing and confirmed less. "Who are you, Uncle Serpent?"

"My name is Napun. Although I do not work directly for SICK,

I am what you would call an outside consultant." Despite his best efforts to control himself, both his gaze and his tone hardened slightly. "You, on the other hand, have been working for someone other than SICK. That makes us competitors for the same information."

She shrugged, one red-striped tentacle rising slightly higher than the other. "So you're right about that. So what? Personally, SICK makes me sick."

"I did not seek you out to engage in a debate on the morals of international politics or commerce or the prime movers thereof. Your opinions are your own and I am willing to respect them. While we may serve different masters, we do so from the same perspective. We are hirelings for the same purposes, you and I."

She made no effort to disguise her surprise and contempt. "What? I don't think so, old man."

He sighed understandingly. "I have spent a lifetime disproving disrespect." He glanced around. "I would rather not have to do so yet one more time in such crowded surroundings. However, you may rest assured that I will do so if necessary. But there is no need for that. Think of me what you will." He leaned slightly forward. "I am prepared to pay for whatever knowledge you may have gained regarding the present whereabouts or intentions of the two named Namericans. As you have doubtless already been paid a likely half of what your own employers promised you, what I can offer should more than make up for what you have lost on this particular project."

This time she did not dismiss his words out of hand. "I lost a colleague. Boo wasn't only a fellow employee, she was a friend." Lindiwe made a spitting sound without actually expectorating, revealing a melded tongue that had been maniped so that it was fully prehensile. A younger man might have found that distracting. Not Molé. "As for our team 'leader,' she was forced on us by the—by our employers. She was an arrogant out-of-town Natural bitch who thought she knew everything, and now she's dead." Her gaze met Molé's without flinching. "So some good came out of it."

"I care nothing for such individuals. They are more expendable than stale bread. As to your friend, I am sorry." He considered. "I will double your employer's death benefit."

Lindiwe's stare narrowed. Around them a radically melded assortment of humanity danced, leaped, osculated, fondled, cursed, and engaged in caressing and touching with a variety of limbs and digits both human and maniped. As he waited for a reply Molé ignored it all, from the pounding goolmech to the suggestive gestures to the occasional bemused stare that briefly flicked in his direction.

"What makes you think we learned anything?" Lindiwe asked him. "We were making progress, yebo, but we had to get out of there fast. The place was booby-trapped to the ult." She shuddered mentally at the memory. "Misleading tactiles, poisonous spiders— there are reasons why people leave sangomas alone, and they have only occasionally to do with old superstitions."

"*Did* you learn anything?" Emotion-deprived at the best of times, Molé continued to speak as calmly as if placing an order at the bar.

Lindiwe found her gaze distracted by a pair of two-meter-tall local males each of whose heads had been severely maniped to resemble that of a horse. One man boasted a black mane and tail while the other's maniped accoutrements were a Scandinavian blond. Both wore very little, the better to emphasize their additional stallion melds. These extended to regions beyond head and hair. At the moment they wore the expressions of men alone and not wanting to be. But first she had to get rid of this persistent old man.

"We—the European—had just opened files in the sangoma's box when the spider flood arrived. She thought they were illusory.

They weren't. They killed her before she could do much in the way of digging."

"But you got away."

"I ran like hell. The door was secured so I went out a window."

"You ran. You are a coward." The way Molé voiced it the word hung in the air as a cold statement of fact, not an accusation.

Lindiwe was young but not so inexperienced as to be so easily provoked. She ignored the implication. "The bite of *one* button spider can kill. I prefer to say I cut my losses rather than that I ran."

Molé did not pursue it. There was nothing to be gained by doing so. "You say that Chelowich had just begun to open the sangoma's files. I presume there were some that related to the visit of the two Namericans. I know it is difficult to read and comprehend while running (once again his tone was not accusatory) but were you able to see or learn anything? Anything at all?"

Get rid of him, an increasingly stimulated voice inside the tentacle woman's mind insisted. Conversing among themselves, the impatient stallion Melds were threatening to desert the vicinity of her table.

"You keep saying you'll pay. How much?"

Molé named a figure. "No negotiations. You know it's more than you deserve."

She pondered, then nodded brusquely. "Half upfront. To prove that you're more than just a babbling senior citizen. The rest after I tell you everything I saw."

Now it was the old man's turn to hesitate. He disliked spending his employer's money on goods unseen. But this worm-armed woman was his only serious lead. He had been completely honest when he had told her that tracking down the sangoma, who had gone into serious hiding, would take time and effort.

"Communicator?"

Smiling, she drew it from a purse. As her device processed the proffered payment she turned her smile on the taller of the two nearby equine Melds. He neighed encouragingly and added an additional flourish with a becoming toss of his mane.

As soon as the amount had been verified and entered into her account she placed the handheld device back in her purse and secured it. "Several sentences flashed in the box field before it went dead, but I was moving fast and yes, I was scared, so I didn't exactly linger to read at leisure. In fact, out of all of it I just remember one word, and that only because it had been highlighted several times."

Though quietly displeased, he reserved judgment. "What was the one word?"

Rising, she let her left tentacle slide around the back of the blond horseman and her right around the waist of his contrasting companion. The pair of flexible limbs continued to coil around the exposed muscular bodies until they reached manip-hardened abdomens. Both men looked startled at the unexpected ministrations. Then the blond smiled down at her, put an arm around the back of her head, drew her close, and kissed her. Pulling away, she grinned up at him, then over at his equally agreeable and expectant companion.

"Want some sugar, pony-boys?"

Finding himself abruptly ignored at the table Molé raised his voice slightly. "I just paid you a lot of money for one word. I will have it, please."

The dark horseman, who weighed well over a hundred kilos, sneered at the elderly figure. "I gives you one word, *ikhela*, and I no charge you for it." He proceeded to deliver himself of two syllables.

The newly bonded trio of tentacles, tails, and temerity laughed uproariously. Molé quietly pushed back his chair, stood, and calmly addressed the speaker.

"I venture to say that your dick is considerably bigger than your wit." His gaze shifted to Lindiwe. "The word. And if that is indeed all you have to offer then I must insist on a partial refund of what I have just paid you."

Her lips parted in astonishment. The gall of the little ancient! "Are you *threatening* me, old man?" She looked first at the blond, then at his companion. "Can you believe it? This old fart is threatening me."

Leaving her in the embrace of his stablemate, the dark Meld came around the table. Even without the hooves that had replaced his feet he would have towered over Molé.

"Time to go, *Gogo*. Nothing left for you here now but more words. You keep pester this arm-woman and you will get angry ones, and maybe also clip-clop upside the head."

Molé sounded tired. "I did so not want this to be difficult."

He jumped. Or more properly, he sprang.

To their credit the two equine Melds reacted smartly. A professional, Lindiwe responded even faster. In a conventional brawl that would have been enough. Attracted to the action despite the club's disorienting deluge of sound and light, other patrons could have been forgiven for considering the fight uneven: one unprepossessing old man against three much younger and bigger Melds. Sympathetic onlookers could have told him that there were easier and less painful ways to commit suicide, which was what he appeared bent on.

Few of them were close enough to see the chromatic flash of cutlery that erupted from the oldster's hands and elbows. While unable to clearly perceive the cause of all the blood that explosively filled one corner of the big room, startled spectators had no difficulty discerning the results.

As Molé completed his leap and landed behind the blond, the big horse Meld went down as if his bones had been soaked in acid. With both his femoral artery and jugular sliced, even advanced emergency medical procedures would have been hard pressed to save him—and they were not available. Efficient as always, Molé did not waste time in contemplation of his accomplishment. Bloviation and the striking of heroic martial arts poses were for melodramatic popents, not real life. He engaged with the second big male before his first victim's spurting torso struck the floor.

Exposing body armor fashioned from dense maniped bone, the startled dark-haired Meld parried his much smaller assailant's thrusting hands. That left him vulnerable to attack from Molé's feet. Pushing off on his right foot and making full use of maniped muscles, the frozen-visaged old man kicked out with his left foot. A curving razor the full width of his foot snapped out from his shoe's leading edge. Propelled by muscles both natural and enhanced, this weapon embedded itself in the horse Meld's abdomen just below the navel all the way up to Molé's ankle. As he dropped back toward the floor he twisted his body sideways. His left leg followed suit, as did his left foot. Landing cleanly on his right foot he dropped into a defensive fighting stance. Though not necessary given the blow he had just struck, this fresh posture was the consequence of a lifetime of skill and training.

The remaining equine Meld looked down at himself, swaying slightly, and took a tentative step backward. His elderly assailant forgotten, the man dropped both hands to his stomach and pressed hesitantly inward. Turning and staggering toward the front of the club he kept both hands against his lower belly while he devoted his full attention to keeping his now revealed intestines from spilling out onto the floor.

Having managed to avoid her interrogator's initial attack Lindiwe had pulled a pair of handguns. Contrary to the more common fictional depictions of such confrontations they were different makes and models, the better to maximum the potential results. Each had been customized to be held and operated by tentacles instead of hands. Taking careful aim at the old man she fired twice.

First one slug, then a second, penetrated Molé's shirt and the toughened skin of his chest beneath, knocking him backward. Slightly slowed, both then struck the internal organic fibrous armor plates that had been grafted to his ribs and sternum. Manufactured of gengineered keratin grown from Molé's own body (so that its natural defenses would not reject the internal grafts) and reinforced with carbon nanofibers, the plates stopped both shots as well as absorbing much of the shock. Even so, the impact was enough to cause his heart to miss a beat, but it quickly stabilized. His specialized and enhanced internal defenses moved quickly to englobe the fragments of the bullets to prevent infection. They would render the metal shards harmless until they could be removed.

Lower level adepts like this snake-arm never learn, he told himself as he fought to regain his footing. When dealing with an attacker always aim for the head. The body, even a small body, has too much available space in which to plant defenses.

Her second sidearm fired poison darts. Unable to penetrate his toughened assassin's epidermis they bounced harmlessly off him and fell to the floor.

By this time he was moving sideways and had one of his own weapons out. Increasingly aware of the toxic confrontation that was escalating in their midst, Natural and Meld patrons alike had begun to scatter in all directions. The rising mad panic provided a percussive counterpoint to the pounding, throbbing goolmech that continued to pour into the club from hidden projectors. In the distance by the entrance a pair of two-hundred-kilo lods with low brows and bald skulls covered by sensor caps were trying to force their way toward the scene of the ongoing confrontation. Their progress was hampered by the crush of screaming patrons battling to reach the exit and a concurrent need to avoid squashing as few customers as possible.

As two more shots and a second flurry of ineffectual poison

darts came his way, Molé threw himself toward the floor. Shells and the plastic feathers that made the darts fly true shot over him as he fired his own weapon while still falling. His response of choice consisted of a single small pellet fired from the end of one maniped finger. Penetrating his target's skin and lodging in her flesh, the swiftly dissolving pellet delivered a rapidly dispersing measured quantity of modified histrionicotoxin that had been synthesized from the body of *Dendrobates azureus*. The consequences of this dosage of maniped lipophilic alkaloid took more time to manifest themselves than would a bullet or a fatal charge of electricity, but he did not want to kill the female hireling outright. Dead people were a notoriously poor source of information.

Exhibiting no adverse effects from the pellet that had lodged in her gut, Lindiwe was still trying to get a clear shot at her tormentor. The fact that he was much faster on his feet and hands than she expected was complicated by the play of ceiling lights and wandering glowlos that played havoc with her vision. It took a moment or two before she finally spotted him hiding behind a table that had been overturned by other patrons in their haste to escape. She smiled to herself. No thicker than the radiant fibers from which it had been spun, the vit screen oval tabletop would pose no barrier to the slugs from the more traditional of her two sidearms. Pocketing the poison dart pistol she gripped the heavy plastic gun with the ends of both tentacles, ignored the pornographic offerings that were continuing to stream across the upturned table, and fired.

Unfortunately for her aim, by the time her tentacle tip depressed the electronic trigger she was already falling backward. The shot slammed harmlessly into the ceiling, sending plastic and insulate flying. Fully alert but now completely unable to move, she landed hard on her back.

As she stared helplessly upward a figure came into view. One hand scratching at the back of his head, her elderly assailant gazed down at her speculatively. There was blood on the front of his torn shirt where her earlier shots had struck home, but otherwise he seemed none the worse for wear for having taken two direct hits to the torso. He was so close. All she had to do to finish him off was incline the muzzle of the pistol still gripped in both rubbery limbs slightly upward and depress the trigger with the tip of one tentacle. But though they held tightly to the weapon her cephalopodian limbs would not respond.

Bending over her the old man studied her face. He did not appear especially angry nor was he breathing hard. He circumvented his inability to pry the multiple coils of her locked tentacle tips off her gun by sliding a concealed blade from the left side of his left hand and simply sawing them off above where they gripped. Quivering like dying snakes, the bleeding ends continued to cling to the weapon even after they had been severed from her body. He tossed the mess aside and looked back down at her.

"You are externally paralyzed," he informed her unnecessarily. "You cannot even close your eyes." She looked on in horror as a small aerohypo emerged from the end of another of his fingers. "I am going to give you a small localized dose of the antidote. In addition to your heart and lungs, which for the moment continue to function, this will enable you to move anything from the neck up. You'll be able to blink and moisten your eyes, to move your tongue, and to talk. If you tell me what I want to know I'll give you enough of the antidote to allow you to recover fully within five minutes. It's a very unique toxin. The ability of the natural world to find ways to kill is still superior to that of melded man."

"What . . . ?" Her tongue and lips felt thick, as if they had been coated with liquid rubber. Both were still far from functioning perfectly, and coordination was an increasing problem. "What do you want . . . ?"

"The one word. You say you remember seeing one word repeated inside the sangoma's box projection before you fled her establishment. I paid you for it. A lot for one word. You can keep the subsist."

"You'll—you'll give me—the antidote?" Breathing was growing increasingly difficult. She feared she was on the verge of swallowing and choking on her own tongue.

"Of course." He looked up and to his right. The two bouncers were drawing near, having forced their way through most of the remaining crowd. "Quickly, please."

She told him. He frowned.

"Are you certain?"

"That was all I—saw. From the file. And like I told you, I saw it—several times. Enough so that despite everything, it stayed with me."

He nodded. "Very well. I believe you. I also need to know who you were working for. Who hired you and your deceased friend and the incompetent woman Chelowich?"

Capable of movement, her eyes met his eyes. "That was not—part of the agreement."

He started to rise. "We can renegotiate—if you wish to take the time."

"No, no." Her eyes widened. "It was the Yeoh Triad!"

He nodded thoughtfully. "Unpleasant people. Very persistent, few scruples. Knowing of their interest now adds urgency to my undertaking." For the first time since he had presented himself at her table he gave her an honest smile. "Pun is intended."

Trembling inside, she stared up at him. Her chest was starting to hurt, as if one heavy weight after another was being layered onto her sternum. Despite the paralysis it felt as if little needles were being inserted into her lower throat. Needles with legs that were crawling upward. "The antidote!"

He straightened. "I'm terribly sorry. I seem to have forgotten to bring some. In my profession I don't have much use for antidotes. You see, as far as my employers are concerned, I am the antidote. To foolish interlopers like yourself."

Stepping over her immobile body he started toward the entrance, heading straight toward the approaching lods. She tried to scream after him, her tentacles and their bleeding amputated ends lying like expired anacondas against the floor.

"You—promised! You . . . !"

He glanced back at the helpless figure that was part octopus but still mostly woman. "Don't worry. The toxin is still spreading through the rest of your body. It won't hurt when it reaches your heart. Unless it begins to affect your lungs first. That might be painful." Turning away he ignored her increasingly frantic mix of curses and screams.

Finally he could relax. After missing his quarry in Florida and then in Sanbona he would no longer have to stress himself to track down the thieving doctor and her pathetic Meld companion. Because he knew where they were going. In one word, the Yeoh Triad's surviving (for another moment or two, anyway) hireling had told him so.

"Namib," she had said.

Surprising and unexpected as it had been to hear, the one word was enough to make the remainder of his task easy. He could now take his time.

What they were attempting was impossible, of course, but if he had learned one thing about his targets it was that their resolve far exceeded their common sense. It was admirable, if self-defeating. He would react accordingly.

Namib. He shook his head. The world was full of crazy people. He knew this to be so because in his career he had met far more than his fair share. Prior encounters notwithstanding, Dr. Ingrid Seastrom and the man who called himself Whispr had to be the oddest as well as the most determined pair of fools he had ever dealt with. All because of a little storage thread that his employers desperately wanted returned.

Not for the first time he found himself wondering what was on it. Then he released his curiosity like a little boy letting go of a kite. Someone who had mastered his particular skill-set labored daily under a constant cloud of concern. There was no need to add to it by wondering about matters that did not concern him.

His path blocked, he halted.

The two bouncer lods were now directly in front of him. Each was enormous, their eyes almost disappearing into the flesh of their engorged faces, marbles sinking in pudding. Even their cheeks were muscled. They looked like overstuffed baby toys. If either of them got a solid grip on him they could pop him like a grape.

"I'm leaving now, gentlemen. My preference is to do so quietly."

Displaying natural oriental features, the older of the two lods would have made a fine Buddha stand-in had he not been employed to subdue mayhem on a nightly basis. The figure confronting him in the now nearly vacant club was small, elderly, and deceptively self-confident. Looking past the patron's patient, almost grandfatherly visage, the bouncer's gaze rose to take in the overturned fixtures, the sliced and diced blond horse Meld, and the utterly motionless tentacle woman. A glance to his left showed a wide trail of blood leading to where a second horseman had collapsed on the floor only meters from an emergency exit. As if trying to escape the claustrophobia of his gut, entrails dribbled out between the Meld's spread fingers.

The two bouncers exchanged a look. Wordlessly they stepped aside, two mountains giving way in recognition of reality. Without glancing to either side, Molé took his leave through the valley between. Both lods tracked him with their eyes until he, like the rest of the evening's shaken clientele, had funneled out through the main entrance.

"He looked awfully old," declared the younger Meld.

"No," insisted his superior. "Not old. Experienced. The two ain't always the same." Turning back to the room that was still under assault by waves of numbing contemporary music he waved a thick arm. "Let's get this mess cleaned up."

Within the hour the House of Nasty was back in business as if nothing untoward had ever occurred within its unhallowed walls.

5

Ingrid woke up fast when Whispr screamed. It was a piercing, shocked sound the likes of which she had not heard before. In the course of their association her companion had done plenty of shouting, but this was the first time she had ever sensed true terror in his voice. Naked fear reverberated around inside his throat like a ball bearing caught in a pipe.

Sitting up sharply she looked to her left. A hasty glance at his communicator, which had been placed on the ground between them, indicated that it was almost two in the morning. Feeling that lightning (or in this case flood) was unlikely to strike twice within the same week, and taking their usual care to conceal their heat signatures from possible passing SICK searcher drones, they had sought shelter at the bottom of a sandy dry creek bed beneath another jutting sandstone overhang. With no clouds in evidence overhead or hovering ominously above the mountains off to the east they felt that a repeat of the flash flood they had survived earlier was unlikely.

Then what had prompted Whispr's ear-vibrating screech?

"What is it, what's wrong?"

Having shot from beneath his thin but warming cover he was now standing stock-straight in the center of the ravine. Moonlight unadulterated by haze or atmospheric pollution of any kind cast the impossibly slender Meld as a character out of Sleepy Hollow. Shaking visibly he raised a stick arm and pointed.

"Ghost! It's a ghost!"

He was pointing at her.

Dropping her gaze to the front of her own blanket she saw nothing. Then movement, intermittent and rapid, caught her eye. Whatever had awakened her companion was making its way across her covered ankles. Barely visible in the reduced light, its outline confused her at first. Then she identified it, and having identified it, understood the reason for her companion's panic. Having done far more reading about their intended destination than Whispr, she was able to recognize the intruder for what it was, and promptly relaxed. But not entirely.

The dancing white lady spider was poisonous, and it certainly was as *pale* as a ghost, but it was not aggressive. Having migrated north from South America, far more dangerous arachnids now infested the lowlands of her home county in southeastern North America. Fascinated, she tracked the spider's pallid progress until it disappeared into the depths of the overhang. A nocturnal hunter, it was unlikely to retrace its steps and trouble them again. Turning, she smiled reassuringly at her still trembling associate.

"It's just a white spider. It won't bother you." She snuggled back down beneath her cover. "Go back to sleep."

He continued to hesitate. After several minutes of hard staring during which he failed to pick out the fast-moving and now vanished arachnid's path he finally returned to his sleeping pad and with considerable reluctance slowly slid back down into a prone position.

"Easy for you to say. It didn't go tiptoeing across *your* face. What if it had been something more dangerous?"

"Then *I* would have screamed." She rolled over onto her side. "I've seen a lot worse on a biosurge's table."

Whispr was muttering to himself. "White spiders. Black mambas. What's next—green scorpions?"

She did not reply. Muffled in a dearth of sympathy, he closed his eyes and once more bemoaned his situation. Why was he here, halfway around the planet, trudging through open desert in expectation of imminent demise when he could be back home in Savannah, riffling tourists and sharing tall tales and short toddies with his friends?

The answer had not changed any more than had the question. Because "back home" offered no prospects, no future, and no friends. Because back home the cops were looking for him. Because he had chosen to risk all for a chance to find the pot of gold at the end of a rainbow that probably terminated in hell. And because he had grown far, far too fond of a Natural woman who was so beyond his station that his train never even stopped there.

Every breath of wind caused him to open his eyes sharply. Every imagined touch, contact, brush, and crawling sensation made him look down or flutter his covering. It was the middle of night-morning and he was never going to go back to sleep. Not pills, not singsong, not anything was going to erase the tickling memory of the ghostly scuttling shape that had forged a methodical path across the angular topography of his face. He shuddered at the remembrance.

Ten minutes later he was sound asleep.

WHEN AGAIN HE FELT scratching sensations he held himself still. Blinking, he noted that the sun was almost up. This time he wouldn't panic. This time he would not scream, no matter if a hunting leopard was pawing at his hip. Whatever the cause, he

realized quickly that it was having more impact than the comparatively delicate touch of the dancing lady spider. As he grew more and more awake he realized that someone was trying to tie his hands behind his back.

They had been jumped by wildlife of a different kind.

Struggling, he saw that Ingrid was lying nearby on top of her bedding instead of beneath it. She had been bound at ankles and wrists and padded tape had been slapped over her mouth. Her wide eyes were eloquent with fear. Still trying to wrestle with his unseen assailant a single horrifying thought crossed Whispr's mind and chilled his blood.

Molé had found them.

If the elderly assassin succeeded in binding him as well then he and the doctor were both dead. The only difference from falling off a cliff was that if they were suitably restrained Molé would take his time with them. That would be very, very bad. The assassin was serious evil personified. Whispr knew he had to fight back, had to get free. But though much stronger than he appeared to others he proved no match for the hands that were securing his arms. Even as he fought he was thinking that the parameters of the desperate struggle made no sense. Yes, Molé was strong and tough. But he was not big. The sheer weight pressing down on Whispr suggested someone far more substantial than the elderly killer they had encountered in South Florida.

Twisting his body as he tried to free a hand, he finally glimpsed his attacker. It was not Molé. Nor was it a representative of company security.

Satisfied with his handiwork, the panting freewalker straightened and stepped back from his prisoners. Enough light now penetrated the arroyo to reveal the unmistakable features of the Meld who had sought engagement as a guide as Whispr and Ingrid had been leaving Orangemund. The fleshy winglike water storage sac

attached to his back sloshed audibly as he turned to check on her. Whispr used the lull to anxiously search the ravine in both directions. Unless others were concealing themselves farther down the gully or up top, their attacker was alone.

"Been following you ever since you left town." Quaffer's gaze flicked back and forth between the two bound figures. "Thought I might've lost you in the flood. Glad you made it out."

"Your concern is touching." Whispr continued to fight with the plastic loop that had been used to secure his wrists behind him.

Off to one side Ingrid had managed to struggle into a sitting position. The tape having finally slipped away from her lips, she glared at their captor.

"What do you want, Quaffer? Are you planning on selling us to SICK?"

The manta-backed Meld looked shocked. "Hell no! I don't want any more dealings with the company than you do." He indicated their surroundings. "If they find me here they won't have to make any deals. They'll just shoot me. And you too, of course. But you are not foolish people—at least, not entirely foolish—and I am sure you already know that." He leaned toward her, the water sac that was part of his back shifting fluidly.

"I don't want to hurt you. As I said back at town, I want to help you."

Jerking his head toward his left shoulder, Whispr gestured with his chin. "How about helping us out of these ties?"

The guide spoke without looking in his direction. "Certainly, stick-man. I will be pleased to do so. But not just yet." The multiple overlapping folds of his forehead slid toward Ingrid so severely that she marveled they didn't slide off his bald skull. "First we must come to an agreement. I want a share."

Whispr looked away, rolled his eyes, and said nothing. "A share of what?" Ingrid inquired blankly.

The tiny deep-set eyes glittered in the brightening morning light. "Don't play the stupid with me, woman. The same thing we discussed on the dirt outside Orangemund. No more games, no more lies." He waved at their surroundings. "Such things are meaningless out here. In the Namib only the truth survives. This is the Sperrgebeit. A company searcher could come by at any minute and we will all be as good as dead. But with my help you will survive. And with your help all this difficulty and suffering will be made worthwhile."

"That still doesn't tell me what you want from us," she protested.

He sounded honestly bemused. "I cannot figure out if you are strong or stupid. Myself, I think, inclines to the latter." His voice rose. "A share of your diggings, of course. In return for my guidance and protection." A wide grin spread across the almost hairless face. "It will be worth your while to engage me."

"Diggings?" Torn between fear and confusion, Whispr's expression was as twisted as his tone. "You mean diamonds?"

"No," the much bigger man responded dryly. "I mean cattle droppings. Of course I mean diamonds. There is nothing else in the Sperrgebeit worth digging."

Lying bound on the ground Whispr started to chuckle. His characteristic straight-faced laugh only served to infuriate their captor, but the slender Meld couldn't help himself. Having this water-back idiot confront them outside Orangemund with such a ridiculous challenge had been unsettling. Finding that he had trailed them all the way out into the emptiness of the Namib on the basis of the same misguided premise was irresistibly hilarious.

Quaffer found it less than amusing. Approaching the prone captive he drew back his right foot. "Shut up! Shut up or I'll kick your head in!"

Preceding his response with a hurried cough, Whispr swapped

hilarity for dead seriousness. "Listen to me, freewalker. I'm a poor streetie-sweetie from urban Namerica. The only diamonds I've ever seen are the ones locked up in arcades behind heavy security, secured in museums with even stronger security, or bouncing on the bodies of the rich who are too well protected for a street scavenger like myself to even think of riffling. Stones that are flashed by lesser citizens I don't try to apprehend because it takes an expert with specialized techrap to tell a real stone from a fake. I learned that early on. Hellup, these days stealing stones pays less than stealing bones. There's a market for morrow marrow because you can't fake genuine organics. A rock, on the other hand, is just a rock. Easy enough to synthesize. I expect there are always those willing to pay for guaranteed real, though, or there'd be no mining here."

The guide listened to this so stolidly that Whispr was unable to tell if his logic had made any headway. At least the freewalker's foot descended without making contact with the slender man's spine. Such hesitation suggested that perhaps a word or two had penetrated the solid node balanced atop of the man's neck.

Sensing vacillation on the part of their captor, Ingrid hastened to chime in.

"Whispr's telling the truth, Quaffer. We're not here after diamonds. We don't know anything about diamonds. I don't even own any diamonds myself." She hesitated. "We can't give you shares in a nonexistent mine."

The big man mulled over his captives' words. Both Meld and Natural had spoken without being pressured to do so. Their expressions were earnest, their voices sincere. And yet, and yet . . .

"If you are not after diamonds," he said slowly, "then *what* are you doing in the Sperrgebeit?"

Whispr was quick to jump on the guide's indecision. "We told you, back outside Orangemund. We're scientists and we've come out here to . . ."

Suddenly angry all over again, Quaffer glared down at him, his fury more a product of frustration than antagonism. "Don't tell me you risk your lives to come to this place in search of wildlife! Don't insult my intelligence again!" The foot drew back, farther this time. Whispr closed his eyes and waited for the blow.

"All right, I'll tell you! Don't hurt him!"

Both the man on the ground and the Meld standing over him turned in Ingrid's direction. The restraining plastic band digging into her wrists, she implored their captor with her eyes.

"I'll tell you the truth. But it isn't what you want to hear."

"Try me." Lowering his booted foot for a second time, Quaffer stared at her out of eager, beady eyes.

"Don't do it, doc! Don't tell . . . *ummphh!*"

Aimed at Whispr's stomach instead of his head the forceful kick did no permanent damage. But it did shut him up. Holding his boot in reserve, the freewalker nodded tersely at Ingrid.

"Go on—talk."

"You're right. We're not here to look at wildlife."

Quaffer smiled contentedly. "Of course you're not. Now tell me something I don't know."

As best her restricted circumstances permitted, she nodded toward the gasping Whispr. "My friend is my assistant, and I am a scientist. A practical one." She took a deep breath. "We hope to sneak into a SICK research facility located at Nerens."

Recovering from the punt to the gut, Whispr's eyes grew wide. Had his intellectually brilliant but socially naïve companion finally gone over the edge? Now all their captor had to do was call SICK security and turn them in. No doubt there was some kind of standing award for those who exposed intruders into the Forbidden Zone. Except . . .

If Quaffer notified the company of their intrusion he would also have to explain what *he* was doing in the Sperrgebeit. They might let him off, they might pay him a reward—or they might execute him along with those he had exposed. Just to ensure everything remained nice and clean and that once back in Orangemund the wayward guide did not reveal to others of his ilk the safest route inland. No one would question the company's actions in such a case. Their ruthlessness and methods were long-established and well known. Certainly such an extreme response would be unfair to the guide. Satisfaction carried to the grave, however, tends to wither as fast as flesh.

To his credit the freewalker Meld did not reject Ingrid's explanation out of hand. He ruminated quietly for several moments. Then he walked deliberately over to the doctor until he was standing next to her recumbent form.

"I give you credit, woman. That is the most outrageous pretext for risking one's life in the Namib I have ever heard. It is so outrageous that I could almost credit it being true. Almost." He leaned over her, his partially depleted water sac sloshing against his spine and expanded supporting ribs. "Why in the name of Mandela's mandala would you even think of trying to sneak into Nerens? Unauthorized entry into the Sperrgebeit means almost certain death. Attempting to infiltrate Nerens removes the 'almost.' Explain yourself to me, pretty woman!"

Gazing up at him out of recently color-maniped eyes, she was quietly defiant. "You don't need to know."

With his insides churning Whispr waited for the inevitable heavy-toed kick to strike his companion. That it did not was testimony to a combination of Quaffer's uncertainty and his astonishment at being openly challenged by the helpless woman lying at his feet. His reaction, when it came, was unexpected.

He laughed. Out of amazement, and out of a perverse admiration.

"I was wrong. You are not smart, woman. You are crazy!" He

looked over at the anxious Whispr. "And whether you are following or leading, stick-man, you are crazy for being with her!" Lowering his voice he knelt on one knee to bring his face closer to that of his captive.

"Listen to me, red-haired lady. Listen close, listen good. *Nobody gets into Nerens unless they are authorized by the company.* Nobody! People have tried. If you live in Orangemund and you pay attention, you learn that anyone who tries to do so ends up dead or worse." He was nodding as much to himself as at her. "Yes, there are worse things than death." Rising, he placed his hands on his hips and shook himself, adjusting the water in the skin sac as easily as a Natural would reposition a backpack. "I have had enough lies. It is getting warm and I am getting tired. No more lies. No more jokes." He lifted his right foot. But this time he did not draw back his leg to deliver a kick. Instead, he slowly lowered the sandboot until it was resting on Ingrid's upturned nose. A great deal of crushing, shattering weight lay behind the deeply scored sole.

"Where . . . are . . . the diamonds? Where is the mine, or the field, or the alluvial deposit?" His foot descended slightly. Unable to turn away, she felt the pressure. Her sinuses began to scream. As a doctor she knew in detail the succession of physiological events that would follow if he allowed all his mass to follow his foot. The crunching noise and the subsequent copious blood would be the least of it. More worrisome would be the direction the numerous bone fragments would take as they spread throughout her . . .

The boot wavered, moving slightly back and forth, and then slid forward off her face to land in the sand. He was straddling her now and swaying slightly. As he turned he reached for the pistol that was attached to his belt. His hand and fingers seemed to freeze. Hardly daring to breathe, she squinted up at him.

Something was sticking out of the side of his neck. Several

somethings. They looked like green needles. As she stared, another struck him in one fold of his ridged forehead. Reaching up, he plucked it free and gaped at it with a confusion of shock and wonderment. His eyes rose; searching, scanning. Another of the green needles penetrated the left one, just below the pupil.

Screaming and clawing at his face, he stumbled backward and tripped over the body beneath him. She was grateful that he landed nearby and not on top of her. As he rolled in pain and dug desperately at his punctured cornea a hail of pale green needles peppered his body. Water began to seep from his back sac where they pierced the aqueous manip. Soon he stopped screaming and stopped digging. More moments passed before he stopped for the last time.

As Ingrid lay on the ground breathing hard, a small scrabbling noise drew her attention away from the body of the guide. Squinting against the still rising sun she was able to make out shapes gathering along the upper edge of the ravine. More and more appeared until there were several dozen of the upright figures staring silently downward. Each carried a hollow reed that had been strengthened with treatment from vegetable resins and a quiver full of needles slung across its back. A few wore small pouches slung over one shoulder or the other. Their hair ranged from brown to gray and on to white, but their eyes were universally black. None stood much taller than the other.

None stood much taller than a foot.

She was dreaming, Ingrid told herself. That had to be it. There was no other reasonable explanation. On the other hand their tormentor was dead. The freewalker Quaffer lay nearby within arm's length, motionless and studded with green needles. Moments ago he had been alive and delivering very real threats. Now he was unmoving and harmless. The indisputable cause of his condition stood lining the rim of the ravine and staring down at her.

A glance showed that Whispr was equally mesmerized. But despite the belligerent guide's evident demise her friend was not as sanguine about their prospects as was his companion. The creatures had killed Quaffer. They could with minimal effort kill him and his equally helpless companion.

They began to chitter among themselves. Then one that was slightly bigger than his companions descended into the arroyo. Small clawed feet effortlessly found footholds where a human would simply have fallen back to the bottom. As it approached Ingrid she lay perfectly still, not wanting to do anything to alarm it. Not that she could do much with her hands bound behind her and her ankles locked together by plastic strips.

The slender mammal performed a quick circumnavigation of the doctor, staring and sniffing, while its companions watched intently from above. Scrambling up onto her chest it rose up on its hind legs and stood as comfortably as any biped while it studied her face. The black nose at the tip of its long snout quivered. When it yawned she had a glimpse of small but very sharp teeth.

Whispr could stand it no longer. "What is it?" His gaze swept the line of armed figures that dominated the rim of the little canyon, their eyes intent on the two bound shapes below. There were more than thirty of them now, each grasping a miniature blowgun. "What are these things?"

Her attention fixed on the face of the furry being standing on her chest, Ingrid swallowed before replying. "I've seen nature vits of them. I think they're meerkats."

A response was immediately forthcoming—but not from any source she would have anticipated. It arose in the form of an intelligible squeaking from the enchanting lightweight whose strong supportive tail was presently aligned with her cleavage. Each word was enunciated with the painstaking care reflective of the effort that had gone into forming it. At the same time sunlight glinted off the bits of crudely clipped nanocable that emerged from the back of the diminutive speaker's skull. The trailing wires imparted a faintly Rastafarian look.

"Yes—meerkat."

6

"They can talk!" So flabbergasted was Whispr that for a moment he forgot he was bound and incapable of more than the slightest movement. "Talking weasels—here!"

The subject of his amazement turned to look at him. "Why not—here?" The tiny paw not clutching the blowgun gestured upward. "I, called Nyala, can talk. Other friends—cannot."

Hopping down off Ingrid's chest the meerkat landed on all fours and scurried over to the mountainous body of the big freewalker. As she trotted across the sandy bottom of the ravine Ingrid could see that the quiver on her back was filled with more of the minute needles that feathered the corpse. Approaching with caution, the creature who called herself Nyala sniffed gingerly of the body. Jumping onto the chest she quickly explored the dead guide's length from ribbed forehead to booted feet. Coming back around the torso she paused beside an open hand, opened her jaws, and sank needlelike teeth into the extended thumb. Whispr winced as blood leaked. The test was conclusive.

Quaffer was not faking.

Returning to Ingrid's side the meerkat leader looked up and let loose a stream of chatter. Immediately the flanks of the gully filled with members of her mob who easily handled walls so sheer that they would have defeated any human's efforts to climb out. Swarming over Whispr and Ingrid they began chewing carefully and energetically. While a fascinated Ingrid observed the frenetic activity in silence, it moved her companion to be considerably more vocal.

"That's it . . . get the ones on my ankles . . . hey, that's a finger, not a strap . . . !"

Within moments they found themselves free to sit up. While the rest of the mob retreated to a safe distance the meerkat who called herself Nyala remained close to Ingrid, watching as the human rubbed her wrists to restore circulation. Blood flowing once again and their nemesis from Orangemund reduced to a harmless mass of dead flesh off to one side, she found herself in solemn conversation with the desert-dwelling mammal. The meerkat's habit of standing on two legs while propping itself up with its tail gave it the incongruous appearance of a small, sunken-eyed, sharp-snouted primate. Recollection of her elemental zoology reminded her that it was not a primate but a member of the mongoose family. She did not wonder at its ability to speak: only at its comparative fluency.

Plainly, it had been expertly magified.

Animal magification was a long-established analog of human melding. Though it was only supposed to be applied to fully domesticated animals or those that had been specifically bred for the purpose, exotic animorph pets were widely available on the black market. Parrots that could sing as well as speak were all but ubiquitous. Cats that could respond to verbal commands with purring answers were a perennial holiday gift. Even some of the higher reptiles like the iguana responded well to advanced magification. And of course everyone knew of the famous and long-established Ciudad Simiano Reserva in Central America that was home to the descendants of true primates who had been illegally magified so that they possessed actual intelligence.

But the mongoose was no primate. Yet it displayed an intelligence level on a par with several of the old-world monkeys. Ingrid continued to rub at her left wrist.

"Why did you come to our aid? Where have you come from? How—how are you able to speak with intelligence?"

"Many questions." Leaning back on her tail, Nyala checked the condition of her mob before replying. "Must go slow. Thinking makes—head hurt."

Whispr let out a grunt. "Never thought I'd have something in common with a weasel."

"They're not weasels, Whispr," an irritated Ingrid corrected him. "They're mongooses."

"I'll tell you what they are." Sitting on the sand he turned to face the nearest line of dark-eyed saviors. The movement caused a couple of blowguns to be raised part way in his direction. "They're damn welcome, that's what they are." He eyed his left wrist. "I didn't think anything had teeth sharp enough to bite through a restraint band." Swiveling on his skinny backside he directed his gaze at the meerkat standing beside Ingrid. "Why *did* you help us out, furball?"

On the verge of responding, Nyala was momentarily distracted by the appearance of a small beetle that was attempting to make its way between her and the female human. Dropping to all fours she darted directly at it, snapped it up in her jaws, chewed briefly, and swallowed. Neither Ingrid nor Whispr was unsettled by the display. With the advent of worldwide food shortages, insects and their kin had become a major protein source for humankind. In a turnabout from thousands of years of history locust swarms were now looked forward to with eager anticipation by large segments of the planet's population. Having finished her unexpected snack, the meerkat Nyala explained.

"Come—from Bethlehem."

Their pint-sized rescuers were not through delivering shocks, Ingrid realized. "I can't believe that. Bethlehem? All this way? You crossed the whole continent? And if you came from there why do you speak general English and not . . . ?"

Having responded more judiciously to the claim, Whispr had crawled to his pack and extracted his communicator. To conserve its remaining power, in lieu of an energy-hungry projection he opted to study the small screen directly. When he found what he was looking for, he interrupted.

"They may be smart," he explained, "but they're not super-weasels. They can't defy distance. Turns out there's a Bethlehem in South Africa." Lifting his eyes from the device he gazed admiringly at the row of curious faces staring back at him. "Still, it must have been a helluva hike from there to here."

Nyala gestured at her companions. "Some run, some steal ride on machines. Namib our home, ever. Taken as infant cubs were we. Raised and . . ." She struggled to form the words for which she was searching, finally surrendered and settled for a single one. It was more than adequately expressive.

"Experiment," she finished helplessly.

Ingrid nodded understandingly. It was just such illegal intelligence-enhancing gengineering that had produced the ancestors of the apes of Ciudad Simiano. Nyala's limited ability to speak and think proved that such prohibited research was still being carried out. She gestured diplomatically in the direction of the alert and watchful mob that was arraigned around their leader. Bored by the hard-to-understand human chatter, a couple of them were taking tentative nibbles of the dead Quaffer's fingers.

"But the others can't talk?"

Proving that she had absorbed more than just minimal speech, Nyala responded with a negative shake of her head. "All can think. Some experiments more effective than others. Some others . . ." Her little voice trailed away. Ingrid kept very quiet. Then the meerkat straightened. "Others not have successful layright—larynx manip. Only me." In a gesture Ingrid found inexpressibly touching, the meerkat tilted her head forward until she could place a small black paw between her ears. "One other thing also make difference. Experiment people say I—genius."

Whispr nodded understandingly. "So because of that this, uh, tribe, they chose you to be their leader?"

"Meerkat mob leader always a female," she snapped back at him. "I chosen because I best to help others survive. Not because can think far and speak human. This is Namib home. More useful here is meerkat chatter than human growling."

"I could almost agree with you," Ingrid murmured fervently. "You still haven't said why you helped us."

"Remember me being many times tied. Remember fighting back. Remember being—hurt." Dropping to all fours Nyala padded over to Ingrid, stood up, and put a paw on the back of the doctor's hand. It was tiny and soft. Small bright black eyes stared deep into Ingrid's own. "Tying against will is wrong." She glanced toward the lump of the freewalker's body. "Hurt others is wrong. And—is important for species survival dominant females stick together."

Ingrid found herself starting to choke up. Whispr was encumbered by no such emotional upwelling.

"Dominant fem . . . ?" He shrugged. "Whatever." Raising a hand, he pointed toward Quaffer's body. "I'm guessing you punctured the subgrub with about fifty or sixty of those little needles. Even though the biggest of them is only maybe a couple of centimeters long, the freewalker dropped like a friend of mine who once ohdeed on redruzz."

Slipping her paw off Ingrid's hand Nyala turned toward the male human. "Needles are Codon spines dipped in scorpion venom. Meerkats eat scorpions. Poison is—strong, but we are immune."

Whispr was nodding. "Okay. Now I know why he went down. Maybe you could let us have a few of those spines? They'd come in real useful in a close quarter fight and . . ."

"No!" Nyala dropped to all fours and scurried away from him. "Humans have enough things to hurt already." She looked back up at Ingrid. "We make mistake in saving you?"

"No—no, you didn't, and we're more grateful than we can say." Ingrid glared across at her companion. Perceptive enough to realize that he had stepped on some very small toes, this time Whispr offered no comment. "My friend—it's just that there are so many dangers out here in the Namib and he likes to be prepared for anything."

Standing up, Nyala indicated the freewalker's carcass. "That is worst kind danger anywhere everyplace, and Namib is mostly safe from it. You stay in Namib, you avoid that kind worst danger."

Ingrid smiled appreciatively. "If that's an invitation, thank you. But we can't stay. We have things to do. Places to go."

"Death to meet," Whispr muttered, breaking his brief silence.

Ingrid glared at him again, but Nyala was not disturbed. "We all have death to meet. Meerkat by cobra or leopard or jackal or bird. Human by gun or bomb or evil words. I prefer some day be taken by eagle. Is honest death and one creature feed another. When humans kill each other, no animal benefits from it—not even humans. You are wasters of the world."

Ingrid felt compelled to demur. "I recycle religiously."

"Other things. Not self. Only artificial doings, to make yourself feel better." Nyala turned and barked something to her mob. "We will help you. We claim kill."

As the two travelers looked on, the mob swarmed over Quaffer's body and bent to work digging into a raised spot on one side of the soft ravine bed. Sand flew high and far enough to force Ingrid and Whispr to turn their heads away and shield their eyes with their hands. Occasional quick glimpses revealed what the meerkats were up to: they were preparing to bury the body.

"This—this isn't necessary," Ingrid told Nyala. "The desert scavengers will take care of him."

"We desert scavengers, too," the meerkat leader informed her. "We—recycle. Not for meat, but for body's water. All fluid precious here."

Ingrid had a vision of a dozen meerkats taking bites out of the sand-covered corpse's back and lapping up the outflow from the fleshy maniped water sac. The image rendered Nyala and her companions somewhat less cuddly.

"I give you gift of participating. You may share," the meerkat declared.

"Thanks." Ingrid smiled wanly. "We have water with us, we know the location of the water holes ahead of us, and in an emergency we have devices that can pull water from the air."

Nyala stared at her. The energy being displayed by her mob was truly prodigious. Already Quaffer was disappearing beneath a blizzard of expertly flung sand and soil.

"So much smart. So much stupid." Turning away from the human, the meerkat matron scampered over to the guide's corpse to supervise the final bits of the ongoing burial.

Normally, Nyala told Ingrid as evening descended, meerkats obtained all the moisture they need from the assortment of snakes, lizards, insects, arachnids, and the occasional small bird they consumed. But when other liquids became accessible they did not hesitate to avail themselves of the source. The stored water that flowed from the maniped back of the dead freewalker must have struck them as surprising as the flash flood did the two human visitors days earlier.

Having sipped from the fleshy storage sac of the nearly buried guide until their bellies bulged, they sprawled themselves out on the sand like so many miniature intoxicated guards. As it grew darker the only sound in the sheltered ravine was the occasional lap-lap of a tiny tongue, like a butterfly tap-dancing, as another of the mob took one last drink of the precious fluid that was of no further use to the intruding desert Meld.

Normally Whispr tried to sleep as close to his companion as she would allow. Not this night. Finding semi-shelter beneath a partial overhang he rolled himself up in his blanket with his back pressed tightly against the rock wall. Though he was loathe to admit it, while the weasels or mongooses or rats or whatever they were had undeniably saved them from Quaffer's single-minded madness, he was more than a little mistrustful of the sharp-toothed little vampires. Anything that could bite through a restraint band could bite through a neck. The meerkats' partial demolition and rapid interment of the freewalker had done nothing to mitigate his wariness.

So he lay awake watching for the unheralded approach of small eyes in the darkness. The only advantage their eerie bipedal presence conferred was that he was so busy keeping an eye on them that he forgot all about the possible presence of far more noxious natives such as scorpions and dancing white lady spiders.

Perhaps naïvely, perhaps out of empathy, Ingrid felt no such concerns. In the lonely vastness of the Namib where the only human beings they had encountered since leaving Orangemund were a half-mad hermit and an even madder diamond hunter, the magified meerkats seemed more human than any of their recent contacts. While only the leader of the mob could speak, all of them were imbued with a depth of compassion that arose from having been ripped from their homes and families and transported to a far-off research facility where their brains and nervous systems could be experimented upon for the ultimate amusement of other mammals boasting bigger bodies and smaller souls. Where they made Whispr nervous, they fostered in Ingrid Seastrom only empathy and curiosity. The former was the doctor in her, the latter the scientist.

"What will you do now?" she asked Nyala by the glow of a small portable light. Standing in its shadows, the leader of the mob was picking her teeth with an unpoisoned Codon spine.

"What we have done since returning here from Bethlehem. Raise our families, play, eat, survive. What our kind has always done."

"You're not afraid those who were experimenting on you illegally will try to track you down and take you back?"

Nyala let out a rapid chittering sound. It might have been meerkat laughter. "None of us embedded. No trackers planted in us. There was—no need. We could not escape. And if we escape, where we go? Certainly not all way back here. Not all way back—to the Namib." Her tone grew darker. "It be easier for them collect innocent lives of others to destroy."

Lying wrapped in her blanket, her head resting on one hand, Ingrid studied the dominant female. "Doesn't that bother you?"

"Meerkats not like humans," Nyala told her. "We fight all time. For territory, for hunting rights, for best burrow-digging places."

"Sounds like humans to me," Whispr called out from his chosen sanctuary on the other side of the gully.

Nyala ignored him. "What happen to other meerkats not concern me. Only my mob concern me. My mob and my children. Pass on genes."

Ingrid considered thoughtfully. "I thought we were more alike than that, you and I."

"Warm blood not everything." In the most humanlike pose she had displayed since first putting in an appearance in the ravine, Nyala put her right paw over her heart. "What here is everything." She looked around. "Not good be caught out at night outside burrow. Too many eaters of meerkat."

"I'd think the presence of Whispr and myself would make anything smaller than a leopard hesitant to come close."

"Yes, is true." Nyala nodded agreement. "Human stink frighten off most everything. No burrows here. I go find patch of warm sand. I wish no moon to you, woman."

"My name is Ingrid."

"In-gred. Yes, Ingred. You sleep. Always good have nice sleep before sunrise. Maybe sun bring food, maybe sex, maybe fight. Maybe death."

THE HEAT WOKE HER. Something was wrong. Constantly adjusting to both the ambient external temperature and that of her body, the biothermosensitive blanket was supposed to keep her comfortable even in extreme conditions. Blinking in the darkness, as her eyes adjusted to the starlight she quickly saw the problem. And smiled to herself. Lying back down she told herself firmly that there was nothing she could do. She would just have to deal with the increased temperature.

Smothered beneath thirty snoring meerkats, she soon fell back into a deep, contented, and very warm sleep.

FOR THE DOCTOR FROM Savannah the following morning dawned crisp, clear, and—except for her mercurial Meld of a companion—alone.

Sitting up fast she first checked the opposite ends of the gulch before letting her gaze travel to the winding rim above. There was nothing. No piercing jet-black eyes, no quivering nostrils, no inquisitive stares returned her gaze. The only movement came from a speckled lizard poking its head out of a crack in the rocks. In the absence of warming sunshine it swiftly withdrew. Something large and black-winged soared past high overhead, checking to see if the two figures that had been slumbering on the sand were alive or dead. The reality of Ingrid's movements sent it soaring away disappointed.

Across the way Whispr was also starting to wake up. When he saw her sitting up and intently scanning their surroundings he struggled to shrug off the last vestiges of a sleep that clung to him like old cobwebs.

"What is it, doc? Something the matter?"

"They're gone." Disappointment as well as resignation colored her reply. "All of them."

Slipping free of his blanket Whispr rose to his feet and stretched, a human scarecrow pushing slow fists skyward. "The weasels—sorry, mongooses. They're gone?" Scratching himself, he performed his own morning inspection of the narrow gulch. All was quiet, still, and exactly as might be expected of such a tranquil scene—provided one ignored the recently raised mound of freshly excavated sand and dirt off to one side. As he began fiddling with his gear he noted that a hopeful Ingrid continued to eye the ravine's rim.

"You miss 'em, don't you?"

She nodded. "They were—charming. And that Nyala: certainly the most interesting illegal experiment I ever met."

He grunted as he pulled out a breakfast envelope and carefully added water from his pak. As the liquid reacted with the catalyst in the packaging material the dehydrated contents rapidly began to heat.

"Haven't made the acquaintance of any illegal experiments myself. Though I have met one or two Melds who should have been." He gestured with his quickly warming, expanding breakfast. "Aren't you hungry? Better eat something even if you're not. More walking today." He shook the bulging envelope gently, the better to mix and evenly heat the contents. "You'll need the energy. Never know in a place like this when a meal might be your last one."

Ignoring his characteristic pessimism she continued to scrutinize the rocky overhangs even as she prepared her own food. Sipping a mix of hot cereal, milk, sugar, and reconstituted berries, he sat and watched, unable to understand her fascination.

"Look," he finally said, "I know the little cat-rats saved our butts." For emphasis he nodded in the direction of the unprepossessing mound beneath which lay the body of the freewalker Quaffer. "But they're gone, and I for one don't miss 'em." He made a rude noise. "Sure they were heavily magified, but they were also too close to full wild and they had too many teeth. Not to mention their little nightymare poison darts."

Ingrid was shaking her own breakfast to life. "Well, I do miss them. I've never heard of a nonprimate being raised to true sentience, not even illegally. It would have been enthralling to get Nyala's perspective on so many things." She spoke wistfully. "Who knows? Maybe they could even have helped us get into Nerens."

At this Whispr smiled and began shaking his head. Her brows drew together as she challenged him.

"What? What'd I say?"

Setting his empty biodegradable food container aside he chuckled briefly before meeting her eyes. "Doc—Ingrid—you have more knowledge of science in your pretty little pinkie than I do in my whole besotted brain, but I have more in common with street folk." He gestured upward, toward the sand and gravel plain that was cracked by the ravine. "Those mere cats, they were kinda like little

subgrubs. A gang permanently on the run from the authorities."
His laughter faded. "Don't get me wrong: I'm thankful as hell their
leader decided to get all noble on us and vape the freewalker. It was
getting bad squeeze there for a few minutes and I don't like to think
what would've happened if they hadn't showed up. But spine-
tickling one Meld is one thing. Exposing themselves to the authorities, even private security such as SICK's, for a cause that
doesn't involve them, is more of a risk than your typical street snarks
are willing to take. Even," he concluded, "if the snarks in question
happen to hold a patent on cute."

Casual pondering of her companion's heartfelt observations left
a reluctant Ingrid no choice but to agree with his judicious assess-
ment of meerkat motivation. Despite all he and she had been
through together she was still not in a position to challenge the
wisdom of someone who held an advanced degree in the acumen
of the street. Downing the last of her liquid eggs Benedict, she set
the empty package aside and shouldered her pack. After adjusting
the straps she took a moment to ensure that the pressure-sensitive
inflatable pads were correctly positioned. Bending, she picked up
her wide-brimmed thermosensitive hat and nodded in his direction.

"All set. Let's go." She squinted skyward. "Nerens won't come
to us." A hand gestured up the gulch. "We keep on straight?"

Whispr checked their remaining communicator, glanced up,
checked it again. "It's something like ten k's to the next permanent
water hole. About half along this creek bed, the rest exposed up
top."

"Then we'd better get moving." Making a final adjustment to
her pack's position, she started past him.

"Hey, slow down, doc! You'll burn out before lunch." He hurried to catch up to her. "You're still having regrets about losing your

pets, aren't you? Don't think about it." He tried to lift her spirits. "Maybe we'll run into the mob again."

"Yeah, that's likely," she mumbled.

They hiked in silence for nearly an hour before he spoke up again. "This affection for the little critters, doc: it wouldn't have anything to do with you not having kids, would it?"

Hemmed in on both sides by layers of ancient sandstone she looked at him sharply, then shook her head. "We've spent a lot of time in each other's company, Whispr, but I swear there are times when I just can't figure you. Like right now I can't decide if you're being perceptive or just utterly ignorant of the meaning of the word 'tact.'"

Her pointed retort did not faze him in the slightest. Words never did. "You didn't answer my question."

"And because of your attitude, I'm not going to."

Lengthening her stride, she deliberately moved out ahead of him. He shrugged and maintained his pace, content to follow. Not that he really gave a damn one way or the other about how she might have answered. Then why had he asked the question? No wonder she baffled him.

There were too many times when he baffled himself.

UNLIKE THE BRIEF BUT intense deluge that had nearly drowned Ingrid in a previously negotiated ravine, the rising sand-storm announced itself visually but not audibly. More alert to the unexpected and blessed with better distance vision, it was Whispr who wondered aloud at the changing color of the horizon.

"If we were back in a big city in Namerica I'd say that was smog." The longer he gazed at the darkening phenomenon the deeper became his frown. "But there can't be any smog out here. There are no big cities. Hell, there aren't any cities. According to all the

maps and Ouspel's instructions there's nothing out here but Nowhere."

He looked over at his companion. Clad in loose-fitting desert
gear, Pollocked with dirt, and sweating profusely, she still roused
sensations in him that burned through protein better invested elsewhere. "So what is it?"

Shielding her eyes with one hand, Ingrid squinted into the distance. "Whatever the cause, it seems to be intensifying. Let me
have your monocular."

Halting beside her, he stood patiently while she dug through
his pack to find the single-lens magnifier. Peering through it, it took
only a moment for her to ascertain what was coming their way.

"Shit," she said concisely as she put the compact optical device
back in his pack.

Whispr was not shocked, but he was mildly surprised. Ever
since their first meeting the doctor's language had been decorous
tending to the excessively polite. Rough travel and hard experience
were wearing her down. To his level, he told himself. That realization ought to have pleased him. Perversely, it did not. Though the
passage of time was rendering her more approachable, he found to
his surprise that he preferred her on her pedestal.

"Sandstorm," she told him. "At least, that's what I think it is. I've
only ever seen a sandstorm in nature vits."

"Same here." He stared at the burgeoning yellow wall that was
approaching rapidly from the north. "Not something you see in
Savannah." He began searching their immediate surroundings.
"Guessing from the speed at which it's moving it should hit here
inside an hour. It's right in front of us, we can't outrun it, and we
can't go around it. We're gonna have to hunker down somewhere
and ride it out." He grunted. "Your cat-rats would probably just
shrug and wait it out in burrows. Feel like digging?"

She held up her hands. Physician's hands. Normally soft and sensitive, long days of difficult travel had turned them hard and tough. They were not miner's or road worker's hands, not yet. On the other hand (so to speak), digital decor like fingernail polish was a distant memory. Staring at her upraised fingers she saw that she needed a manicure. Her whole body needed a manicure.

The flat, sandy plain across which they had been walking offered little in the way of shelter. There were no trees; nothing taller than knee-high succulents. Both of them picked up the pace until they were almost jogging.

"Can we make it to the next ravine?" she asked anxiously. By this time the sky ahead had been subsumed in yellow grit. She could hear the approaching storm now; the faint howl of a meteorological golem. Abrasive grit driven by weeping winds was scouring the landscape. Sitting and waiting it out on flat ground would not be pleasant. Walking through it would be impossible. As she looked on it seemed to gain speed toward them; a smooth-faced rolling wall of unforgiving geological obfuscation.

"We can try," Whispr told her. He picked up the pace until he was running across the flat surface.

According to Ouspel's map they were very close to safety. They had made good time across the flats. Furthermore, the next concealing gully that spilled out of the foothills ran northwest. Besides offering shelter from the oncoming storm it would have the added benefit of bringing them closer to their goal. He found himself visualizing its sheltering walls. All they had to do was reach it, scramble down inside, and wait for the tempest to blow over. They could rest and regain their strength from the long hike and final dash across the plain. They could . . .

They didn't make it.

The outburst did not come upon them gradually, like a rainstorm. Scouting for the airborne sand that filled the body of the storm, zephyrs of increasing strength buffeted them as they frantically sought last-minute cover.

"Over here, doc!" A madly beckoning Whispr directed her toward a slight depression that was fronted by several smooth-surfaced boulders. A few scraggly Euphorbia formed a loose hedge around the depression. They had chosen the site to put down roots and propagate because water occasionally collected in the low spot, or perhaps was found deeper below the surface. It was not much of a kraal, but it was better than nothing. The truth of that determination brutally announced itself moments later.

The storm did not hit. It enveloped them, swallowed them, blinded Ingrid with such unexpected alacrity that she could barely make out Whispr's attenuated form even though he was only a few meters ahead of her.

With fine particles of grit stinging her face and threatening to damage her eyes, she stumbled forward. The lethal potential of a sandstorm, a danger that humans had been forced to deal with since the dawn of civilization, made no allowance for her acquired social graces or advanced education. She was in as much danger now as if she had been a veiled member of a camel caravan crossing the Sahara thousands of years ago. She found herself stumbling in near darkness, unable to hear, unable to see.

Where had Whispr gone? Where was the depression? Seconds earlier both had been right in front of her. Now she couldn't see a thing. If she opened her eyes all the way, the sand that was now screaming parallel to the ground threatened to blind her. If she turned her head away to protect them, she could not see where she was going. What she needed was something technologically regressive but highly appropriate for the conditions in which she now found herself: a scarf.

Holding her right arm in front of her face she staggered on.

Surely she should have stepped into the depression by now? If she wandered off in the wrong direction she would be lost in minutes. And what if Whispr was looking for her? Without any idea how long the storm might last, they could become permanently separated.

Shouting his name, she heard nothing. The roar of the storm overwhelmed her best efforts to make herself heard more than a foot or so from where she was standing. Since her own communicator was gone, if they did become separated he would not be able to find her.

How had people located one another in such desolate places before the advent of electronic tracking? Such ancient skills were not taught in today's urban environment. And most of their remaining equipment was with him. She had food and her waterpak, but how would she survive? Alone in the world's oldest desert, beset by ignorance and the inability to find her way, she would die a lonely death, her body picked at by scavengers, her friends and patients back home wondering how and where Dr. Ingrid Seastrom had vanished. She would never be found because no one would know where to search. It might be hundreds of years before curious travelers discovered her bones. Assuming that the desert hyenas left anything to be found. To her immense surprise, she started to cry. Again.

It was amazing how easily and copiously the tears spilled from her eyes. They flushed some of the grit that had accumulated there but otherwise didn't make her feel any better. Worst of all, she thought as she sobbed, her demise would all be for naught. She would not even have the comfort of learning the secret of the thread before she died. As for Whispr, despite his street survival skills he would probably perish as well. Of course with the thread gone, secreted on her person, there would be no reason for him to continue to Nerens. If he turned back immediately instead of trying to find her body he might have a slim chance of making it back to now distant Orangemund.

Unable to see where she was going, blinded by yellow instead of black, she tripped over something and went down.

"*Farko*, doc! Watch where you're going!"

She threw herself against him, heedless of whether she might have suffered an injury in the fall. A bigger woman would have been able to wrap her arms around his willowy melded form twice over. After a moment's hesitation he gently placed his own thinner but stronger arms around her and held her close. She continued to cry until she remembered where she was and what she was doing. Pulling away from him, she tried to hug the ground. The clump of boulders and the sturdy wind-whipped Euphorbia provided just enough of a windbreak to send a good deal, though not all, of the blowing sand flying over her head.

She was forced to wipe continuously at her sand-struck eyes. Her tears turned the accumulating grit to a kind of clenched particulate muck. As she periodically dug out the dirt she decided she didn't need a Q-tip—she needed a spoon. Eventually she remembered to apologize to her companion.

"I—I'm sorry I fell on you, Whispr. I couldn't see anything. I didn't even know if I was going in the right direction. I shouted, as loud as I could, but I guess you didn't hear me."

He had to raise his own voice to pump out an audible reply. "I can hardly hear you now, doc." Tilting his head to one side and raising up slightly on an elbow, he tried to see beyond the rocks. Ferociously whipping sand quickly drove him back under cover. "Still can't see anything, either." Reaching down, he removed his waterpak and took a long drink, careful not to spill a drop. He wiped his lips with the back of one forearm before resealing the container. "Might be here for a while."

"How long is awhile?" She lay prone next to him.

He sniffed and dug into his rapidly filling nose. "How should I know, doc? I don't know anything about sandstorms. Minutes, hours. Days." He nodded at the peculiar nearby plants. "Look at these guys. They might be hundreds of years old. Just sitting out here, nothing to see, nothing to do, hoping that in between storms like this their spines are deterrent enough to keep off the plant eaters." He shook his head. "I farking hate this country! A day in Savannah or Charleston is better than an eternity out here."

"Maybe not if you're a plant," she countered.

"Well, I wish I was one right now. One with deep roots." As he slid lower he let his gaze drift upward, blinking against the wind and sand and blowing gravel. "My mother—don't look at me like that, I had one—used to say that some good comes out of everything. Even though we're stuck here out on the flats we shouldn't have to worry about company searchers or patrols. Even machines will shy away from this kind of weather. Grit'll choke their intakes." He closed his eyes.

She peered at him in disbelief. "Don't tell me you're going to try to *sleep* through this?"

His eyelids fluttered but did not open. "I once slept through a free ten-band spatially multiamped technopulse concert in Jackson Park. This is nothing." He went quiet.

Having little else to say and no one to say it to, Ingrid tried to emulate her companion's sangfroid. She had only limited success.

7

"Goddamn storm!"

Volksmann wrestled with the controls as the floater lurched to port. Not an aircraft, it was unable to rise above the furious winds. He was in no position to object to the choice of transport since he was among those who had from the beginning vetoed the suggestion that an aircraft be used for the intrusion.

"You can't take a plane or a chopper into the Sperrgebeit," he had explained to his superiors in Guangzhou via closed satellite link. "SICK security would pick it up immediately. And ground transport will show up on their searcher drone sensors. The only thing that has a hope of working is a fast floater. Keep low to the ground but above it, get in fast and get out fast. And it's still going to be risky as hell."

"If a floater has a chance of getting in and getting out," Hsing Pa inquired reasonably from Triad headquarters, "then why are such attempts not made more often?"

"Because there's nothing to be gained from just getting in and getting out." Volksmann was patient with the older man. "You have to have a worthwhile reason for going in beyond being able to boast that you did so. Every such incursion I know of involved prospectors. A ten-minute visit isn't long enough to find and mine diamonds. It isn't even long enough to locate a site. Especially when eight minutes of it would have to be spent looking over your shoulder. But it's plenty of time to land, kill two people, take what they have, and leave."

Hsing considered. "Will you need that much time on-site?"

Volksmann had shrugged. "Five minutes. Another five as buffer."

The Triad operations chief nodded once. "Since we are not entirely sure what we are looking for, you should bring everything out. Including the bodies in case there is something of significance secreted within their persons."

"That's what I figured. I don't anticipate any problems." Volksmann had spoken with confidence.

He had not, however, anticipated having to navigate at night in the depths of a sandstorm.

They could have set the floater down and waited it out. But lingering in one place for any length of time might expose them to passing satellite coverage, or bring them to the attention of a drone. Now he had no choice. He and his team were committed.

Though they had been strapped into their seats for less than an hour, the five associates in the passenger compartment behind him were already grumbling like new Melds who were convinced they had overpaid for bad work. Releasing himself from his restraints Volkmann's second in command came forward, staggering as the floater pitched from side to side in the sand-shot slipstream. Dropping into the empty codriver's seat he gripped the armrests firmly and squinted through the cockpit's curving polycrylic windshield.

"How long we have to keep arguing with this bitch, Karl?"

Grim-faced, the squad leader kept his attention focused on the floater console's instrumentation. He had no choice, because he couldn't see a damn thing outside.

"If the last position the Triad's satellite buy-in gave for them is accurate we should be just about on top of them."

Rocking back and forth in his seat, Xiau grinned. "Hell, man, you set down on top of them and we won't even have to shoot! We'll just scrape 'em into a couple of body bags."

Volksmann shook his head tersely. "Personally I wouldn't have any problem squashing them, but we can't do that. We might bust whatever it is we're supposed to bring back."

"Any idea what that is? Must be something big serious for the Yeoh to risk sending a full squad into the Sperrgebeit."

"I don't have a glueclue, and you know better than to ask. You know the instructions. Bring them out alive if possible, dead if not, along with everything in their immediate vicinity that's not native, down to and including any bodily excretions." He made a rude sound. "But you're right about one thing: must be big serious."

A powerful gust caught the floater and slewed it to port. Volksmann cursed under his breath as he fought with the controls. Commentary of an equally colorful nature rose from the men and women seated in back.

One of the dash readouts spoke up, pleasant but insistent. The floater's driver growled.

"What's wrong?" Untrained to interpret the floater's sputtering commentary, Xiau had to rely on his boss for an explanation.

"Sand's getting through the filters. We don't have any choice now. We're going to have to set down, wait for the storm to let up, and do a manual clean-out. Forecasting can't predict for sure when this will stop." Volksmann glanced at another readout. "We're close—real close. Even with the delay we should be right on our target and up and out of here before morning. Back in good ol'

Alex Bay before sunrise. That's all that matters. That and picking up the two meats." He grunted. "We'll be fine as long as we don't hang around long enough to be visible in the 'Geit in the light."

Xiau nodded understandingly. "Me and the others, we didn't get a lot of jobbo detail. A twofold pickup and sitewipe is all we were told. Should we be looking for any trouble?"

Volksmann felt he had acquired sufficient control as the floater began to descend to spare a glance for his number two. "Targets are a street Meld, male, and a physician, female. The Zaniwars of Spring '49 this ain't."

Leaning back in his seat Xiau rode the bucking floater as it hit the ground, bounced once, and finally came to rest between low scrub-covered dunes. A smattering of sarcastic applause punctuated by a few choice expletives sounded from the passenger area.

"Suits me. Nothing I like better than a soft objective that doesn't fight back. Have to wonder what a lady doc is doing out here, though." Gazing through the windshield, Xiau saw nothing.

As Volksmann shut the floater down the steady burr of the engine was replaced by a staccato rapping, as if the vehicle had come under simultaneous fire from a thousand pellet guns. Driven by the wind, sand spattered against the front and sides of the transport. While the flying grit was potent enough to flay skin, it did not penetrate the tough polycrylic windows or the composite body. Neither the storm nor the darkness intimidated Xiau. He had survived far more cogent and deadly attacks.

Relieved to be at rest, the remainder of the squad gratefully unbuckled themselves from their travel harnesses. Men and women whose noxious profession was not sanctioned by any legal body joked and swapped playful insults as they stretched and availed themselves of the transport's supply of refreshments. Once outside and on the ground this promised to be an easy job. The fact that half a dozen of them had been contracted for the mission showed the importance the Triad placed on its successful conclusion. None of the six expressed the least doubt as to the outcome even as they wondered why so many of them were deemed necessary to carry it out.

Someone brought the tired Volksmann a hot cup of synthetic civet mocha, heavily sugared. It was a good team, he mused to himself as he drank. Once given the assignment he had brought them together himself. Better to overpay for additional competent help than leave anything to chance.

There had been no predicting the sandstorm, of course, but the rough conditions would result in only a momentary delay. In fact, if the last reading they had taken on the position of the targets was correct, he and his people could probably just step out of the floater and walk up to their quarry while they slept. For certain they would be bundled up and resting while they waited for the storm to subside. The last thing they would be expecting to encounter under such conditions was company. The scenario would play out precisely as Volksmann liked it.

No muss, no fuss. A quick in and quick out, long before their presence could be detected by roving searcher drones. SICK, Inc. security was excellent, but it was not omnipotent.

His attention was drawn to movement in the passenger compartment behind him. Relieved to be able to set aside their restraining, confining harnesses, the members of his team were standing, stretching, and joking about the storm.

"I don't like it when there's more ground in the air than underfoot," muttered Chenwa. Long and lanky, he let his melded left arm twitch back and forth across the floor. Half tentacle and half whip, it could pop out an eye with a single snap.

Presenting the inoffensive appearance of a French grandmother, the diminutive elderly woman standing next to him and joining him in gazing out one of the floater's windows was neither. Her name was Isgard Fleurine, she was in her late twenties, and she had chosen to undergo the maniped old age meld out of pure professionalism. No one expected a grandmother to be able to scale sheer walls with her bare hands—or throttle a fully-grown Natural. Volksmann knew she was quite capable of that and more.

The remainder of his people were an equally eclectic mix of Naturals and Melds. Each one brought different strengths to the team. With luck no exertions out of the ordinary would be required. With luck he ought to be able to carry out the mission all by himself. It had been given to him because he always fulfilled whatever task the Triad assigned to him. Experience had made him a firm believer in backup. As far as Meyer Volksmann was concerned there was no such thing as overkill.

"I need some air." The speaker was a partial Meld named Hideki. With his thick glasses (he had stubbornly refused the melds that would have rendered them unnecessary) and short, squat stature he looked like an accountant or pharmacist. In other words, plainly harmless. In his career, harmless Hideki had killed more people than most who opted for employment in certain stressful professions. He glanced questioningly toward his boss.

Volksmann was no barking martinet. You couldn't be and still maintain control of so many edgy personalities. "If you want to stick your ass out in this, Hiro, go ahead. Just don't go far." He checked a readout. "It's still hours until sunup and I don't want to lose anybody. We're *very* close to target. When this *verdammt* storm stops I intend to conclude the mission as quickly as possible and get the hell out of here." He did not blink as he met individual stares. "Anyone not back on board at that time is welcome to try walking out."

Hideki bulged his eyes and fluttered his fingers. "Oooo—I'm all shaky-scared!" A couple of his companions laughed. Fleurine giggled.

Volksmann ignored them. Though this was regarded as a fairly simple, straightforward mission, a degree of tautness still ran through every one of the participants. Not from concern over their innocuous targets but because a chance encounter with feared SICK security was a real and far more serious concern.

In the end only Xiau joined the voluble Hideki in stepping outside. As they emerged, both turned their faces away from the howling wind. Blowing sand peppered their exposed necks. The smaller man straightened his glasses, whose special lenses were wirelessly seamed to his own optic nerves, stretched, and took a deep breath.

"Ahh . . . fresh air!"

Xiau did not inhale deeply. "It's good to be out of that slay locker, but fresh?" He wiped steadily accumulating grit from the back of his neck, above the collar. "You could plant this stuff."

Hideki smirked at his colleague. "You have no appreciation for Nature's wonders."

"Maybe if I had a baleen nostril meld like you I could appreciate it more. Your throat and sinuses are gunk-protected. And since when did you develop an appreciation for Nature?"

"It has always been a part of me." The internal optics balanced on his nose flexed suddenly, reporting movement that was not wind-borne. Tensing, he turned in the relevant direction. As soon as his glasses allowed him to identify the source of the unexpected motion he relaxed. "Here, I'll prove it to you."

Preternatural reflexes that were a combination of biosurge-enhanced muscles acting in concert with his lenses allowed him to pull his sidearm, raise it, aim and fire all in one continuous motion. Despite his own perceptive skills Xiau was barely able to track the blur that was his colleague's gun arm. On a ridge among the scrub, something unseen squealed in pain. Straining to penetrate the storm, Xiau saw nothing and said as much.

"What the hell are you shooting at?" He cast an uncomfortable glance in the direction of the floater. "Volksmann will be pissed."

"Aw, levity a little, will you. Ever seen one of these?" Hideki held up his pistol for his associate to admire. Fully chromed, it glistened in the light shining out through the floater's windows. "The shells are tapered penetrators, make hardly any noise, and there's no muzzle flash." He gestured with the collapsible barrel. "It's not like we've got an audience. Our target isn't going anywhere and a company searcher would have to be perched on your head to notice anything."

Shielding his eyes, Xiau continued to peer in the direction of the low ridge. Brush fringed it like a Huli's hair. "I still don't see what you were shooting at."

"That's because I shot it, wallet-head." Suddenly he pointed. "Hey, there's another! See it there, popping up and down?" Raising his weapon he took aim for a second time. "This is like an antique shooting gallery. Very obliging of the local fauna to supply a means for alleviating our boredom. Mine, anyway."

Sure enough, a second shot produced a second scream. This time Xiau, his attention focused in the right direction, clearly saw something small and slender disappear as the burst from his colleague's gleaming weapon struck home.

"Nice shot. Wonder what it was?"

Hideki shrugged, hoping another play-target would present itself. Disappointingly, the ridge remained clear. He finally holstered his pistol.

"No idea. Looked kind of like a big rat." He pushed his glasses a little farther back on his nose and the internal optics immediately realigned themselves. A short flick of pain behind his eyes indicated that the momentarily interrupted contact had been reestablished between the technology on his nose and the nerves in his head. He no longer even noticed the occasional discomfort. "I guess the other rats got the message." He sounded disappointed. "This little outing is making me hungry. I could do with an ability bar before we go to work."

Xiau nodded, the two small deaths his companion had inflicted already forgotten. "From what Volksmann says, the whole thing should only take a few minutes. Seems like a waste of money, six of us for this."

Hideki nodded toward the floater. "Yeah. I imagine Volksmann just needed one backup. Everyone else is dead-weight."

"Including me?" Through the darkness and blowing sand Xiau eyed the other man sharply.

"Especially you. You're just a paid kiss-ass anyway."

"Ah, but a very well paid kiss-ass. Be careful my kiss-ass doesn't suggest cutting your subsist."

"That wouldn't be a . . . *son of a bitch!*"

Expecting to locate the source of the sudden excruciating pain, Hideki looked down at himself as both hands plunged toward his lower body. The foot-long length of sharpened and polished bone that had been rammed into his groin was shocking in its whiteness.

Even more shocking was the presence of several giant rats clinging to the end of it.

As he drew his own sidearm it struck a stunned Xiau that the creatures were not rats. Even cloaked in darkness and partially obscured by the horizontally whipping sand it was evident they were something completely different. They were, he quickly decided, clones of the small shape that the seriously wounded Hideki had casually blasted from the top of the scrub-covered ridge. They were also clearly hostile, unexpectedly treacherous, and needed to be dealt with swiftly. Next to him Hideki had dropped to the sand and was still clutching at himself. Blood poured from between his fingers and he was screaming like a baby.

Experience and highly trained reflexes came into play as Xiau took aim at the nearest of the murderous creatures. He would kill all of them and see them served to poor Hideki on a platter, skewered and well seasoned. But despite his skill with a gun he was having trouble drawing a bead on any of the little assailants. The damn things moved like little cheetahs. Not in a straight line, either. They zigged and zagged unpredictably, scampering about like small soldiers who had been taught how to keep themselves from being targeted. One bullet and then a second tore into the sand and soil, sending gouts of grit vomiting into the air that the wind whipped away as rapidly as they rose.

A voice sounded from the floater as the door opened and a figure appeared in the opening.

"What the shinobi is going on out there?"

Something hit Xiau in the left thigh. Wincing at the sudden sting but not daring to look away from where his weapon was tracking, he started backing toward the floater as fast as he could, sweeping the darkness with the muzzle of the gun he now held tightly in both hands. A second thumping pain struck his leg, just above its predecessor. Compelled to look down, trying to peer through the whipping sand, a glint of metal caught his eye. The two pieces of salvage that had been thrust into his flesh had been beaten and pounded with rocks into a pair of crude knife points. Spreading stains surrounded the wounds. Somewhere in the distance Hideki's screams had given way to moaning sobs that were barely audible above the steady roar of the storm. Xiau turned toward the floater and yelled.

"I'm hurt! Hideki's down! I need help!" Professional that he was, Volksmann's second in command fought through the pain as he half limped, half dragged himself toward the transport. As he drew near he was relieved to see that a couple of his colleagues had piled out and were hurrying toward him, weapons drawn.

His relief was short-lived. With a mixture of disbelief and horror he watched as the man and woman who were running to his aid went down. Held tight by multiple tiny hands, the wire that tripped them in the darkness and blowing sand was nearly invisible. Like the two chunks of crudely reworked sharpened metal sticking out of Xiau's left leg, the wire had been salvaged from one of the innumerable wrecks that littered the southern Namib.

Gun in hand, the woman rolled over and got off one shot into the night before she was swarmed by several dozen furry shapes. At the same time, her companion was being assaulted by what appeared to be giant muscular mice. Trying to blink sand away from his eyes, Xiau looked on aghast.

Some of the attackers wielded small knives and spears. Others stood off at a distance and puffed on one end of what looked like wooden straws. Each time one of the spine-darts they fired struck the downed assassin she twitched. Unable to use her pistol at such close quarters, she set it aside and began striking and pulling at the chittering creatures that covered her body. But as fast as she could break a neck or throw one aside, others took their place. Meanwhile a handful of the attacking animals dashed in and, before she could react, picked up her sidearm and carried it off.

Her larger male companion was having better luck. Having managed to struggle to his knees despite the swarm of biting, stabbing assailants clinging to his back and flanks, he was firing his napistol into the night. Packed with highly compressed napalm, each shell produced a geyser of orange flame where it struck. Small flaming shapes raced in all directions while the wind swept the acrid stink of burning fur and flesh through the air.

Sinking their teeth into his right ear and wrenching back, two of the attackers tore it away from his head.

Shrieking in anguish he rose and flailed madly at the side of his skull. Clinging to his wrist, another of the little monsters attacked the hand holding the wildly waving napistol and bit down hard on the trigger finger. Incredibly sharp teeth punched all the way to the bone. Instead of letting go of the gun, the man's finger contracted reflexively and the weapon fired again. Unfortunately for its pain-crazed owner, the muzzle was pointing up and at him as his body reacted. The shell entered his open mouth and detonated. Opening like the petals of a red flower, a ball of expanding flame replaced his head.

Chenwa appeared in the floater's doorway firing a pistol with one hand and snapping his maniped whip. The latter cut one meerkat on the ground in half as two others standing atop the dome of the parked transport dropped a third of their number onto the assassin below. Holding a foot-long porcupine quill tightly in its front paws, the plunging meerkat drove it straight through Chenwa's right eye. His lower jaw dropped along with his gun, the deadly whip-limb went limp, and the contract killer slowly toppled forward onto the sand.

Preparing to follow Chenwa outside, Volksmann had quickly changed his mind. Whatever had possessed these addled animal denizens of the Namib to wage war on his people he did not know. What he was certain of was that he wanted no more of it. All the approbation and monetary reward in the world were useless to someone lying dead in the desert. Making sure that Chenwa's body was clear of the doorway, he touched a switch and watched as it cycled shut.

"Get us out of here!" Isgard Fleurine, the twenty-something professional executioner with the grandmotherly meld, stood facing the doorway holding two sidearms aimed in its direction. There was panic as well as determination in her voice.

Volksmann needed no urging. Racing to the front of the transport he threw himself back into the pilot's chair and ran anxious fingers over multiple controls. The floater's systems immediately came back online, the light from the various screens and readouts raising his spirits considerably. The absence of the driver's heads-up didn't concern him. What mattered now was to get off the ground. Once the compact craft was in the air and hovering a safe three or four meters above the surface the maddened hordes of homicidal rodents, or whatever they were, would be reduced to impotent chattering.

With the floater's automatic maintenance system having cleared the intakes of the bulk of ingested sand and grit, the transport rose smoothly to its maximum operating altitude of five meters. That was more than high enough for safety. Panting hard but beginning to breathe normally, Fleurine had holstered her weapons and was moving to join him. Safe from attack she leaned forward to peer down through the sweeping transparent front of the craft. Volksmann noted that the sandstorm was finally starting to abate.

"Four dead," he muttered. "Murdered by indigenous rodents. *That'll* go down well with the Yeoh."

She put a reassuring hand on his shoulder and he reminded himself that this was a woman in her twenties who had only chosen to look eighty. A meld like that suggested a damaged personality, he knew. But then, both fit her job description. He was glad for the company.

"Unexpected death comes with the territory. You don't have to go into detail in your report, Meyer. I'll back you up." She wore a lopsided grin, simultaneously sensual and wolfish and greedy. Her eyes were not eighty. "This way I get to collect payment for six, so don't expect any tears from me."

Turning on the floater's landing beams Volksmann used them to search the ground off to his right. The earth there seemed to be moving, a veritable flowing pavement of brown and white bodies. Many of them were looking upward and throwing things in the direction of the transport. Spines, rocks, bits of metal: anything they could pick up. But their forelegs, while strong for their size, were short. Very little of the thrown material reached the floater's underside. The few bits of metal that did rise to the transport's height made tiny pinging noises as they bounced off the tough composite body.

"Excitable little pointy-nosed bastards, aren't they?" Moving away from the pilot's seat the female assassin pulled the larger of her two sidearms and opened a port in the canopy. "Not that I'm into revenge or anything—it's unprofessional—but hang here while I roast a few dozen of them. Wouldn't want the rats to think they won anything."

Volksmann licked his lips. "Because of the storm we've been stuck here longer than I like. We need to pick up our quarry and start back before SICK security makes the changeover to the more active daylight shift."

"Sure, sure. I only need a couple minutes, *mon père*." Leaning slightly out the port, the surviving member of his team started to take aim. "I got a bunch of them huddling together. Just let me take them out and . . ."

A snapping sound cracked above the dying wind. Volksmann didn't flinch at the sound of the gun going off. When he finally did turn to have a look he saw that it was not Fleurine's weapon that had discharged. Turning, she gazed back at him with a blank look on her faux elderly maniped face. Her mouth was open and her expression one of surprise. When the blood from the hole in her forehead started to trickle into her eyes she blinked. Without speaking a word she fell forward onto the floor of the floater.

A stunned Volksmann gaped at the petite form, then whipped around to peer out the windshield to his left. Light from the underside of the floater illuminated ground that was swarming with still more of the milling, chattering creatures. Many of them were pointing at the transport with tiny black paws. His searching eyes finally located the cluster that had been overlooked by the too-eager Fleurine.

He recognized a pistol that had belonged to Shakovsk, who had tried and failed to help Hideki and Xiau. Propped up on a rock, it was supported by a densely packed knot of the creatures who kept it balanced and steady. Its lethal barrel was aimed upward and straight at the hovering floater. A worn, chewed, but tough strip of old leather had been passed behind the trigger guard and looped over the trigger itself. Six of the creatures clung to each end of the strap, looking for all the world as if they were engaged in a serious tug-of-war.

Standing on its hind legs well behind the gun and gazing up at the floater was a single representative of the species. For an impossible instant Volksmann had the absurd sensation that he was looking into the eyes of another intelligent being. Then he flinched back just as the gun went off again.

The shot smashed through the windshield, missing him by centimeters. As he lurched to one side his right hand dragged across several controls. Responding to the anomalous mixture of inadvertent manual commands, the floater went into a wild slew to starboard. Before Volksmann could recover and countermand the accidental instructions, it had smashed into the ground.

Dazed but conscious, he pulled himself upright in the pilot's seat and began working the instrument console. The engine whined and the floater skewed sideways, but would not rise from the ground. Something had been seriously damaged in the crash. Preoccupied with stabbing and pressing at various controls, it took him several minutes before he grew aware of a new sound. It reminded him of the flying sand that had scoured the transport as it battled its way northward through the storm. But the noise that had begun to reverberate through the sides and roof of the floater was not coming from blowing sand.

It arose from the rapid-fire patter of hundreds of tiny feet.

Whirling, he flung himself out of the pilot's chair just as several dozen armed meerkats began scampering down the windshield in front of him. Utilizing their minuscule instruments of death they started scraping and stabbing at the transparency. To his relief he saw they were unable to so much as scratch the tough polycrylic. The hole that had been made by the second shot from the recovered pistol was not large enough to admit even the smallest of the attackers. He was safe inside the floater. At least, he was until he had to deal with SICK security, which would surely locate the downed craft as soon as the sun was up and the storm had fully subsided. There was water and emergency rations to sustain him. Not to mention his own weapons. He almost smiled. Unless his inexplicably organized assailants could muster enough strength to carry the floater off, he was safe.

His biggest remaining concern, he realized, was how the hell he was going to explain this to SICK's people and to his superiors in the Triad. Even in times when extraordinarily magified animals were commonplace, what had befallen his expedition made no sense. Magified mammals were harmless. Maniped pets did not attack their masters.

"Bad human," piped an unmistakably small voice. A chill went down Volksmann's back, displacing the confidence that had braced him only a moment earlier. He turned.

He had forgotten to close the port Fleurine had opened.

There were at least a hundred of them inside now. Some rested on all fours. Others stood upright on their hind legs in disconcertingly humanlike poses. Dozens of bright black eyes were focused on the transport's remaining occupant.

Volksmann looked to his left. His personal sidearms lay in a compartment underneath the main instrument console. It would only take a matter of seconds for him to pull them out and start firing. But he did need those few seconds. Proffering a winning smile, he looked down at the furry creature who was standing slightly apart from the others. It was she who had voiced the two astonishingly clear words. He found it unsettling to hear himself talking back to the creature.

"This has all been a mistake. A stupid, regrettable mistake. I'm sorry for what has happened, but somehow I'll make it right. I know that some of your—people—have been hurt. But all my people are dead. It's all been a big misunderstanding." As he spoke he was leaning slowly to his left. His hand extended toward the compartment that contained the guns.

"Not all—your people, dead." The articulate meerkat spoke with a solemnity that belied her size. "Is one people still alive. You."

"Well, yes, that's true. What do you propose to do?" Volksmann's straining fingers were almost to the handle of the compartment. Pull, grab, and shoot. With so many of them crowded together he would not have to worry about taking aim.

The meerkat's voice never changed, never varied in volume or tenor.

"Rectify."

Volksmann's fingers closed convulsively on the handle of the under-console compartment and yanked. Before the concealed drawer had stopped sliding forward he was already reaching for the nearest of the pistols inside. Had he been facing others of his own kind he might have had a chance. But no human boasts reaction time as fast as a meerkat. Just as no one was around to hear the screams that issued from within the downed floater.

In any event, they did not last for very long.

One of the nice things about a modern Gatling gun, Het Kruger reflected as he watched the familiar lonely terrain slip by beneath the company floater, was that they could be massaged to accept pretty much any type of projectile that would fit the muzzles. Traditional solid bullets, explosive shells, armor-piercing rounds—just about anything that could be contained within the rotating barrels could be spat at an incredible rate of discharge toward a target.

Take the floater in whose copilot's seat he was presently sitting, drinking tea with his booted feet propped up on the instrument console. The two electrically powered amidships guns, one facing to port and the other to starboard, could spew explosive shells at thousands of rounds per minute, sufficient to disable or destroy anything short of the most heavily armored military hardware. To an outsider they would surely seem to constitute overkill for simple company security—which was precisely the point. Kruger called them his "bouncers"—a hoary old term still used to refer to individuals charged with keeping order in bars and clubs. Be they Natural or Meld, the best men and women engaged in that ancient profession never raised a hand in anger. Their mere presence, or the firm delivery of an appropriate word or two, was usually enough to defuse a potentially unruly situation.

Similarly, the sight of the floater's starboard and port multibarreled weapons was usually sufficient to convince even the most heavily armed intruders that they were seriously outgunned and that their best chance for survival lay in surrendering their arms. While on Kruger's watch the heavy weaponry had only been fired once in anger. Two minutes after they had been unleashed, it was impossible to separate the bodies of the intruders from the floater in which they had been traveling. His own forensic specialist had taken one look at the mess and declared his inability to identify any of the remains.

Instead of explosive shells, the single forward-mounted Gatling fired darts filled with a powerful soporific. The contents of one or two was usually enough to put even a big lod Meld to sleep. If weapons had to be used Kruger much preferred this quieter and more humane method of taking down illegal visitors. For one thing, the chance to question live intruders provided information that could be added to the facility's security bank. Names, places, facilitators, could all be stored for reference against future intrusions. For another, cleanup was infinitely easier and less time-consuming.

The particular intrusion he and his team were presently on their way to confront had been detected by the company satellite that stayed in synchronous orbit over the central and lower Namib. Able to complete a full high-resolution scan of the region every several days, it was not perfect. But it did make it impossible for any vehicle bigger than a kid's shufslide to remain in the area long enough to do any harm. It was theoretically possible for a well-equipped intruder to get in fast and get out fast without being picked up by Nerens-based security. If an intruder was willing to risk their life for some vit and a few pictures, Kruger could only admire them. That was real dedication and he did not concern himself with such transitory violations.

It was those who came hoping to spend time in the Sperrgebeit that set the facility's, and his, alarms to ringing. Most of them were after diamonds. Some came seeking rare animals they could sell on the black market. A thousand-year-old *Welwitschia mirabilis* was worth a great deal of subsist to wealthy plant collectors. While industrial espionage was also always a possibility, in his tenure as chief of security he had never encountered an interloper who had entered the Sperrgebeit with that in mind. Few outside the inner circle of the SAEC even knew there was a research and manufacturing facility at Nerens. Those who did had no reason to suspect that it was engaged in anything other than mining studies.

Early morning in the Namib was beautiful no matter where one happened to find oneself, no matter which direction one looked, no matter what time of year it was. It helped to have an appreciation for the beauties of desert terrain. Not everyone could tolerate such a lack of greenery. Kruger loved the peacefulness and the solitude, the banded colors of the rocks, the way the wind coiffed the crests of the barchan dunes. The money.

His work consisted mostly of running routine checkups of procedures and equipment that never went wrong. It was repetitive but satisfying. Another man might have been bored to death. Not Kruger. Having seen plenty of action in his youth he was more than content to enjoy what amounted to an exceptionally well-paid semiretirement. True, at the facility he was occasionally exposed to sights and sounds that puzzled and confused him, but interpreting their meaning was not his job. Having survived being shot at for real, he knew that shooting other people while ducking fire was a scenario far better played out on a vit immersion than in real life. Bullets burned, getting hit hurt, and losing body parts even in a day and time when they could nearly always be replaced or substituted for was not nearly as exciting or invigorating as some of his younger and less experienced colleagues supposed.

So he was gratified when word came from his scanner operator that there was no sign of movement at the location they were speeding to investigate.

"Dead quiet ahead, sir," the woman told him. With her right hand she slightly adjusted the perception helmet that covered her entire head. The three slender part flesh, part metal tentacles that emerged from her left shoulder were plugged deep and wirelike into the console in front of her.

"Nothing at all?" Kruger spoke softly into the tiny vorec mike suspended in front of his mouth.

"Nothing, sir. There's a floater there all right. Imaging people were right about that. I've got it on reflective now. The silhouette is sharp enough for me to analyze the composition—but nothing's moving. No heat signature from the vehicle and nothing bipedal in the immediate vicinity. It's—quiet."

"Maybe they're sleeping." The port-side gunner stroked the back end of his weapon as if he were caressing a cat. "If so they're gonna get a nasty wake-up call."

"Take it easy, Raki." Kruger recognized the tone. Like so many of his ilk the younger man was bored. Rotation was a problem in every department at Nerens, including Security. The isolation, the lack of things to do, the restrictions on individual movement both outside the facility and within, tended to result in rapid burnout among the personnel. Few stayed more than a year. Even fewer were on track to remain in their posts until their recruitment period was up. Among employees he was something of a dinosaur. Occasionally the strain of fulfilling an employment contract combined with the remoteness and desolation caused an employee to crack. Like that unfortunate Ouspel fellow, for example.

As the floater turned due west he found himself wondering what had happened to the vanished employee. It was likely that he had fled on his own, propelled by his own personal psychosis. If so then he would have perished out in the vastness of the Sperrgebeit just like everyone else who tried to leave the facility without going through formal discharge procedures. Somewhere hyenas were gnawing the technician's bones.

"I have target on my screens, sir." The pilot's limbs gently adjusted instrumentation and the security craft slowed. "Orders?"

With a sigh Kruger sat up straight in his seat and pulled his legs off the console. Time to go to work. "Sipho, where are you?" The security chief knew he could have answered his own question simply by checking one readout on the console in front of him, but it was always good procedure to have verbal confirmation of your backup's position.

"Coming around from the southeast, Het." The voice in the security chief's earpiece was clear and devoid of distortion. "ETA in approximately five minutes. You want us to go in or stand off?"

"Stand off and stay airborne but move in close enough to establish visual. So far we've got nothing. I don't like dealing with nothing. It implies concealment."

"You think they're waiting for us?"

Kruger considered. "There's no way they can know that their presence here has been discovered. I doubt they're expecting company so soon after entering the Forbidden Zone. One of my gunners thinks they may be sleeping in. It's possible, especially if they had to ride out yesterday's sandstorm. That doesn't mean they're not equipped with automatic alarms, or for that matter, automated weapons. I'll go in first, make the usual circuit, give them the usual warnings. Then we'll see."

"*Minaqonda*—got it."

The second armed company floater was just visible hovering on the eastern horizon as Kruger's craft topped the last low rise and the target came into view. One did not need the security chief's practiced eye to tell that something was wrong.

The shredded bodies half buried in the sand were proof enough of that.

"Circle," he directed the pilot. "Distant but within range. Gatlings powered up." Sobered by the sight of so many motionless human forms being slowly claimed by the desert, none of the floater's gunners cracked wise. They kept their hands on their triggers, the electrically powered weapons ready to run riot at the touch of a switch.

"I've got nothing moving, sir." The scanner operator's fingers and tentacle tips efficiently worked her console. "No heat signatures, either. Individual reads are cold."

"Might be somebody alive inside and shielded." Kruger was thinking out loud. Given the presence of so many dead on the ground outside the downed craft it seemed unlikely anyone had survived within, but one of the hallmarks of his administration of security at Nerens was that he was always ready for the unlikely.

"Close pass," he ordered tersely.

The floater pilot performed a second circumnavigation of the silent transport. The scanner's follow-up report was as void of life as its predecessor. As the security craft gradually orbited in closer and closer to the crash site, Kruger was able to make out details without the aid of supplementary lenses: the hole in the vehicle's windshield, the open port, and the main doorway gaping wide. From the spray of sprawled corpses that fanned out like palm leaves from the vicinity of the portal he could tell that those inside the downward craft had managed to get out. The question that nagged at him was what, if anything, had managed to get in? He was close enough now to be able to see where weapons had been dropped beside bodies.

What had happened here? Had the intruders fallen to arguing among themselves, with fatal results? His interest was purely personal. From a professional standpoint the intrusion had conveniently resolved itself.

"Find a level spot and set down near the intruder's front end," he told his pilot. "Raki, you stay at your gun. The rest of you make sure your sidearms are charged and loaded and get ready to disembark." He directed his last words to a console pickup. "Sipho, move in close but stay aloft."

Nothing challenged him or his subordinates as they raced quickly down the ramp that the pilot deployed from the side of the company floater. Outside the armored transport the air was utterly motionless. A common-enough atmospheric condition in the Namib, and one that was especially appropriate given the grisly scene that was spread out before the wary security personnel. Standing in dead air Kruger slowly took stock. It seemed as if the carnage had even intimidated the wind.

Naturals and Melds, men and women alike had been felled by unknown adversaries. The identity of the latter soon became apparent. Spreading out to count the bodies, Kruger and his team came across a number of far smaller corpses scattered among the deceased humans. Broken, smashed, half incinerated, several of the deceased meerkats still carried quivers of poison-tipped spines on their backs or clutched weapons improvised from bone and scavenged, coarsely reworked metal and plastic. As if the presence of their embattled dead was not proof enough, the ground was covered with thousands of tiny footprints.

A shuffling Maranon joined the security chief as Kruger nudged a huddle of dead meerkats with his right foot. There were half a dozen of the small twisted bodies in the pile. They looked as if they had met their end at the same time, cooked with a single shot. A practitioner of Brazilian mechcandomblé, Maranon was visibly uncomfortable in the presence of so many unexplained undersized fatalities. Dead humans, Natural or Meld and in any number, did not trouble him. Armed meerkats were something outside his experience, and it showed in his voice and expression.

"What the hell, Mr. Kruger, sir? I mean, what the *hell*?"

As a scientific explanation of the lethal biological anomaly that was spread out before them, the subordinate's observation left much to be desired. Viscerally, however, Kruger found himself in complete accord with the other man's remark. Raising his gaze he began to scan the surrounding landscape, searching for any sign of movement. Especially small mammalian movement.

"This is unusual," he commented with characteristic understatement. "Decidedly out of the ordinary. There will have to be a report." Lifting his wrist, he spoke into the communicator that was strapped to his lower forearm. "Sipho, we've got a real anomaly here. Remnants of a massacre the likes of which you won't believe. Set down and deploy your people in a defensive perimeter around the site. Tell them to—tell them to keep an eye out for meerkats."

Incredulity was prominent in the other man's reply. "'Meerkats'—sir?"

"Yebo, meerkats. Someone, somewhere, has been engaged in some extreme magifying. At least we won't have to deal with the intruders. They've already been dealt with."

"Dealt with, sir?" came the other man's voice. "By whom, sir?"

Kruger hesitated a moment. "By the natives. And not the ones you're thinking of. As soon as you set down come on over and you'll see for yourself."

Lowering his arm and breaking the connection Kruger resumed hiking away from the downed floater. Several of the dead humans had so many Codon spines sticking out of their bodies that they looked like desert succulents themselves. One still clutched her pistol in a death grip while the rest lay weaponless. Either they had panicked and abandoned their floater while it was under attack and the rest of the intruders' guns lay inside, or else someone had carried their weapons away.

Could a meerkat aim and fire a weapon designed to be utilized by a human? Kruger pondered the possibility. Even a small gun would be too big, too heavy, too clumsy. But several agile meerkats working in tandem, now . . .

Having not enjoyed a single comforting thought since setting down in this haunted place he looked forward to returning to the comfort of his apartment and office back in Nerens.

At least his report would be able to include a full description of the intruders. Though individually they were a flutter of aliases, there was more than enough information in their floater computer to mark them as operating on behalf of the Yeoh Triad out of Guangzhou. What the Triad was looking for in the Sperrgebeit, Kruger had no idea. Maybe someone had given them a line on a diamond deposit and this team had been sent to check it out. That made sense, the security chief told himself. If they had entered the Forbidden Zone only to validate information and then leave, they could reasonably assume they would be able to do so before he and his people had time to respond to their intrusion. The lack of any mining gear on the downed floater lent further credence to such a theory.

Of course their incursion might have nothing to do with diamonds or mining. Since he had been deprived of anyone to interrogate, their true motive remained open to speculation. That was now a matter for SICK intelligence, not him. He made sure that his personnel recorded everything as they wandered among the sandy killing field. Otherwise no one back at the facility was going to believe them. Murderous meerkats—oh, certainly! That Het Kruger—what a joker!

But it was no joke. There was nothing funny about a septet of corpses. He found himself wondering if the encounter that had taken place here represented an isolated incident or was a precursor to a brand-new security issue. He would have to find out what poisons were effective on meerkats. Or had these heavily maniped specimens been magified to the point where they knew enough to recognize and ignore baited traps?

All matters for speculation, he told himself as he turned back toward his waiting floater. The ethics of animal magifying, the how much and what kind, had long been hotly debated. Its practical aspects were less frequently addressed. Here was a perfect example of how such biological manipulation could get out of hand. In the old days security at the facility had just been a matter of dealing with invasive species. Now people were developing their own invasive species in labs and illegal manip centers.

It had been stated with confidence by the appropriate international regulatory bodies that the Ciudad Simiano in Central America represented the end of such thoughtless research and experimentation. His expression twisted. He would have liked to have been able to show some of those self-satisfied, overconfident politicians around this particular patch of the Namib.

Meerkats were smart, social, and adaptable. So were rats, who were even more adaptable and far more procreative. The weapons on their broken little bodies proved that the meerkats who had done battle with the intruders had been given at least a minimal intelligence boost. What if some deranged biosurge or gengineer somewhere decided to do the same for a few rats?

He shook his head at the shortsightedness of it all. You couldn't stop the magifying of animals. Too many people wanted their "special" pets. There was far too much money to be made in the underground market, selling yodeling lemurs and cooing cats and dogs who could speak a few programmed phrases. Greed would always outweigh danger. The Sperrgebiet was proof enough of that.

Aware that Maranon was shadowing him, he turned abruptly.

"Are you following me, mister?"

"I'm watching your back, Mr. Kruger, sir." The other man spoke with deference as he shifted his rifle from one arm to the other.

A small smile played across the security chief's face. "No, there's more to it than that. You're afraid, aren't you?"

If Kruger expected a sputtering denial it was not forthcoming. "Yes sir, I'm afraid." The Natural's eyes darted nervously over the surrounding silent terrain. "These meerkat creatures aren't normal. They live in burrows, in tunnels. They could be anywhere, even right under our feet right now, waiting for the right moment. Waiting for us to relax so they can pop up and fill our legs with toxic darts."

"Well then, you can stop worrying, Maranon. I've seen enough here and we've recorded enough to prove to the others back at the facility that we're not liars. Analyzing and trying to make sense of what happened here is a job for the bio-boys, not us. We're pulling out." He clapped the other man on the shoulder. "Go on, get back to the transport. And for pity's sake, quit worrying about cousin mongoose. I haven't seen anything alive bigger than a bug since we got here. However they did this, or why, any killer weasels are long gone."

"Yes, sir. Thank you, sir." Maranon smiled and nodded, grateful that his boss had chosen not to demean him.

After he gave the general order for departure Kruger waited while the rest of his team pulled back to the two waiting floaters. Alone once more on the desert floor he took the time to stroll slowly around the perimeter of the confrontation. Aware that the members of his team would be watching and monitoring his progress from inside the two floaters, he knew it would bolster their spirits to see their commanding officer making a final inspection of the impossible battlefield without any immediate backup. It should settle a few nerves. That was his job, too.

Satisfied that there was nothing more to be learned unless he left a detachment behind to conduct a more in-depth study, he broke into a jog toward his floater. An explanation for what had taken place here would be forthcoming in its own good time. He looked forward to it. Unlike many of his subordinates he did not make jokes about the desert. He had a healthy respect for its vast empty spaces and the many secrets it doubtless still contained. Much as he would have liked to know exactly what had transpired in this place he felt no need to rush to judgment. Sometimes it was best not to pursue things in the Namib too closely or in too much haste lest a camouflaged sand cobra jump up to bite you in the ass.

Climbing back into the transport he gave the order for both crafts to lift off and return to Nerens. Settling himself in one of the seats in the back he helped himself to a cold Tusker and reflected on the morning's work. Though he was returning with a mystery in tow, at least he could assure his superiors of one thing.

The trespassers had been dealt with down to the last Meld and no other intruders were left alive in this sector.

Despite her unease, despite her fears, and despite the steady, unrelenting howl of the storm and the particles of wind-borne grit that assaulted her face like a thousand tiny biting gnats, Ingrid Seastrom had fallen asleep. Exhaustion is ever the tortoise to the hare's pain.

She woke up choking on sand. Spitting and wiping at her mouth, she sat up and found herself staring at a sky of such untrammeled Prussian blue that it seemed a glaze on the ceramic bowl of heaven. In that perfect-toned firmament nothing moved: not a breath of cloud, not a stirring of wind, not a whisper of wings. Speaking of Whispr . . .

While she brushed sand off her legs she looked to her right, then to her left. Twisting her tired body, she looked behind her. No Whispr. Only eastern mountains and western plains, rills and runs and rips in the rocks that were millions of years old. Her heart started to beat faster—and in the complete and total silence she felt she could hear it.

What if he had decided he would be better off on his own and had taken off while she'd slept? What if he had finally surrendered to his nagging paranoia and decided to return to Orangemund and thence home? He had the only functioning communicator. On the communicator was the only copy of Morgan Ouspel's instructions on how to get to Nerens—and how to return safely to the Orange River. If he had abandoned her then she would have time enough only to contemplate her own imminent demise.

But he wouldn't do that to her—would he? Not to the doctor who had removed the police traktacs from his back. Not to his partner in exploration. Not to the woman he childishly and transparently wanted to possess. Not to Ingrid Seastrom, M.D., beloved of all her patients and . . .

There was no point in shouting her frustration because there was no one to hear her.

Standing up allowed her to take in a good deal more of the barren landscape. Squinting against the harsh sun she located more mountains, more scattered brush, more dunes and cracked gravel pans. But no Whispr. No companion. No other motile living thing.

Which way to go? Which way to run? Orangemund lay far to the south now. She *might* be able to remember the way back, might be able to retrace her steps. But shorn of specific directions she was unlikely to make it. Nerens was nearer now and she knew its general direction, but without Ouspel's map and details she might stumble right past it. Even if she found the place she would not exactly be assured of a hearty welcome. To the east lay the Kalahari, to the west the undrinkable Atlantic. She had no choice. Grim and resigned, she started off in a northwesterly direction.

A dozen steps and as many silent curses later she tripped over her companion.

Except for his sideways-turned face he lay completely buried in the sand. His pack lay nearby. Whether he had dropped it, set it

down, or flung it away in a fit of madness she had no way of knowing. It lay open to the elements, its precious contents scattered by
the wind.

Carefully she brushed sand from his cheek and neck. Then she
smacked him on the upturned side of his face hard enough to make
her palm sting. He sat up so fast that she had to backpedal quickly
to avoid being knocked down.

"Wha . . . huh?"

"I'll give you 'wah-huh' you pathetic, insensitive bastard! I
thought you'd run out on me! I thought you'd left me here to die in
the desert while you bone-scooted your miserable scrawny ass back
to Orangemund! I thought . . . !"

"Aw, you missed me," he cooed, interrupting her tirade.

She was ready to continue, stopped, stared at him a moment,
then looked away. "I felt so alone I would've missed a pustulant
iguana. I was *scared*."

"Okay, okay. I'm here. Wish I were elsewhere, maybe, but still
here. You can relax now knowing that you won't die alone and that
you'll have company when you do so. Sorry if that doesn't make *me*
feel any better."

Her heart rate slowing, she looked down at him. "What happened? Why'd you move?" Her expression contorted. "Usually
when we turn in for the night you can't get close enough and I have
to kick you away."

Busy shedding the rest of the diminutive dune that had accumulated atop his body, he didn't meet her eyes. "I thought maybe
if I sat upwind of you with my back to the storm I could keep some
of the blowing sand off your body, help you to get some sleep. I
think that I did. Then I fell asleep. And fell over."

"I don't remember passing out, either," she muttered. "Fatigue
will do that to a person."

"Unfortunately," he added as he turned and pointed, "I made

the mistake of putting my pack next to me. I should've put it under me, or at least remembered to secure all the straps and seals. I didn't think the wind would be strong enough to move it, much less pick it up and dump it somewhere else."

Together they walked over to where his pack had stopped. Some of the food was missing. The wind had probably carried it halfway to the Makgadikgadi by now, she thought regretfully. Fortunately all of the special supplements required to keep Whispr's melded digestive system functioning properly remained. Between the two of them they had enough packaged nutrients to keep going for at least another few days. His waterpak was still in working order. And though the force of the wind had sucked it outside the backpack, they found his first-aid kit lying nearby, intact and still sealed against the weather.

Their relief at recovering so much food and drink turned to despair when they finally located his communicator. Wind-driven grit had penetrated the protective housing. No matter what command he tried to enter and irrespective of the contacts he touched, the small screen remained blank and the integrated tridee projector would not light. Nor did the battered device respond to verbal command.

"Can you fix it?" She stared hopefully at the compact glassine rectangle.

His laugh was as bitter and sardonic as any she had heard issue from his willowy throat. "I suppose I should be flattered that you think enough of me to even ask that question, doc. Much as I'd like to say yes, you got me wrong. I just steal these things." He brandished it at her. "I don't fix 'em." A wave took in the distant mountains. "It's no problem, though. We'll just amble over to the nearest shop and buy a replacement."

"That's what sustains me through all this," she growled back at him. "Your mordant wit."

He started to bark a rejoinder, then unexpectedly broke into one of his irritatingly ingratiating grins. "Being angry's healthier than being scared. Go ahead and bitch at me all you want. I can take it. I'm used to being a punching bag."

She sighed and shook her head. "Why can't you just stick to one psychological state—sarcastic or pitiable? I never know which way to jump."

He gestured anew. She was unconscionably gratified to see that his arm was pointed in the same direction she had been preparing to go when she'd thought he had run out on her.

"Might as well jump that way. Without a map, directions, or GPS we don't have much choice. Or we have a wealth of choices. Depends on how you want to look at it." His eyes met hers. "Now getting to Nerens is about more than finding out what's on the thread. Now it's about finding food and water." His eyes widened. "You still *have* the thread, don't you?"

She started. In all the confusion and confliction she hadn't . . . Reaching inside her shirt she felt for the small storage compartment that had been sewn into the inside of the left cup of her brassiere. After a moment's searching, the tips of her fingers closed around an unyielding cylinder. Finding the storage capsule's seal intact she let out a sigh of relief.

"Still here."

He exhaled with relief. "For a moment there all I could think of was having to dig through a few dozen square meters of sand with my bare hands in search of something smaller than a finger joint." He gestured at the debris-strewn ground. "Let's see if there's anything else we can salvage." His grin returned, crooked as ever. "At least if we get hit with another sandstorm we won't have to worry about losing all our supplies. Because you already surrendered some to the flood, and me to the storm. Heck of a way to lighten a pack."

"Can't argue with that logic." She made herself smile back at him. "You can't lose what you've already lost."

They searched the immediate surroundings for nearly half an hour without finding anything. The sand had taken everything except his first-aid kit. He was glad to still have it. The sand had nearly taken her companion.

She was glad to still have him.

HIKING THROUGH HEAVILY ERODED hills instead of across a flat plain offered more opportunities to keep under cover and away from the prying eyes of any company searcher drones. It also offered shade from a sun burning through a cloudless sky. But it also made for slower going. Ironically, in a world awash in helpful electronics they now found themselves navigating by the light in the sky.

It helped that both of them had poured over Ouspel's map and instructions so many times that much of it remained in memory, though they no longer had a communicator with which to confirm their decisions. They did not speak of what would happen if they missed Nerens entirely and continued trudging northward. Beyond the SICK company outpost there were no towns or scientific stations, and the east–west road (the only east–west road) that connected the towns of Lüderitz and Keetmanshoop was farther from Nerens than the SICK facility was from Orangemund. Miss their target destination and they would surely die in the desert.

Even in the most complex world, she reflected as she marched alongside Whispr, life could ultimately be reduced to simplicities.

Actually, there was a simple way to avoid getting lost. All they had to do was head west until they hit the sea and then turn north. But with company diamond mining sites scattered all along the coast and Nerens being supplied from the sea, the chances of approaching the facility undetected via a coastal route was essentially zero. They had no choice but to try to sneak in from the wide-open east. From the desert where no one ventured except fools and the deluded.

Which am I? she wondered. Recently she had told others that she was a scientist. Plenty of fools and the deluded belonged to that profession. Surreptitiously she eyed her slender companion as he trod silently beside her. At least Whispr harbored no such illusions. He was here for the promise of subsist and nothing more. His ruminations were not troubled by elevated hopes. In a way, she envied him. There was something to be said for the peace conveyed to the soul by a complete lack of curiosity.

Worry was being pushed into the background by weariness as they topped a low rise and a sheltered riverbed came into view. They had encountered and crossed many such, but this one was strikingly different. For one thing, it was preponderantly green instead of brown and yellow. Not for the full length of its meandering course, nor heavily so. But there was tall brush, and clusters of reeds, and even a few scattered ivory palms lording it over lesser desert vegetation. A trio of distinctive ungulate shapes with towering horns paused to stare in the direction of the new arrivals before breaking into a gallop for the nearest ridge. As the two tired travelers watched, the three gemsbok disappeared over the rocky crest, still moving at a lazy trot as they vanished.

Conferring, Ingrid and Whispr agreed that this little desert paradise was one of the last main water holes that had been marked on Ouspel's map.

"I even remember the damn name." Whispr had to restrain himself from plunging headlong toward the inviting garden. "Kokerboom Oasis."

"Then we're not far from Nerens." Her reply was tinged with barely controlled excitement.

"That's right. We can look forward to being taken prisoner any day now." He was licking his lips as they descended the slope on which they had been standing and started across the soft sand and gravel of the largely dry river bottom. "I've already decided what I want for my last meal. Assuming SICK allows the condemned a last meal."

The sight of water oozing out of the sands among the greenery was so inviting that she determined to forgo the dubious pleasure of arguing with him. It formed a pool, not a river, but in the absence of humankind the water was clean and potable. The sensation of it sliding down her throat was indescribable. No liquid derived from a waterpak could taste half so sweet.

As soon as she had drank her fill she laboriously removed her boots and self-inflating socks, rolled the legs of her pants up to her knees, found a suitable rock, and plunged her limbs into the water. It was just deep enough to allow her toes to touch bottom. Curious centimeter-long silvery fish, an amazing presence in so remote a place, finned over to investigate the pale sausagelike intruders that had immersed themselves in their isolated paradise.

She looked toward her companion. Wiping the last invigorating droplets from his lips, Whispr was gazing into the high reeds as he unlimbered his backpack.

"Why don't you come and join me?" she urged him. "It'll lower your body temperature and in ten minutes you'll feel like you've spent a weekend in Bermuda."

"Thought I heard something," he muttered.

She shook her head sadly. Whispr's perpetual state of watchfulness had certainly helped him survive a range of dangerous situations, but it also made it impossible for him to relax.

"What could you have heard? There's nothing here." She gestured at their gardenlike surroundings. "The oryx have gone. Although I suppose there could be reptiles. Lizards or snakes." She kicked her feet back and forth, splashing the cool, soothing liquid. "I don't even care if it's a viper—I'm willing to share and I'm not moving."

Someone moaned.

Her stated resolve immediately forgotten, Ingrid scrambled to slip back into her boots and socks. Advancing cautiously, a bent-over Whispr had entered the reeds and was moving in the direction of the sound. By the time Ingrid was back on her feet the moan had been repeated. Louder, and larded with words unknown to her. But from the country research she had done prior to disembarking in Cape Town she thought she recognized the language. The clicks and glottal stops were too distinctive to be anything other than the language of the original indigenous inhabitants of the Southern African desert.

Then they found the creature and she thought she was mistaken. Until it spoke again.

Lying panting and bleeding among the reeds was the most radical Meld Ingrid had ever seen—so extreme that at first she thought it was an antelope or some other small four-legged creature that had been magified to look human. Only as she moved slowly closer was she able to see for certain that it was a maniped human being. Even Whispr, who had encountered some truly radical melds in Savannah's underground, was taken aback. What lay before them was more than the usual cosmetic manipulation. The how of it was not in question. The why of it left them utterly bewildered.

Looking up at them, the creature—the person, Ingrid corrected herself—gasped a pair of sentences in her peculiar click-tongue. In the middle of her speech and without warning she abruptly switched over to English.

"You are not—company?"

"No." Now that her professional as well as personal instincts were aroused Ingrid felt no compunction about moving closer. "We're—explorers. We mean you no harm."

Dark doe eyes widened and the feminine voice strengthened slightly. "You are not—SICK security?"

"Hell no," Whispr assured her. "We don't want to see them any more than you do."

Ingrid was kneeling beside the injured—woman. Long bloody gashes streaked her left leg and buttock (haunch?). She wore very little, no more than the equivalent of a bikini top and a short skirt. But the dark fabric was synthetic tough. It imitated animal hide but had not been fashioned from it.

"What happened to you?" Without giving the woman time to answer she added, "My name is Ingrid. This is my friend and traveling companion, Whispr." As she reached toward the nearest gash the woman Meld pulled away. "Be at ease, relax." Ingrid smiled. "I'm a doctor. A real doctor."

"Doctor?" Her puzzling condition notwithstanding, the woman had a right to be surprised at encountering a self-proclaimed physician out in the middle of nowhere.

"Yes, a doctor." Ingrid adopted her professional mien. "Now, what happened to you?"

"I was gathering certain plants. Medicinal plants that grow along the river. I remember coming here to drink." Raising her head slightly she nodded upstream. "Leopard, he also came to drink at the same place, at the same time. He surprised me. I surprised him. We argued." A hint of a shy smile appeared on the dark sweat-stained face. "Leopard always win that argument."

"But you're still here," Whispr observed admiringly. "You're still alive."

A slight nod. "He struck at me out of surprise. I fought back." Reaching down, she touched her waistband and Ingrid saw a leather sheath. It was empty. "Mr. Leopard, he now wears my knife." Convinced she was not about to be shot or arrested, she struggled to sit up. "I am called !Nisa." Her name began with a sharp click of tongue against palate.

"Easy—go easy." Putting an arm behind the young woman to support her, Ingrid looked back at Whispr. "First-aid kit." He nodded and disappeared back into the brush.

Cleanser was followed by antibiotic. As she applied sprayskin from Whispr's kit Ingrid was afraid the small travel bottle would run out before she could close the last of the leopard's wounds, but there was just enough to complete the work to her satisfaction. He regarded her efforts disapprovingly as she set the empty container aside.

"Nothing left for us."

The Ingrid Seastrom who replied was not the same Dr. Ingrid Seastrom who had left Savannah weeks ago. Her response was curt. "So don't get cut. Anyway, if somebody shoots you, a travel dispenser of spray isn't going to close the wound."

"How reassuring," he grumbled.

"Prognosis is all part of my job. No extra charge." *I'm starting to sound like him*, she thought a little wildly. Bracing herself, she got both arms under the injured woman's shoulders. "Can you stand?"

A pause, then, "Yes, I can stand." With the doctor's help !Nisa proceeded to rise from where she had been lying.

Ingrid initially thought the woman's back locked on her when she was halfway erect. Then, as she stepped clear, she saw that the woman actually was standing. She just wasn't standing like a normal human. Or even like a normal Meld.

She was standing on all fours.

In that posture the full extent of her radical meld became clear. Her wrists had been maniped so that the heel of each hand was hardened like a hoof. While still as prehensile as ever, both hands could also serve to support the woman's upper body as efficiently as any feet. As for the latter, the ankles had been broken, radicalized, bone-ladled, and reset so that both feet faced permanently forward. !Nisa's legs had been strengthened and every muscle tuned and maximized for running. Her hip joints had been swiveled (that was the only way Ingrid could think of them considering how they were presently positioned). The neck had also been strengthened, given a greater backward arc, and lengthened like that of a melded runway model.

As she contemplated the remarkable reworking of the woman's body Ingrid wondered if it was even capable of standing erect anymore. No Meld she had ever seen or even read about had been maniped to this extreme. Had she first encountered !Nisa from behind she would have thought she was looking at an animal.

It wasn't just an animal meld, either. Those were to be found aplenty. Standing before her was an earnest attempt to reimagine a human being as a full-fledged quadruped. It was an extraordinary example of the biosurge's art. The next step, she supposed, would be to try a complete reversal of bipedal evolution.

"Why?" she heard herself ask. "Why do you look like this? Who made you look like this?"

"There is a fine clinic in Gaborone." Twisting her head and neck completely around, !Nisa leaned back and showed that she was as capable as any antelope of nibbling on her bruised and damaged hip. "We own it. My people. It is to enable us to be more of what we have always been." Leaving the treated wounds, she looked up at her new friends. "We are the San. The people of the desert."

"Are you saying," an aghast Whispr asked her, "that there are *others* like you?"

"We are the San," !Nisa replied simply. "One day we are all to become like this." She turned. "Come and I will show you." When they hesitated she kicked out with a hand—or was it a foreleg? "Come—are you afraid?" She cast a meaningful glance skyward.

"It is day and we are exposed here. Would you rather go with me or with a company drone?"

After recovering their backpacks Whispr and Ingrid followed the remarkable—and unsettling—Meld upriver. !Nisa explained as they followed the slow-flowing stream that often vanished into the sands.

"For a long time my people were mocked, derided, even hunted by those who invaded our ancestral territories. White, black—it made no difference. All looked down on and despised the San. Before the advent of the SAEC, the last tribe-country that ruled this land tried for many years to make the San live only in cities or on reservations. Neither is for San. In cities we die. On reservations we cry. But like this"—and she gestured down at her bent-over, four-legged self—"we can try. Always the San have lived in these deserts, the Namib and the Kalahari. We live here still. But to live as in days of old we no longer can. Always we have been told by others that we must change. So we change." She grinned. "But not as others would have us change. This time, these days, *we* decide on how to change!"

Over the course of the next several hours Ingrid and Whispr were forced to do more actual climbing and scrambling than they had since leaving Savannah. Despite the injuries she had incurred from the claws of the leopard, the tumbled boulders and awkward heights proved no obstacle to !Nisa. Traveling on all fours with greatly maniped leg muscles, she had no difficulty leaping from one ledge to the next. Patient with her charges and ignoring Whispr's constant cursing, she led them up a side canyon and away from the main river.

Still wondering if so severe a Meld was capable of standing on two legs, Ingrid got her answer when they were confronted by a pair of young men who seemed to materialize out of the rocks that flanked both sides of the trail. Though equally as radically maniped as their guide, they stood on their hind legs. They also held rifles in their melded fingers. His hands rising reflexively into the air, Whispr nodded at the nearest gun.

"I suppose you're going to tell me that's a traditional San weapon?"

!Nisa spoke to the guards in her own remarkable language. They promptly lowered their weapons. "We are traditionalists," she told Whispr. "Not fools."

Now advancing escorted by the pair of guards they continued upward into the foothills. Unable to hold their weapons and proceed on all fours, the two men had slipped the rifles into long woven holsters slung across their backs.

"What do you need guns for?" Ingrid asked curiously. "Out here, in this empty place?"

"The desert is only empty to those who do not know how to look. Because we are again become one with the Namib does not mean we must feed ourselves with bows and arrows. Had I brought my own gun with me I could have dealt better with the leopard and would not have needed your help. But then you would not be seeing this place now." Sitting back on her haunches she gestured ahead.

The hanging canyon was a small paradise high up in the foothills. Where the slope flattened out, the winding trickle of a tributary they had been following expanded to form multiple pools. Surrounded by high rock on all sides, the little valley boasted a surprising amount of vegetation. Traditional hunter-gatherers, the San did not farm the well-watered soil. Nor did they erect or have need of structures. Caves and overhangs provided ample shelter. Their lifestyle did not demand a full reversion to ancient times, however. Traditional culture had its limits.

Sheets of amorphous solar cells colored to match and blend with the surrounding terrain provided power. Small camouflaged satellite pickups allowed for the reception of the same vit programming one would find in Cape Town—or for that matter, Savannah. Noiseless refrigeration allowed food to be stored and kept despite the extremes of temperature experienced in the Namib. Concealed in a large cave near the back of the community were not one but two veiled floaters.

"In Sperrgebeit this kind of formal settlement is quite illegal, of course." !Nisa pointed out one surprise after another as she led her guests through the village. Nearly naked children broke away from monitors and projections that depicted everything from courses in advanced desert zoology to linguistics and floater mechanics in order to gape at the strangers. !Nisa continued to enlighten her two visitors.

"Those of us who have permission to live outside developed areas have reclaimed and been granted traditional parts of the Kalahari and the Namib. Our ecologically sound communities make no imposition on the animal preserves and offer educational and recreational facilities for tourists who wish to experience the desert regions and learn about our history and way of life." Her tone hardened.

"But other lands that have always been home to our people are officially off-limits. Sperrgebeit is one such place. As you can see, it has not stopped us from resettling territory where our ancestors once roamed freely."

"What'll you do if company security finds this place?" A young girl offered Whispr a biodegradable plastic glass full of fruit juice. Finding it surprisingly cold, he downed it greedily.

"We will argue for our rights to remain here. Do not let either our melded appearance or our choice to live with as little clothing as possible fool you. In addition to the best biosurges, we have fine solicitors on our payroll. And if we cannot win rights to live in places such as this legally, we are ready to fight for what we believe belongs to us."

Using the back of a skeletal hand to wipe fruit pulp from his mouth, Whispr shook his head sadly. "You can't win a pitched battle with the SAEC." He indicated the idyllic surroundings. "One armored floater full of company mercenaries would take this whole valley out."

!Nisa nodded. "From a military standpoint you right." Raising a hand off the ground, she gestured toward a well-concealed cluster of antennae. "But it would all be broadcast, live and worldwide. We have excellent uplink facilities here. Resulting outrage would be very bad for the company. So we have a number of weapons with which to fight.

"Meanwhile we live here quietly, peacefully, and undiscovered as we honor the ways of our ancestors. On reaching adulthood, many of children you see here will go off to soches in the cities to learn how to live and interact with other people, Naturals as well as Melds. Not all will choose return. But enough will come back to live as I do in order to maintain connection that we have worked hard to reestablish with the land and with our traditions."

Exhausted from the climb, Ingrid looked around for a place to sit down. Arriving out of nowhere a teenager with a collapsed chair approached her, sat back, unfolded the chair, and invited her to relax. Murmuring a thank-you she lowered herself onto the supportive fabric. Clearly she, Whispr, and their interaction with !Nisa was being studied. When her companion requested similar seating, a second chair was quickly provided.

"Now then." Settling herself back on her haunches and idly licking a hand-foot with her melded tongue, !Nisa confronted her guests beneath the shade of the massive stone overhang where they were sitting. Ingrid noted that the two armed lookouts who had escorted them uphill had recently been joined by two similarly equipped older men. "You must tell me what brought you to this place where no one comes."

"We did tell you," Ingrid began. "We're explorers who . . ."

!Nisa raised the hand she had been cleaning. "Please, doctor. You are too far from anywhere and too lightly equipped to be engaged in desert exploration. Fools do not deceive the company on a daily basis, and we San are not fools. I indebt to you for treating my wounds and for helping me, but not to extent of endangering all that we have made here." Leaning forward, seated on her haunches, and resting foot-hands on the ground, she embodied both sheep and shepherd in a single vision. "What are you doing in the Sperrgebeit?"

Her tone and her expression hinted that further obfuscation on the part of the visitors might result in a serious downgrading of the hospitality they had so far been shown. So despite Whispr's frantic eye-rolling and gesturing Ingrid proceeded to tell their host the truth. By the time she had concluded the story, her attenuated companion was on the verge of passing out from frustration. But !Nisa looked satisfied.

"That is an extraordinary tale. Too extraordinary to be an invention, I think. You actually *want* to get into Nerens?" Ingrid nodded vigorously, but their host still found it hard to believe. "Not for diamonds, but to learn what lies on a single storage thread you have bring with you?" Once more Ingrid gestured affirmatively.

"You might maybe get in," one of the armed men standing on four legs behind her commented, "but you never get out again."

Twisting around she looked back at the speaker. "They're our lives. It's what we choose to do, no matter how crazy it sounds." She turned back to !Nisa. "Of all people the San should appreciate that."

"You argue plausible. We will let you go."

"Right." Whispr was on his feet fast. But Ingrid hesitated.

"Can you help us? Help us to get inside the facility? If we can just get past perimeter security I think I can convince any workers we meet that we belong there. I *am* a doctor. People, even those who are usually suspicious, tend to believe what doctors say."

"People like me?" !Nisa smiled, then turned serious again. "This *Nerens* we are talking about. Is true my people have no love for the company, or its minions, or the constant patrols whose attention we work to avoid. But at same time I see no compelling reason why we should risk even one of our own to assist you on what is plainly insane desire to sacrifice yourselves on altar of SICK security."

"Where have I heard that sentiment expressed before?" Whispr muttered under his breath.

Ingrid mustered all the determination she could. "!Nisa, you're proud of your children, of how they go out into the world to get a proper social education and then, how some of them at least, return to adopt again your traditional way of life. Well, I happen to know that someone or something connected to this thread and to SICK is doing things to young people. To young adults who have suffered through bad melds. It's possible even some young San might be among those who have received certain unauthorized nano-implants."

The men behind her moved closer. Several other villagers who had paused to watch came nearer. Had they been listening all along? Nothing in this place, she reflected, was half as primitive as first appeared. She rushed on.

"I don't know what these implants do. I do have reason to believe that they're connected to the thread somehow because both the thread and the implants are made of the same unique material. We believe that the material, and maybe also the thread and the implants, originate or at least are worked on at a secret research facility in Nerens."

"Nerens all about diamond mining," put in an older man who had just wandered over. "Nothing else there."

"No," Ingrid corrected him firmly. "The diamond mining may be real, but I believe it's a cover for this facility. My friend and I have dedicated ourselves"—Whispr made a rude noise but was ignored—"to getting inside this place and learning what the thread and the implants are all about. Maybe you're right—maybe we won't get out"—another distinctive nonverbal comment arose from her companion—"but we've come a very long way through very difficult circumstances to try." She sat back. "Won't you—can't you—help us? If not for our sake then for those of the children whose futures are somehow being tampered with."

An older woman standing behind !Nisa spoke up. By now quite a crowd had gathered around the visitors and their guide. "How do you know that is happening? You just admit that you don't know what these implants do."

"You're right, I don't," Ingrid confessed. "But I do know that people operating out of benevolent motives don't put unauthorized devices into the brains of unknowing young people who are just trying to get bad cosmetic work fixed. Devices that vanish when anyone tries to study them. If these implants are intended to do good, why would those who install them do so secretly and without notifying the patient?"

"And SICK behind this?"

Sensing the mood change in her growing audience and not wishing to have to parse her explanation, Ingrid simply nodded agreement.

Several older villagers moved to consult quietly with !Nisa. Whispr and Ingrid could only wait in hopeful silence as their hosts debated her request. Would they risk exposure of their little paradise to assist a couple of lost strangers, even if they believed that the intentions of the two Namericans were benign? Or would they force them back down to the desert floor and turn them loose to be discovered by company security? It had been a while since she and

Whispr had been at the complete mercy of others and it was not a sensation Ingrid enjoyed revisiting.

When finally the conference broke up and the elders wandered off without so much as looking in the visitors' direction, she could not help but wonder if her request had even been discussed. !Nisa quickly resolved her uncertainty.

"Wherever the company establish an enterprise it likes to be able to say that it provides jobs for locals. Often these are low-level, low-paying positions. At Nerens some of these are always reserved for the San. Hiring some of us make them look good. Sometimes San employees sent to Cape Town to provide reassuring vitops for visiting media." Turning to her left she strained to see deeper into the village. "So someone have gone to fetch Gwi."

For the first time in a very long while the normally pessimistic Whispr felt a tickle of sanguinity. "This Gwi person—this is some-one who has actually worked inside Nerens?"

!Nisa nodded. "The research division of which you speak may be unknown to outside world, but is hard to keep secrets from the San." She turned thoughtful. "Maybe SICK does not care what we know because they understand that except for our clinic and con-tacts in Gaborone we have little contact with the outside world. Or perhaps their people think that because we choose to live and meld ourselves this way that we are stupid throwbacks."

"I can't believe this." Seated before their host Ingrid reflected on all that she and her dour companion had gone through to get to this point. Now, here, in the Forbidden Zone of the Namib, they were for the first time about to meet someone who had not only worked inside Nerens but might possibly know something about the research facility itself!

No, she corrected herself. This would be the second time. She had momentarily forgotten about the refugee employee Morgan Ouspel. But other than providing them with instructions on the best way to make it through the Sperrgebeit and panicking at the sight of the storage thread (a "distributor" he had called it), he had either been reluctant or unable to supply anything more in the way of explication save for some nonsensical babble about a "big picture" and its "painters." Would a modern bushman who had worked at the facility know more? Or at least prove more transparent in his comments?

Gwi was a surprise in more ways than one. Not only had he not undergone the extreme quadruped meld favored by his fellows, judging by his appearance he had not yet been subjected to a single manip. Short like all of his people, he was nearly as slender as Whispr despite being completely Natural. In place of the skimpy traditional attire favored by his relations he was clad in buff desert pants whose camo pattern changed according to how the sun struck the chameleon material. This was complimented by a yellow-beige shirt whose pockets were stuffed with the kind of mini-electronics one might expect to find on a sophisticated youth out for a skate in Cape Town or Joburg. Sand-repelling sandals shod his otherwise bare feet. Among his four-footed relatives he looked almost as out of place as the two Namericans.

In contrast to his appearance, his first words were not encouraging.

"I don't know why I'm talking to you two except that Auntie !Tana told me to do so." His expression as he studied them over the rim of photosensitive shades was disapproving. "She said something about you trying to help mis-maniped people my age."

When it came to lack of tact Whispr was more than a match for the newcomer. "You've worked in the facility at Nerens?"

"Not exactly." The young man turned his critical gaze on the much taller Meld. "I *work* in the facility at Nerens."

The correction shut Whispr up, but only for a moment. "C'mon—you expect us to believe that company security lets you travel freely back and forth between the facility and the outside world? We have it on *excellent* authority that nobody is allowed out unless they've first been properly 'debriefed.'"

A thin smile appeared on the younger man's face. "Who said anything about 'freely'? I'm San. This is my country, and in my country I come and go as I please."

Ingrid wanted to believe him. Wanted to very badly, because if he was telling the truth then it presented the kind of opportunity she and Whispr could hardly hope existed.

"How can you get in and out of the facility without being picked up by Security? And why would you take that kind of risk?"

He shrugged. "I take the risk because I know I can do it. I like to visit my relatives. And there's another reason." When he lowered his voice Ingrid realized it was not for their protection but for his. He didn't want any of his friends or relatives to overhear. "I'm a musician. As a boy I started here in the village playing modern reproductions of traditional instruments. Just like San language, San music is full of unique rhythms and sounds. I've been to Gaborone and played in clubs there. I want to go to Harare and Mombasa, to Mauritius and Antananarivo, and expand my musical horizons." His voice filled with enthusiasm. "I want to compose, and to play full bandwand!" His right hand gestured. "But I need a sounding meld." He indicated their surroundings; the peaceful valley, the busy village.

"I love my people, and my family. But a good sounding meld costs real subsist. My people have happiness, but not a lot of money. What they manage to accumulate is used for melding. There is a communal pot, but the subsist in it is not for the use of would-be musicians. That's why I took the job at Nerens. So that when I slip away from there to come here for a visit, I can take some time along the way to look for diamonds. To pay for my gear and the travels I hope to take."

"Find any?" Whispr automatically asked.

Gwi's excitement faded somewhat. "One or two. Poor quality. Not worthless, but far from enough to pay for the music meld I need. So I keep working, and I keep looking. All I need is one good-sized gem-quality stone. That's all, just one."

"Get us into Nerens and I'll pay for your meld," Ingrid told him without hesitating.

He frowned as he eyed her up and down. "You? What are you, this man's mistress? Or a wandering hooker from the Cape Flats?"

Ingrid flushed so violently that Whispr worried she would faint. "I—am—a—*doctor*! And this hair, this body, is just a temporary camo qwikmeld. I don't normally look like this. In my natural state I am . . ." She caught hold of herself. "I really am a successful physician, Gwi. Ask !Nisa. While I see that your people have access here to many modern conveniences I suspect that a credit card processor isn't among them. But I promise you: if you help us to get inside Nerens I will pay for whatever meld you want, no matter how elaborate."

"I know she doesn't look like it at the moment," Whispr added tactlessly, "but she really is a doctor. Good one, too."

Gwi pondered their responses before replying coolly. "How can you pay for my meld if you are dead? Or do you expect me to get you out of Nerens as well?"

"Just get us in. Of course," she added with a knowing smile, "if you do want me to pay for your body work then I suppose you *will* have to get us safely out again."

The young San pursed his lips. "You trouble me like lice. What proof do I have that if I help you to do this thing you will not simply shaft me once you are safely outside again?"

Ingrid spread her hands wide. "We have no communicator and our food is running low. Without your help or that of your people there's no way we can get out of the Sperrgebeit, much less the greater Namib." She gestured beyond him. "We saw that you have floaters. Get us into Nerens and out again, then take us to the nearest town that offers banking access. I'll transfer the subsist while you watch. If you want, you can bring some armed friends of yours. If we don't fulfill our side of the bargain you can take compensation on us however you wish."

Whispr looked alarmed. "Hey now, wait a minute, doc! Leave us maybe discuss this between us before you go promising my blood and bone on your behalf!"

"Too late." Gwi looked satisfied. "It is a bargain, Ms. . . . ?"

"Alice," she told him. "Call me Alice."

"Ah," he murmured, nodding. "Because I am about to take you through the Looking Glass, yes?"

"Uh, yes, sure—that's it. And don't mind my friend Colin here. He gets nervous whenever he thinks about actually being inside Nerens instead of just talking about it."

"Then he is smarter than he looks." Amusement faded from the young man's voice. "There is a real possibility that once inside, you will be discovered. Then you will die. As for myself, I am prepared for such an eventuality. One who dwells in the Namib lives each day side by side with death. But I will keep you alive as long as I can." He turned to leave. "I will see to it that your packs are topped up with additional food. You will need to carry your own gear. I will guide you but I will not porter for you."

"That's understandable." She rose. "Don't worry about me, Gwi. I'm tougher than I look. I'm tougher than I was."

"You will need to be."

"Just a minute." Whispr bade the other man pause. "You haven't told us what it is that you do at Nerens, inside the facility. Are you a scientist?"

Looking back at him, Gwi smiled. "The only scientists among the San are in Gaborone, and a few who work in Joburg. The jobs

SICK makes available to my people at Nerens are of the more mundane variety."

"Yet you still think you're clever enough to get us inside?"

"Much of my work is with the facility sewerage system. So I think I am clever enough to get you inside, stick Meld, since I work with shit every day."

As a suddenly grim Whispr started toward the younger man Ingrid hastened to interpose herself. "I believe you, Gwi." She looked sharply at her companion. "Just like I believe we won't get a kilometer from here if we start fighting before we've even started." She turned back to their new guide. "The part of the facility we need to get into involves something called the Big Picture."

Gwi eyed her blankly. "Never heard of it."

It was the response she had expected. An honest answer but a discouraging one. They were going to have to find out everything for themselves.

"So despite how smart you are there are areas of the facility that you're not allowed into?" Whispr queried mockingly.

Gwi replied as if addressing a child. "Of course. I specialize in general sanitation. Why should I be allowed into the Restricted Zone?"

Ingrid perked up. "But you know that such a place exists?"

The young man nodded. "Security there is impossibly strict. If that is your intended destination you will never reach it."

She smiled. "That's where we want to go. That's where we have to go. Where security is tightest. Where casual visitors aren't allowed."

"I can direct you toward it," he told her reluctantly, "but I cannot take you there. It lies on the lowest level of the complex."

"Of course it does." Whispr was nodding knowingly. "It *would* be closer to hell than any other part of the facility."

"You mean you have not already visited that famously warm

place, stick Meld? I would have thought otherwise. Well, not to feel deprived. Once SICK security gets hold of you I am sure they will provide you with a ticket. One-way." Before Whispr could snarl a reply, Gwi turned back to Ingrid. "Let us find you some additional supplies, Doctor Alice. We can leave tonight if you like. Where company searchers may be about it is always better to move at night."

Whispr nodded agreement. "What kind of communicator do you use to find your way in the dark?"

"My GPS is in my hard drive." Reaching up, Gwi touched his head. "In here. Seven thousand years of accumulated intimate, traditional knowledge about this part of the world, learned at the feet of my elders. My communicator is impervious to sand, wind, and even SICK security. All the animal trails are there, all the watering places, all the holes in which to hide from the patrolling drones that will become more frequent the closer we get to Nerens." He paused, then looked again at Ingrid. "You must understand that if we are stopped by Security I will have no choice but to turn you over to them."

Her lips tightened. "I would expect nothing less from a representative of the world's greatest desert survivors."

10

Below him and to his left was the wet emptiness called the Southern Atlantic Ocean. To his right was the dry emptiness called the Namib desert. Nature in its vastness and variety was all the same to Molé, who more than ever longed for the puzzle-piece packages called crowds that filled the world's most densely populated cities. In that regard even Cape Town had its diversions.

That great southern city lay far behind him now, almost as far down the barren, empty coast along which he was traveling as it was possible to go. Quiet, completely controlled anger powered him as efficiently as did the jatropha that fueled the small private VTOL aircraft on which he was the only passenger. Plenty of fury seethed within his small squat frame. He was mad at his employers for sticking him with this assignment. Mad at the foolish mismatched pair who had somehow, impossibly, succeeded in evading him on not one but several occasions. Mad at those who could have helped to bring his chase to a much earlier conclusion. Most of all he was mad at himself for allowing this project to waste, to

burn up, and to occupy time that could have been better spent in-
dulging his simple if unorthodox appetites.

Well, it would be over and done with soon enough, he assured
himself as the plane turned inland and began to descend. Blue-
green below gave way to yellow-brown. Off to port, beyond the silent pilot who was the aircraft's only other occupant, a cargo vessel
was unloading containers inside a single-quayed harbor. In moments the sight fell behind and out of view. In the distance rose
mountains of modest height and forbidding aspect. Molé knew his
topography. Were the plane to travel onward in a straight line it
would have to cross almost the entire continent before encountering anything resembling a center of population. The advances
made by contemporary technology notwithstanding, the west and
center of southern Africa was as inhospitable to man now as it had
been since the breakup of Gondwanaland.

There was no visible landing strip. The VTOL did not need
one. Hidden electronics buried beneath the flat, dry plain guided
the plane down. It was an easy site to camouflage, since the surrounding terrain looked exactly the same as the landing site. Only
when the whine of the aircraft's compact jets were subsumed into
the overwhelming silence and it taxied forward on battery power
alone did a sizable slab of faux rock rise up like a modern draw-
bridge to reveal a sloping ramp that angled gently downward.
Brakes squealing like a saurian hog, the plane slid into the ground
like a spider entering its lair.

Lights came on automatically as the hangar cover descended
behind them. Figures appeared on both sides of the plane, direct-
ing it to a parking place alongside several other aircraft. All save two
were the same size as the private craft that had conveyed him here
from Cape Town. Wings folded up like giant white butterflies, the
two larger planes were executive jets, luxuriously fitted-out and ca-

pable of flying nonstop from Nerens to welcoming metropolises like Abuja, Accra, or even Casablanca.

Thoughts of proper civilized cities replete with the modern amenities he loved depressed him. He forced such images from his mind. All their delights would be open and available to him as soon as he concluded this assignment. When his safety harness released him he rose and made his way to the rear of the plane, picking up his cane as he went. The pilot remained behind, ignoring his passenger as he spoke into the vorec suspended near his mouth. In the course of the flight north from Cape Town the stolid driver had exchanged perhaps two sentences with his passenger.

Must remember to recommend the man for his professionalism, Molé reminded himself as he waited for the door to rise and the plane's integrated steps to extend themselves. He did not wait for the pilot to follow him. The Meld could not. True and dedicated flyer that he was, his lower extremities fit tightly into the aircraft itself. He would have to wait for the landing team to disengage him. He did not fly the plane—he *was* the plane.

The burly Natural waiting for Molé near the bottom of the stairs looked as if he would rather be somewhere else doing something worthwhile. His disappointment as his attention shifted between the reader he was carrying and the old man standing at the top of the stairs was plain. Frowning, he leaned slightly to one side as he tried to see past the single figure that blocked the entrance to the plane's interior.

"I'm here to escort a Napun Molé?"

"That would be me," Molé replied quietly.

Frown morphed to scowl. "Says here that Molé is a tactical operative, senior classification. You don't look like a tactical operative to me—of any classification."

"That is the idea."

When the escort looked up again from his reader there was no sign of Molé. Not until he felt the end of a cane tap him on the shoulder and, shocked, turned to see the old man standing behind him.

"How did—how did you . . . ?"

"I jumped. It is not far." The smaller man's voice tensed ever so slightly. "I could have landed on you instead of behind you. But then I would have needed a new escort. While momentarily satisfying, that result would have wasted time, and I have a chronic aversion to wasting time." He smiled pleasantly. "Would you be so kind as to take me to station Chief of Security Het Kruger? I have an appointment."

"Yes, sure, I . . ." The much bigger, much younger man swallowed hard and tucked his reader under an arm. His tone had become considerably more respectful. "It's a bit of a flight up from the Cape. Wouldn't you like to see your quarters first? Maybe take a shower, unpack . . . ?"

"I have no luggage. Everything I need is in me."

The frown returned, less put-upon this time. "Don't you mean 'on' you—sir?"

"Yes, of course. 'On' me. Mr. Kruger?"

The escort hesitated, but not for long. As he led the visitor from the underground hangar and into the depths of the facility he offered no more suggestions. This was wise.

Molé's curiosity concerning his new surroundings extended only to a characteristic need to map them in his head. He did not care what the facilities were used for, was uninterested in the motivations of the many Naturals and Melds who bustled around him. He was here on specific company business. The rest of company business did not concern him. Diversions were for when his task was done.

They descended one floor in a massive lift large enough to hold a dozen people and several vehicles. More walking and more corridors brought them to a second lift. This one was considerably smaller and descended a good deal farther. Exiting down another hallway eventually brought them to a double door flanked by two guards. Both were large lods hefting large weapons. Molé identified the guns at a glance, casually noting with approval that both were powerful fast-firing contemporary models that would be well suited to defending a subterranean corridor. The escort identified himself to the guards, who in turn identified him to the door. A feminine voice responded via a speaker and the doors parted with a click to admit the visitors. The paired barriers were thick, fireproof, and probably capable of stopping anything up to and including an armor-piercing military round.

A curving desk in the reception area was staffed by a woman in her early thirties. She appeared to be a Natural, though Molé knew better than most how external appearances could be deceiving. Hovering off to one side between a pair of purple couches, a floating holovit whose volume had been turned way down was showing the most recent episode of a popular folk drama from Madagascar. The receptionist looked up from her box screen.

"Napun Molé?" He nodded and she smiled, showing none of the instinctive disdain that had initially been displayed by his younger escort. "You're expected. Go right in." A single door nearby slid aside and Molé stepped through the portal. As he did so it scanned him, even though he had long since been cleared through an assortment of checkpoints. When his escort moved to follow, the woman spoke pleasantly but firmly.

"Not you."

It was a measure of the woman's tone, or Kruger's status, or perhaps both, that the formerly self-confident young man did not try to argue with her. Turning, he departed wordlessly back the way he had come. The outer doors slid silently shut behind him.

Kruger's office featured one full vit wall that was presently displaying a live three-dimensional projection from St. Mark's Square. Excited tourists mingled with locals while a tenor outside the oldest café in Italy strove manfully to project Puccini above the babble of several dozen tongues. Beneath the transparent pavers that were part of Ascended Venice, the waters of the Grand Canal surged restlessly, stirred by passing vaporetto. Wandering into the foreground and indifferent to the presence of the global box or local police pickups, a pickpocket casually riffled a wallet from a woman's purse. The unjudgmental Molé noted that the man wore a live fluctuator on his wrist. Disguised to look like a cheap chrono, its signal would cancel out the proximity alarm embedded in the stolen wallet, rendering it useless. So went the eternal war between the ever innocent and the always opportunistic.

Kruger noted the direction of his visitor's gaze. "You've been to Venice?"

"Yes," Molé murmured longingly, "I've been to Venice. I was once witness to a drowning that took place there. The poor fellow ended up in a canal and I was compelled to perform CPT on him."

The security chief frowned. "Don't you mean CPR?"

"No." Molé smiled thinly. "CPT. Cardiopulmonary termination." Without changing tone or expression he added, "I like cities in general. It is where I am most comfortable. City people are generally accommodating of the elderly."

Kruger nodded without comment, tracking his guest carefully as the old man settled himself into the chair on the other side of the desk. "You don't move like you need that cane you're carrying."

"Kind of you to say so. I manage my affairs well enough. Unlike you, it would seem."

Kruger instantly dispensed with the false conviviality he was obliged to display toward visitors. From here onward their conversation would proceed on a purely professional plane. That suited him just fine.

"What's that supposed to mean?"

Molé had draped the cane across his lap. "I was informed that you recently lost some of your people here."

The security chief stiffened in his chair. "An unfortunate incident involving unexpected hostiles that took place far outside the facility. Procedures are in place to ensure it won't happen again. It's nothing that need concern an independent contractor like yourself—colleague."

Molé smiled afresh. "I meant no offense."

"You could've fooled me."

"Seriously, I do not. I am merely curious from a professional standpoint. Speaking professionally, I am sure that you recall our conversation of some weeks ago."

"Well enough." Still only partly mollified, Kruger leaned back in his chair. "I replayed it when I was told that you were coming. I wish I could say that I was looking forward to this, but I dislike interruptions to routine."

"Where that is concerned we are of the same mind—colleague."

Kruger felt a bit better about his guest. "I was expecting someone . . ."

"Younger?" Molé finished for him.

Kruger nodded. "And larger." His own smile was flat. "Merely from a 'professional' standpoint, you understand." Without taking his eyes off his visitor he addressed a concealed pickup. "Danae, will you come in here a minute, please?"

Molé did not react as the door behind him slid open to admit the receptionist. When she stopped very close to his left side and leaned toward him he was compelled to take closer notice of her. Ylang-ylang-based perfume assailed his nostrils. Resting her hands on her knees, she locked pale blue eyes with his. Her voice was a trill composed to run up and down specific parts of a man's body.

"Is there anything I can get you, Mr. Molé? Anything at all? In situations like this I am always at a guest's disposal." Watching from the other side of the desk Kruger said nothing, his expression unreadable.

Molé met her gaze without flinching, without blinking. "Tempted as I am by your practiced offer I believe you would find my personal predilections unpalatable, Ms. Danae. You are quite striking and you have excellent breasts and fine hips. I also note that the power mister situated between the former is doubtless loaded with a suitably potent soporific. I would suggest replacing it with a smaller and less prominent model." Her expression fell and he smiled. "Less volume but less detectable is better. The same goes for the flistol strapped to your attractive and well-toned right thigh. Too much bulge."

She straightened and her winsome smile vanished. "No one else ever noticed them."

"No, that is not necessarily correct," he challenged her. "What you mean to say is that no one else has commented on them. That does not mean they have gone unnoticed. Something not commented upon does not cease to exist. This, for example." His hand shot out and grabbed her between the legs.

Shocked, she immediately brought her right hand down sharply, the edge aiming for his neck. Parrying the blow easily with his left hand, the right swung the cane upward. The tip, from which a needle now protruded, halted less than a centimeter from her left eye. She froze. It was dead silent in the room.

Folding his hands on the desk in front of him, Kruger said quietly, "That'll be all for now, Danae."

Backing away from the visitor, the receptionist grabbed her throbbing wrist with her other hand, nodded, and retreated to the outer reception area. While the door closed behind her, Molé turned nonchalantly back to his host. As the monitors concealed beneath the top of the security chief's desk indicated, the visitor's respiration and heart rate were unchanged.

"She's fast. And she is decorative. A useful tool, but she needs to learn how to deal with both criticism and the unexpected."

Kruger shook his head. "I think, Mr. Molé, that you are a little more unexpected than anything she has encountered before. I'll speak to her about the concealed weapons."

Molé nodded. "As tests of my competency go, that was relatively unstressful. You must understand that at my age women are at best a diversion, not an inducement. I trust there will be no more games."

"Why have you come here?"

"That's better." Pleased to have the discussion back on a purely professional level, Molé settled back into the chair. Nearly disappeared into it, Kruger thought. "I have come to await the conclusion of an assignment that has already taken far too long."

Kruger remembered their phone conversation. "The two thieves you spoke about. The ones you said had stolen a small storage thread that belongs to the company. If I recall correctly you said you had reason to believe they might be in Southern Africa." His eyes widened slightly. "You don't mean to say that you think they're somewhere around *here*?"

Molé nodded. "I mean to say exactly that."

"*Wunderbaarlik.* Well, if they're anywhere in the Sperrgebeit either my patrols or our programmed searchers will find them. I assure you that if they're within two hundred kilometers of Nerens they'll be located and picked up."

"These are very resourceful people."

"Because they've managed to avoid you for so long?" Molé twitched ever so faintly at the slight, but not so faintly that Kruger failed to note the reaction. *Good*, he thought. That should even up the "nonoffensive" commentary a bit.

"It is astounding what the most ordinary people can do if sufficiently motivated," the visitor responded calmly. "By subsist, by a desire for power, by sex. Although from what I have learned I do not think the last motivator applies in this instance. It is true that I thought I had successfully run these people to ground previously. Twice, in fact. On each occasion they managed to escape me. They will not this time."

Kruger was on firm ground now. "Not if they come anywhere near my security perimeter they won't."

Molé leaned slightly forward. Despite himself Kruger's right hand moved surreptitiously toward a desk drawer when the tip of the unprepossessing cane appeared to incline in his direction. Neither man commented on the security chief's instinctive reaction. Indeed, Molé would have been disappointed had Kruger not reacted.

"Your confidence is reassuring but possibly misplaced. Belying their backgrounds, these two have managed to elude not only myself but others who would like to take possession of the storage thread. Its significance cannot be overemphasized nor its importance to the company overstressed."

"All right, all right; I get it, Mr. Molé. This thread is important and these people are tricky." His heavy eyebrows drew together slightly. "If you don't mind my asking, if they've stolen something that's so valuable to the company, why on Earth would they try to bring it here, where company security is as tight as anywhere on the planet?"

"Of that I am not sure. But having had more time than I wish to consider all the possibilities, I believe they are coming in hopes of learning what is on the thread. They cannot sell it, for example to those other interested parties to whom I just referred, without knowing what it contains. I cannot imagine any other reason for taking such risks as they already have."

Kruger nodded. "That makes a certain twisted sense. To a crazy person."

"They are not crazy," Molé assured his host. "They are driven. These are not always so very different."

"Their motivation is immaterial to me. If they enter the Sperrgebeit they'll be detected and picked up. And if their intent is to try and slip into Nerens itself, the closer they come the tighter they'll find security." He smiled, ready to relax. "Meanwhile, you must be tired from your trip. Bouncing all the way from the Cape to the Namib isn't my idea of a peaceful journey." He nodded suggestively toward the door that led to the reception area. "You sure you don't want Danae to show you the ropes?"

Molé smiled back. It was different from his earlier smiles. "Not unless you already have someone else in mind for the vacancy she would leave."

Het Kruger was not a man whose blood was easily chilled. But with a single expression the old man seated in the big chair before him had managed to lower the temperature in the office by several degrees.

11

From what Ingrid could remember of Ouspel's map and directions Gwi followed a similar though not identical route. After days of struggling through the hostile desert landscape on their own it was almost relaxing to have an actual live guide. That he talked occasionally at night but hardly at all during the day had nothing to do with shyness.

"SICK searchers listen as well as look," he told her when she inquired as to the reason for his persistent silences.

They were traveling almost due west now. Whenever Whispr would question if they were headed in the right direction Gwi would point out a landmark that was familiar to him. Most of what he singled out for attention did not look like landmarks to Ingrid: a twist in a dry riverbed, a single lonely kokerboom tree, the way two hillside slopes came together to form a particular angle: sometimes their guide's "landmark" consisted of nothing more than a discoloration underfoot. All were road signs to the young San.

They were very close to Nerens when he bade them stop and crouch down behind a sandy hillock. A few twisted sprigs of *Sarco-*

caulon pattersonii, better known as bushmen's candle, held forth against the wind from the crest of the sandy bulge. Ingrid looked around anxiously.

"I don't see anything. What's wrong?"

As he swung his small pack off his back and began fumbling within, Gwi put a finger to his lips. "Forget your eyes," he told her. "Listen."

She went silent. An irritated Whispr was about to say something when the sound of distant laughter made him pause. Hints of hilarity odd in timbre, it was deep and drawing near. Staying on his belly, he scrambled to the top of the hillock and peered into the distance, trying to locate the source of the ongoing incongruous merriment. Several minutes elapsed before he could, at the absolute limit of his vision, make out a dozen or so shapes running toward them. Not, not running, he corrected himself. Loping.

Spotted hyenas.

"Magified melds. Components of Nerens security." Gwi whispered tightly without looking up from working with the contents of his pack. Removing a small cylindrical shape from a package, he carefully unfolded its wings, tail, and propeller, locking them in place. Whispr admired the result.

"Model airplane? You're going to fight maniped carnivores with a model airplane?"

"Maybe he has a model bomb." Ingrid no longer had to strain to pick up the excited yapping of the oncoming predators, who made up for their awkward gait with surprising speed and unsurpassed endurance.

"No bomb." Another transparent plastic container he took from his pack contained half a dozen capsules. Flicking open the container's cap he carefully removed one of the pills, snapped the container shut, and replaced it inside his pack. As Ingrid watched he opened a compartment in the underside of the toy plane, slipped the capsule inside, and snapped the lid shut. The deep-throated coughing laughter of the hyenas was very loud now. Whispr eyed their guide meaningfully.

"You better have a gun to go with that toy."

"I work in sanitation, my friend. No one at the facility is allowed to have weapons except Security personnel. But I have this." Using the hillock for concealment he shifted onto his knees and held the small drone high in his right hand.

Ingrid was trying hard not to panic. Being picked up by and having to try to explain themselves to SICK security was one thing; what the patrolling carnivore melds might do to them quite another. With a person, even a lod, you could reason. But magified hyenas . . .

"I am going to release this on 'three'," Gwi whispered. "Before I say 'three' you should take a deep breath, cover your mouth and nose, and try to hold your breath as long as you can."

"I don't underst . . . ," she began.

There was no time to explain even had the San been so inclined. The howling of the pack was nearly upon them. "One, two" — their guide inhaled deeply — "three!" On "three" he released the drone. Propeller whirring, engine whining softly, it promptly shot off at high speed directly toward the oncoming pack. Within moments it had begun to release a vapor from its underside. Too flustered to prepare properly, Ingrid forgot their guide's admonition and took in a breath through her nose.

The stench that assailed her nostrils and sinus cavities hit her insides like a shot of zero gravity.

As she fell forward, cheeks bulging, Gwi threw himself on top of her. Divining the San's purpose and still holding his own breath, Whispr joined him. Together their two bodies managed to smother most of the sound of the doctor's retching. They laid thus for more than a minute, at which point the struggling Whispr had to gulp air. To his great relief he found that much of the stench had cleared off.

So had something else. The maniacal braying of the pack of magified hyenas was receding rapidly into the distance. In another moment it was gone completely.

Sucking fresh air like a diver surfacing on an empty tank, Ingrid rolled over and wiped at her mouth. Whispr's short-lived gallantry did not extend to helping her clean herself. "I'm sorry," she sputtered, her expression twisting in disgust. "It all happened so fast." Sitting up and still wiping at herself, she coughed and spat. "What was—what did you do?" Turning slightly to her left she listened intently, but of the hysterical choir of approaching four-footed death there was no sound. "What about the hyenas?"

"Running for their kennel, I should think." Gwi was rearranging the contents of his pack. "The drone is a simple, inexpensive toy one can purchase anywhere. I like it because it is wholly mechanical. It is powered by compressed gas and made of maize-derived organic polymers. When it runs out of fuel it will land itself. Eventually it will disintegrate under the force of the elements. With the exception of the small gas cylinder that will quickly be covered by blowing sand there will be nothing for a searcher to find."

"But the *smell* . . ." She put her hand over her mouth as mere memory of the noxious odor threatened to once more overwhelm her insides.

"The drone is an antique model of what used to be called, I think, a crop duster. It is designed to spray a fine mist of water. The capsule I loaded into it is filled with something different."

"Essence of skunk?" theorized a curious—and grateful—Whispr.

Gwi shook his head. "Lion urine, concentrated about fifty times." For the first time since the ominous chortling of the pack had been heard he allowed himself to smile. "Traditional enemy of all hyenas. At that concentration the Melds must have thought they were coming up on a lion the size of an elephant." Turning, he crawled swiftly to the crest of the mound. "Gone. Out of sight. Still running, I am sure. They will run all the way back to the Security kennel." He stood and beckoned. "Come. If we move fast we will be able to reach the facility by midnight. That will be an excellent time to enter."

Ingrid would happily have forked over several hundred for a change of clothing. As that was not to be had, she made herself rise and start off in the guide's wake. She had to content herself with the fact that she did not smell anywhere near as bad as the horrible concoction that . . .

A thought caused her to put her own sorry hygiene out of her mind. "Gwi? Tell me: where does one get highly concentrated lion urine?" Before the San could reply Whispr interrupted with a question of his own.

"Never mind 'where.'" Striding alongside their guide he leaned over to catch the younger man's attention. "*How* do you get concentrated lion urine? And I swear, sandman, if you say 'very carefully,' I will personally snap one of those capsules under your nose."

Gwi told them. The explanation made perfect sense to Ingrid. But then, she was a doctor.

I T W A S S O D A R K that she could barely see the crouching shape of the San in front of her. In such reduced light Whispr's slenderness rendered him almost invisible. She was convinced that if any of them was going to show up on a security monitor it would be her own recently maniped self. But no harsh spotlights sprang to life to blind her and no voices, human or magnified, called out to them in the darkness. They were almost to the access well.

"We should have been spotted long ago." As he paralleled their guide Whispr could not keep from marveling at the lack of attention. "I would have thought security here would be impenetrable."

They halted beside the metal cylinder. Thrice Whispr's height, it looked to Ingrid as if a smokestack had been removed from an ancient steamship and plunked down in the middle of the desert. Even in the darkness she could see that it had been painted to exactly match the surrounding terrain. In the distance, still farther to the west, a few lights were visible.

"There is every kind of security you can imagine." Removing an electronic tablet from his pack Gwi held it up to the softly glowing oval seal that was set hip height flush into the curved side of the cylinder. He interrupted the process of entering code only to glance briefly at his chrono. "But everything at Nerens is self-contained and self-sustaining. It has to be. There is no connection to an external grid. There is no grid to connect to for hundreds of kilometers. So every sector operates on an individual sequence. Each sector requires between two and three minutes to cycle between power sources, during which time it is down. Receiving, aircraft monitoring, climate control, sanitation—even Security. This always takes place late at night so as to inconvenience as little of the facility's work and staff as possible." His fingers danced over the tablet he was holding.

Whispr frowned. "I'd think Security, at least, would cover the couple of minutes of downtime by using some kind of backup power."

"One would think that, yes. But since no one has ever succeeded in breaking into Nerens and since outer perimeter security is considered impenetrable, the company does not seem worried about a couple of minutes of downtime in the middle of the Namib in the middle of the night. Perhaps the necessary switching to a backup source for a mere couple of minutes is more work than they wish to deal with. Even in a village, what is ordered by those at the top is not always put into practice by those at the bottom." When he smiled his teeth gleamed in the darkness.

"I break in and out all the time. So do several of my colleagues. We alternate our unscheduled 'holidays' so that no more than one of us is away from the facility at any one time."

"No one misses you at work?" a dubious Ingrid inquired.

"My colleagues cover my work for me. This is Nerens. The movements of visitors, of scientists and engineers, of security personnel and drivers, those are monitored very closely. No one pays attention to those who deal with the facility's waste except others who deal with the facility's waste. It is expected that we will keep tabs on one another. Mine is not a popular department to visit."

The almost invisible door set in the side of the cylinder hummed softly as it slid noiselessly aside. Photostrips painted on the interior wall revealed a molded spiral staircase leading downward. A primitive solution to an internal transport problem, Ingrid reflected. She found its presence, in lieu of a lift, encouraging. The more technologically downscale the area they were infringing, the less likely it was to draw attention from internal security. It was very much the same as in a hospital.

It was crowded with the three of them at the top of the stairwell. As the curved metal door slid shut behind them Gwi beckoned for them to follow as he started downward. He did not have to instruct them to descend quietly. Even so, Whispr could not resist asking one more question.

"You said the power was off to each sector for two to three minutes. What would have happened if we hadn't gotten inside before that time was up?"

Glancing back as he led the way downward their guide's reply was a soft murmur. "Most likely we would now be in custody of company security. Every alarm on the east side of the facility would have gone off at once."

A somber Whispr digested this news. "Just out of curiosity, how much time did we have left?"

Gwi smiled cheerfully back at him. "About ten seconds, I think. No more talk for now, please."

Whispr did not have to be told again. He was envisioning himself and Ingrid being thrown to the ground, wrapped in secure bands, and hauled off to the local version of a SICK interrogation chamber. Ten seconds . . .

Descending the steep staircase was not as bad as slip-sliding over scree and rocks in Sanbona, but by the time the San raised a hand for them to halt, Ingrid's knees and calves were throbbing from the effort. In the dim light and with her thoughts otherwise occupied she had not tried to calculate the distance they had come. She asked Whispr.

"More than a few stories and higher than hell. That's the best I can guess."

"It doesn't matter." Spurts of adrenaline canceled out her exhaustion. "We made it, Whispr. We did it! We're inside Nerens."

"Yay," he muttered flatly. "Whoopee. We don't even know what part of the facility we're in, except that it's far belowground. Getting all the way from Savannah to here was the 'easy' part. Now we have to get from here into the research center. I hope you're ready to play doctor, doc."

She stiffened. "I don't have to 'play' doctor, Whispr."

He sniffed. In lieu of confidence he would proffer fatalism. He found himself wishing for drugs. "You know what I mean. You're going to have to fool people into thinking you're part of the staff."

"Easier than trying to pass you off as a medical assistant."

He smiled. "I can be your ambulatory demonstration cadaver."

"You better hope I don't feel like demonstrating dissection."

"Wait here." Without further comment Gwi started off down a long, dim, high corridor. It was lined with pipes and conduits, some of them of sufficient diameter to easily pass a person down their length. Water dripped from several. A strange, foreign sensation began to drape itself, coatlike, over the waiting Ingrid. It took her a moment to identify it.

She was cold. Here in the center of the world's oldest desert, she was starting to shiver. The temperature did not seem to trouble Whispr. Thin as he was, he ought to have been feeling the chill even more. Maybe, she thought, his fear kept him warm.

Minutes stretched into hours. They sat, they talked, she shivered, refusing to condescend to the obvious by asking Whispr to huddle close or to pull her thin thermosensitive blanket from her backpack lest they have to move in a hurry. She doubted his body gave off any more warmth than his personality anyway.

Relief came in the form of sleep. Lying down on the floor and using her pack for a pillow she was just as cold, but she didn't feel it. Watching her reclining there Whispr was reminded of why he had come all this way. His participation had begun as a quest for subsist. That avarice remained, but along the way it had become laden with affection. Without his company, without his aid, this brilliant stupid woman would by now be dead ten times over.

You've always been a sucker for a nice body and a pretty face, he told himself. That was all it really was, surely: straightforward lust. For money and for flesh. The alternative was too terrible to contemplate. The possibility that he had fallen in love with her.

These uncharacteristically warm thoughts were interrupted as a touch on his shoulder brought him back to consciousness. Blinking, he sat up in surprise. He had fallen asleep on the floor beside her. Scrambling to his feet, he adopted a defensive stance to confront the enemy. In the feeble light he made out a silhouette that was misshapen, lumpy, and short. He exhaled in relief when he saw that it was only Gwi. Their guide had finally returned to them, and his arms were full of clothes.

As he dumped them on the floor a sleepy Ingrid awoke, rubbing at one eye. "What is—Gwi, what have you got there?" While her eyes focused she found herself recognizing a particular familiar design.

"Doctor clothing, I think." The San grinned proudly. "You say you will pretend to be a facility doctor and this Meld your assistant. To make your gambit work you will need appropriate dressing. Here it is." He shrugged diffidently. "I hope they fit."

Whispr gawked at the garments. "Where the hell did you get this stuff?"

"From the general Laundry." He grinned. "High security is not considered necessary for the Laundry department."

Wide awake now, Ingrid was fingering the all-white medical attire. The long overgown would certainly fit her. As for the too-big pants, she would just have to pull them up as high under the overcoat as possible.

Moving to the other side of the corridor Gwi slipped the fastener on a battered storage chest. It was half filled with maintenance materials that looked as if they had not been touched in years. Reaching within he rummaged around until he found a pair of small illuminating headbands. One he handed to Whispr, the other to Ingrid.

"It will not be sensible or convenient to take your own equipment with you. People might ask what a doctor and her assistant are doing inside the facility carrying dirty gear designed for walking in the desert. This is a good place to leave it."

After removing his water bottle and some food bars and shoving them into the interior pockets of the white overgown he had selected, a reluctant Whispr deposited his pack and the rest of his supplies in the chest. Ingrid placed her own battered pack beside his and watched as Gwi closed and secured the lid.

Reaching up to pull off her filthy, grime-encrusted desert shirt, she found her companion staring at her. The more tactful of the two men, Gwi had turned away.

"Look, Whispr, I don't have any particular nudity phobias, and we've certainly spent enough time in each other's company, but I'd appreciate it if you didn't stare, okay? Besides, you should be focusing on getting dressed yourself."

"All right, sure. No big deal." Moving over to the storage box he began stripping off his own dusty garb. Gleaming like square pearls, the neatly folded pure white medical attire Gwi had brought was slipped on in place of his old clothing. As he dressed he stared resolutely down the corridor and away from her.

Keeping his word as he finished dressing proved harder than crossing the Sperrgebeit.

When he finally finished and turned, the sight that greeted his eyes in the dim light stunned him. Standing in the corridor was not the hardened woman in whose company he had recently traversed Sanbona and the Namib. His thoughts sprang backward, all the way back to distant, dearly missed Savannah and a pristine modern doctor's office in an expensive contemporary medical-codo tower. For the first time in a long while he again found himself in the company of Dr. Ingrid Seastrom, general practice physician and respected member of the Southeast Namerica Medical Association.

"You're staring," she said. "You promised you wouldn't stare."

"That was while you were naked and getting dressed."

"You're still looking at me like I'm naked."

He started to say something, realized instinctively that he was likely to only dig himself a deeper hole, and simply nodded as he turned away.

Once more clad in the clean white garb of her profession Ingrid felt unaccountably confident. It was all she could do, however, to keep from laughing at Whispr. Designed to fit a Natural, his white coat hung like a shroud from his thin shoulders. Only a pair of clasps taken from his pack kept his pants from puddling around his ankles. He did not look happy. But then, she mused, that was a constant, a routine reflection of his personality. Snappier clothing would have done nothing to brighten his mien.

Gwi was also looking in her direction, but without the expected glint in his eyes. Impulsively, she grabbed their guide and kissed him. The young San looked startled. Whispr did not react at all. He had long since resigned himself to being Pluto to the sun called Seastrom.

"You've done so much for us, Gwi. You and your people. I—we—don't know how to thank you."

"You helped Auntie !Nisa. You are going now to try and help some young people like me. If you are lucky, sometimes in life you find a thing worth doing." He turned to go. "Now I must leave and report in to my station. My friends will be glad to see me safely back."

"Gwi, wait." She put out a hand. "You're forgetting the last thing. You have to show us where the research center is." She gestured helplessly at their dark, dank, tunneled surroundings. "We're underground and we don't even know how big Nerens is. I don't want to have to talk to anyone, to ask questions or directions, unless we have no other choice."

He looked from her to Whispr and back again. "I don't know where they do research here, miss doctor. I only know the sewerage system and a few other support areas, like the Laundry, that are involved with maintaining the lesser details of everyday life. I don't know any scientists or engineers or technologists. You will have to find this research center on your own." He was sympathetic but firm. "Even if it means asking questions of others."

"Damn," Whispr muttered. "I knew we'd hit a dead end sooner or later."

"Don't say that," she told him. "I told you I'd find a way to pass myself off as someone who belonged here. I still believe I can do that." She shrugged. "In any case, we have no choice. We'll just have to try."

"There is one thing I can suggest that may get you started." Both of them turned back to their guide. "As you would imagine of any modern place located in the Namib, Nerens has very efficient means for controlling its climate. Here it can be very hot in summer and very cold in winter, especially at night."

"Or belowground." The physician's overgown was all that kept Ingrid from shivering.

Gwi nodded. "There are many large pipings like those you see around us for moving warm or cold air. I have always thought it strange that so many run to the north."

Whispr was puzzled. "Why would you find that strange?"

In the near darkness Gwi eyed him evenly. "I never know of anyone to go very far in that direction. Internal security is also very heavy in that direction. But if there is nothing there and not far to go, then why so much security? Sewerage pipes also go north, but once they reach a certain point none of us are asked to clean or check or repair them any farther. This seems strange to me, that only one part of Nerens should have its own sanitation system. Many service conduits go north, but to where?"

Ever cynical, Whispr had a ready explanation. "Maybe they don't go anywhere. Maybe they just cycle back on themselves. Or empty out into a canyon invisible to environmental satellite scans."

"Or," an intrigued Ingrid proposed, "maybe they feed into a

sector that's off-limits to the regular staff because it's a separate facility that's important enough to justify its own discrete maintenance team." She stared up at him. "For security reasons."

He was shaking his head slowly. "I don't like the idea of trying to crawl through a bunch of service ducts for who knows how far only to maybe come out in somebody's bedroom and have them raise the alarm."

"We don't have to exit the crawl until we see where we are," she countered. "From the start you've been skeptical about my ability to pass myself off as a member of the local staff. Here's a chance to maybe avoid at least a few possible confrontations." She turned back to the silently watching Gwi. "How long are the climate-control pipes that go north?"

"Don't know," the San told her honestly.

"You have no idea where they terminate or what lies at the far end?" Once again he shook his head. She turned expectantly to Whispr, who sighed resignedly. By now he had come to know that look all too well.

"We've come all this way to get to Nowhere. What's a little more nowhere?" he added glumly.

"I don't know what you're bitching about," she challenged him. "With your frame, moving on hands and knees through a conduit or a duct will be a lot easier for you than for me."

"Can't argue that." He brightened slightly. "You go first."

She made a face. "Like hell. You're more sensitive to surprises and to when something's not right. I'll follow you." She looked back at Gwi. "Show us one of these climate control ducts that runs to the north. The biggest one you can."

Committed now, Whispr added. "Make it one that shunts air and not sewage."

They hiked a good half a kilometer before their guide paused

beside a suitable conduit. Since it was located deep within the Nerens complex, its service hatch was not security sealed. The diameter of the ductwork itself was more than large enough for them to
enter it on all fours without banging their heads on the composite
ceiling. Opening a small service box attached to a nearby wall, Gwi
removed a pair of illuminands. Ceremoniously, he handed one to
Ingrid and the other to Whispr.

"Goodbye, doctor. Goodbye, reed-man." Gwi shook hands with
each of them in turn. "I wish you luck and that you may find that
which you seek. I will look for you here, at this spot, at the same
time every day until a week has passed. If I do not see you back here
by then . . ." His voice trailed away. "Thank you for helping Auntie
!Nisa." He indicated the beckoning open hatch and suddenly broke
out in a wide smile. "If you had the San meld and could walk on all
fours this would be so easy for you!"

"Thanks anyway." Whispr spoke dryly as he checked to ensure
that his full water bottle was still secure in a pocket. "But I'd rather
bump my head a few times and be able to stand up straight at the
end of the crawl."

"Very overrated, standing." Gwi was backing away. "One day I
think I must have the full four-leg meld myself, when I decide it is
time to return permanently to the land of my ancestors. And after
you have paid me. But not yet. I wish you luck." He waved once,
and then he was gone.

Leaving a doctor and a survivor of Greater Savannah's mean
streets alone to contemplate the darkness ahead of them, the mo-
notonous pizzicato of dripping water, and an open hatch in the
side of a conduit that disappeared into the wall opposite. Whispr
took a step backward, smiled thinly, and gestured at the opening.

"Ladies first."

She stared him down. "We already settled this, Whispr. I'll follow you. You're so skinny I can see around you, whereas . . ." Her voice trailed away as the implication of her own words hit her. "Let's get moving."

With a shrug he put both hands on the sides of the opening and prepared to pull himself in. "What the hell; what difference does it make? We've had to swim, we've had to hike, we've had to fly. We've run on foot and traveled in boats and in cars. We even covered some ground inside a mechanical elephant. Not much we haven't done but crawl."

Once inside the conduit he placed the illuminand Gwi had given him over his head, tightened the band securely, positioned the front part against his forehead, and thumbed the integrated switch on the right side. The device promptly filled the black tunnel ahead of him with pale light. When Ingrid prepared to follow with her identical headband activated he tapped his own and instructed her to turn hers off.

"We don't know how long these things will last. They have indicators, but that doesn't tell us how fast their charges will deplete." He gestured at her forehead. "Keep yours deactivated unless you absolutely need the light." Reaching up, he tapped his own again. "If mine goes out, no matter where we are or how far we've gone we turn around and come back. We can always try again later."

She nodded understandingly. "See, Whispr—this is why I let you lead in situations like this."

"What, in sewers and air ducts? I'm so flattered." Turning his head and aiming his illuminand forward, he began crawling.

The floor of the conduit was smooth, cool to the touch, and reassuringly dry. For nearly an hour they made good progress. After that they had to stop and rest frequently. Despite the protection afforded by their freshly laundered and newly acquired medical attire, knees and palms were beginning to abrade. In the confined space protesting muscles had started to cramp. From time to time they paused to share measured sips from their water bottles.

How many meters had they come? she wondered. Kilometers? How big was the facility at Nerens anyway? She thought back to what Gwi had told them. He admitted knowing nothing about what lay to the north beyond a certain point. What if this conduit had been angling deceptively to the west? It was impossible to tell for certain anymore which direction they were going. For all they knew the conduit ran all the way to the small servicing harbor at the coast. That lay more than a few kilometers to the west. Even if they managed to crawl such a distance by the time they emerged they would be lucky to have enough strength left to shout for help.

"Whispr, do you think we're still heading north?"

He replied without looking back lest the light from his illuminand blind her. "How should I know? I don't have a magnetic directional meld in my head and I'm not a pigeon. I *think* we're still going that way, yeah. If I had my communicator . . ."

"Even if you had your communicator and could use it, internal security might pick up the emissions. You know that."

"And that's why I can't tell you what direction we're going." He paused. "Hold up a minute."

Her knees grateful for the halt, she sat down with her back against the side of the conduit. "I wish I had tea instead of just water."

"I wish I had a magnum of Rogue River brut '48," he growled. "As long as we're wishing." He switched off his illuminand. Once again they were enveloped by a black as complete as the inside of a cave. "See that?"

"See what?" She was almost too tired to care if he actually was seeing something.

"Straight ahead." In the darkness she could hear him moving to one side. "Past and in front of me."

It took her eyes some seconds to adjust. Initially she thought it was an illusion. Crawling forward, not caring now if she was in front of him, she moved toward it. As she advanced, confidence in what she was seeing increased along with the number of photons striking her retinas.

"There's light ahead. And I can hear something. Machine noise, I think. And voices."

Had the conduit been a little bigger they could have advanced side by side. As it was he followed her as for the first time she took the lead. Having finally been granted his earlier wish, he now had no interest in pursuing it. The intensifying glow ahead and the increasing variety of sounds had fully captured his attention.

After all the arduous crawling they finally found their way blocked by a protective screen. Moving as close as possible to the metal mesh they started to peer through the gaps only to find they had to turn away because the light on the other side was so bright. It took their eyes a couple of minutes to adjust. When they were finally able to see where their efforts had led them Ingrid realized it was a good thing the screen had halted their advance. Tired and methodical as their long crawl had been, whoever had been in the lead might have stumbled right on through the opening at the end. That would have been awkward.

Because on the other side of the screen where the conduit terminated there was at least a hundred-meter drop to the floor.

12

"Oh . . . my."

After all they had suffered, after all they had survived and accomplished, her reaction to the sight spread out before them on the other side of the conduit screen was more than a little inadequate. The climate duct did not open onto a research laboratory. At least, not onto anything recognizable as such.

What it did open into had to be what the frightened Morgan Ouspel had called "The Big Picture."

Warmed or cooled air from the duct fed into an enormous chamber whose dimensions were so extensive that she could not see the far side. Pillars of metal and gleaming hospital-white composite rose from the floor far below to pierce the high ceiling. Tubing and cabling ran everywhere, as if the pillars were being squeezed by a thousand chrome snakes. Blobs of unrecognizable composition and purpose linked pillars and pipes. Though muted by masses of muffling synthetics, the music of live machinery echoed throughout the chamber: pounding, screeching, and humming, interrupted on occasion by the crackle of powerful electrical discharges.

Not a single person was in sight. Kneeling beside her, a baffled Whispr could only stare.

"I'll down Freddy's firkin if they're not making something here—but what?"

Try as she might Ingrid was unable to identify any of the machinery that was visible through the mesh, much less whatever industrial process was being carried out. And all of it hidden from the rest of the world deep beneath the "empty" Namib desert. No doubt the facility's emissions were thoroughly blocked and secured from detection by passing military or archaeological satellites. Not that there would be any reason for any individual or company to run anything except a casual geoscan of this part of the world. And probably not even that since a discoverer couldn't exploit a deposit or excavate a ruin found in the Sperrgebeit anyway.

"I don't know, Whispr. I don't know what it's all about. If they are making something here—I've never seen anything like it."

Just like, she told herself, she had never seen anything like metastable metallic hydrogen. Her hand went to her chest and the precious storage capsule secured inside her brassiere.

"It's only a guess, but maybe this is where they make the metal that the storage thread is fashioned from."

She could see him frown in the light coming through the screen. He gestured toward the activity on the other side. "All this to turn out storage threads the size of a hair?"

"Not the threads, no," she corrected him. "The material from which the thread itself is made. And the implants, too."

He remained doubtful. "Awfully big setup for making nanoscale mechanisms."

"Maybe those are made elsewhere, from the metal that's fashioned here." Gathering excitement banished some of her exhaustion. "In the research lab! If this is where they make the metal, maybe the research center is nearby." She peered intently through the mesh. "I can see doors off to the left, on at least two levels. The ready, finished MSMH could go straight from here to a lab to be formed into threads, or implants, or—other things."

Very reluctantly he allowed himself a modicum of optimism. "If we go back and try your staff doctor bluff, at least now we know what direction to go." He nodded toward the screen and what lay in the immense room beyond. "Anybody starts questioning us, now you have a place, something specific, you can talk about, even if in general terms. Description validates presence."

She nodded, her eyes shining in the dim light. "As long as nobody asks me for details."

They started back the way they had come. Not only did it feel as if they were making better time retracing their steps, the lure of discovery helped to motivate them both.

"I didn't recognize anything in that room," she told him as she crawled. "I didn't see anyone, either. Not a mechanic, not a supervisor, not an equipment operator—not a soul."

Whispr was less perplexed. "So the operation, whatever it is, is fully automated. As advanced as that complex looked it wouldn't surprise me if that was the case."

"Still . . ." She sounded dubious. "It's a strange kind of setup. I can't imagine something that big and important being run without any supervision whatsoever. Remember what Morgan Ouspel told us? He said, 'I've seen the Big Picture. It's real, and it moves.'" She looked back the way they had come. "I guess he was talking about machinery. But I didn't see any moving parts, either. Didn't he also say, 'I've seen the Painters of the Picture, and they move too—they are not of God.' I still don't understand what he meant, and I don't see how he could have had a reaction like that to what we've just seen." She shook her head. "There's got to be more to it."

"When we're stopped in a corridor by a security tech who sticks a gun in your face," he muttered back at her, "you can ask them in person."

Muscles shouting and knees aching she waited patiently inside the duct at the end of their interminable crawl while Whispr climbed out the service hatch and checked the subterranean corridor where they had started. Confident it was as deserted as when Gwi had first brought them there he murmured an all clear and she stumbled awkwardly out to rejoin him. After so many hours spent moving in a hunched-over position it took several minutes for her body to reorient itself, for muscles long unused to unwind, and for those that had been overstressed to relax. There was much to be said for the quadrupedal San Meld.

She sat and drained the remaining, carefully conserved contents of her water bottle. Meanwhile Whispr was slowly working his way up the corridor, pausing occasionally to ensure that the way forward remained empty. Each time he came to a steady drip from a valve or the underside of a conduit he would cup a slim, splayed hand beneath it until he had gathered enough of the liquid to smell. Invariably making a face, he would then move on to the next. From where she was seated and resting, Ingrid quietly tracked the experienced scavenger's progress.

Retracing his steps, he paused beneath one drip already sniffed. This time he cupped both hands beneath it, waited until the fleshy basin was half full, and drank. Slowly at first, then with increasing satisfaction. Content, he let the remainder splash to the floor, returned to her side, and extended a hand. She passed him her empty bottle.

"Are you sure it's potable?" she asked him.

"I'm no chemist, doc, but I've had to drink a lot of bad water in my time. This tastes fine, and it's nice and cold. That doesn't mean it isn't nice and cold and full of arsenic or heavy metals or who knows what. But I think it's okay. Right now I'm more afraid of going thirsty than being poisoned." He smiled. "I figure I can afford to take a chance because if anything goes wrong I know where to find a good doctor who works cheap."

After refilling both bottles to the brim he returned and handed hers back. When she slipped hers into a pocket of her pants, he eyed her questioningly.

"Not thirsty?" He nodded toward the conduit they had recently exited. "After all that crawling?"

She smiled. "I think I'll wait to see if you bend in half in the next thirty minutes."

He responded with a lopsided grin. "How very scientific of you. How noble." Fumbling with his too-large pants beneath the overgown he took out a couple of the nutrient paks he had pocketed from his backpack. "Even if you're gonna wait on the water you better have something to eat. No telling when we'll have the next chance." He looked up the dank, dim corridor, back the way he had just come. "After that I think we should get some sleep. We're overdue."

She protested. "I'm fine. I'm wide awake and I'd rather keep moving."

He considered. "Okay. We'll just lie down here and rest for a few minutes. Just long enough to let the kinks in my legs go away."

She reluctantly agreed. Selecting a flat-topped conduit nearby she stretched out atop it. The inner pipe that the outer insulation protected generated an audible hum. Lulled by its soft thrumming and the slight vibration of the smooth surface she lay down carefully and closed her eyes. But only for the few minutes rest they had agreed upon, she told herself steadfastly.

Within five minutes she was dead to the world.

. . .

SHE WAS RUNNING AS fast as she could; arms swinging, legs pumping, chest heaving. Behind her the hideous cackling laughter of the pursuing magified hyenas was growing progressively louder. No matter which way she turned, no matter what thrust of stone she tried to hide behind or stream she crossed, she could not shake them. Terrified, she looked back, only to see slavering muzzles trailing spittle that were like streaks of mercury and eyes burning with expectation drawing closer and closer.

A ravine lay just ahead. Its sheer-sided walls were unclimbable by man or beast. In her youth she had been a decent athlete and she felt she could leap the gap. In any event she had no choice. The nearest hyena, a big male, was snapping at her heels. Gritting her teeth, tensing her muscles, she reached the edge and kicked hard, scissoring her legs and windmilling her arms to gain distance. As she began to descend she saw that she wasn't quite going to make it. Arms extended to the utmost, she reached in desperation for the far rim.

Her bare hands slammed into the gravel-edged far side of the gorge, sending a shock wave of pain all the way up to her shoulders. Her fingertips dug into the rock and dirt. Straining, digging her feet into the side of the drop, she fought to pull herself up. Behind her she could hear the pack croaking its frustration as its members halted on the far side. She had won. She had beaten them, beaten the odds, beaten . . .

Something heavy slammed into her back. She could smell its thick scent, a combination of raw animal musk and the lingering stink of dozens of scavenged carcasses. Wrenching her head around she found herself looking directly into the eyes of the alpha male hyena. Its wet nose was streaking her neck. When it opened its jaws, jaws powerful enough to crack bone and draw out the marrow, she could see right down its throat.

As it snapped at her face she screamed and lost her grip, sending the two of them plummeting toward the boulder-strewn bottom of the gulch. Missing her face as she jerked back sharply, the ragged carrion-stained teeth slammed into her shoulder and bit deep.

Whispr pulled back as she swung wildly at him. He had been shaking her shoulder, trying to wake her up. Now he stepped away, his eyes wide. As she panted hard and sucked at the damp air the last vestiges of the nightmare wisped away like bits of shredded tissue.

"You were dreaming." Laconically he added, "*Bad* dream."

"I know, I know." Hands braced against the cool conduit atop which she had been sleeping, fingers pressing tight against its waking-world solidity, she sat there while her respiration returned to normal. "Thank—thank you for waking me."

His expression changed abruptly, as if he had suddenly realized that he had dropped his characteristic sheath of sarcasm and indifference like a medieval knight shedding his armor.

"Yeah, well, I have to admit it was entertaining while it lasted, but I didn't want you rolling off your first-class bunk and busting your nose on the floor. We got enough to do without having to spend time on cleaning up blood." He looked away from her and back up the corridor.

Still seated on the conduit she stared at his back. For the briefest of moments after awakening from the unnerving nightmare of pursuit and death, she'd had a glimpse of him with his guard down. In his expression she had seen real concern and genuine alarm. Fear not of her but for her. And there had been something else. Something deeper and more profound and far more agonized.

It left her unsettled.

The awkward silence lingered and grew until she finally spoke. "It's okay, Whispr. I'm fine. It was just a bad dream." She pushed herself off the conduit. "It wasn't all bad. I actually slept some." She looked around at their surroundings. In the dark tunnel it was impossible to tell how much time had passed, how long she had been asleep.

Had he slept? Or had he stood guard the entire time, watching the corridor. Watching over her.

"We're not getting any closer to our goal by sitting here," she pointed out.

He turned back to her, recloaked in full facial mask and emotional armor. "Was wondering how long you were gonna sit there and mope. Let's get with it. Doom awaits."

Back to normal, she thought. She was not sure if she should be relieved or disappointed.

They consumed the remainder of the nutrition paks Whispr had brought from his backpack, washing them down with cold water collected from the comparatively unpolluted drip he had found. After drinking they washed their faces and hands as best they could to remove not only the grime they had acquired while crawling through the seemingly endless conduit, but also the dust and dirt that had accumulated during their long trek through the desert. As for their new clothing, thanks to the electrostatic repulsion that was a standard component of all professional medical attire, it remained relatively clean. When Whispr had finished, she gave him a hurried once-over.

"You're the skinniest medical orderly I've ever seen, but I think you'll pass casual visual inspection. Remember, deportment is everything. Just act like you know what you're doing and keep your mouth shut."

"First one's easy. The second—I dunno." Had the circumstances not been so serious he would have grinned. Turning, he started off up the corridor once more. Hurrying to catch him, she put a hand on his arm.

"You can't lead. It won't look right. I'm the doctor. You can walk next to me or behind me, but you can't lead." She waited for the expected sardonic comment.

It was not forthcoming. He simply nodded, looked uncharacteristically sheepish, and fell into step beside her.

"How do *I* look?" she asked him.

"Leading question," he murmured. "Without going into pleasurable detail, I'd say good enough and determined enough that I don't think the CEO of SICK itself would challenge you."

She ignored the compliment. "I mean, do I look like a physician? Or more like someone who's just trying to look like a physician?"

"I dunno what a physician is supposed to 'look like.' Lemme put it this way: if I met you in a hall and you offered me a pill, I'd take it."

Her mouth twisted slightly. "Why do I have the feeling that if you met any woman in a hall and she offered you a pill, you'd take it. But I'm going to take that as a yes." She nodded forward. "Is that a lift over there?"

He scrutinized the rectangular recess in the wall they were approaching. "Looks like it. Better hope it's not key or security-coded or we'll be stuck down here for a day until Gwi comes back."

Halting in front of the elevator threshold he examined the door as well as the wall on both sides. There was no sign of a keypad, security swipe, or retina scan. Just a single simple unmonitored contact pad. At his touch, the door slid to the left and they stepped inside. Ascending one stop, they found themselves staring out at a virtual duplicate of the service corridor they had just left. Ingrid nodded at her companion, Whispr slid a finger across the lift's control pad, and they ascended another level. Though more brightly lit and not as crammed with machinery, the second floor up presented yet another, cleaner version of the two levels they had already visited.

It was when the lift door slid aside to allow them egress to the third level that they were shocked by such unaccustomed brightness they had to fight not to turn away or reach up and rub at their eyes.

When her vision finally cleared, Ingrid saw that one corridor ran straight away from the elevator while another crossed from left to right directly in front of them. In contrast to the dank warren of automated maintenance passageways they had just scrutinized these halls were teeming with people. Naturals and Melds alike moved purposefully in all three directions. Preoccupied individuals strode past conversing couples or small groups with the ease of experience, secure in the knowledge that they would find their intended destinations without even having to look up. Their confident attitudes stood in contrast to those of a doctor and her assistant who remained standing in the elevator. Ingrid and Whispr had not seen so many well attired people in one place since leaving downtown Orangemund.

Nearly as slenderized as Whispr, a Meld clad in loose gray engineer's coveralls stepped into the lift. Giving the motionless Ingrid a furtive nudge and following close behind, her companion edged her out into the passageway. When the engineer did not bother to look in their direction as the lift doors slid silently shut behind them, Whispr realized they had passed their first test.

Unmoving among dozens of pedestrians the two intruders stood bewildered, uncertain which way to go. Realizing this was bound to lead to awkward questions the longer they lingered, Whispr leaned down to murmur in her ear.

"Move, doc. Start walking. It doesn't matter which direction. We can't keep standing here with our thumbs up our asses. Somebody'll notice. Then somebody'll comment. Then . . ."

He did not need to elaborate further. Striving to make an educated guess based on the direction of the lowermost service corridor they had just left and the climate duct through which they had recently crawled, Ingrid turned to her left and broke into a slow but even stride.

After the long days spent traversing the Namib, every face was a surprise, every sound a revelation, every smell a shock. She had to force herself to avoid making eye contact. She didn't know any of these people and she didn't want them to know her.

"Any idea where we're going?" Whispr had adopted the perfectly blank expression he utilized when in the presence of police.

"North," she told him. "I hope. If this passage doesn't break off at an angle or start to curve we *should* be walking in the same direction as the big room we saw from inside the duct."

"And if we're not?"

"We'll stop someone and ask for directions to the main research center." She was only half joking.

Several hundred meters on, the corridor she had selected was still running straight and true—and hopefully in the right direction. While she continued to avoid looking directly at any of the facility staff she was well aware that a number of them had glanced in her direction in hopes of establishing a connection. Each time this happened she found herself damning her most recent and excessively colorful cosmetic meld.

Two approaching men were not to be denied. One was a science Meld. Maniped neurological storage created a smooth but not unsightly bulge on the back of his neck while each of his fingers boasted an additional joint, the better to help with manipulating intricate scientific equipment. His associate was a Natural, middle-aged and mildly attractive. It was he who confronted her, sidling sideways just enough to block her path. Behind her, Whispr tensed. Though they had no weapons, as a professional riffler he was confident he could handle these brainjuicers without so much as a knife. The problem would not be putting them down: it would be what to do with them afterward.

As was often the case, it developed that he was worrying overmuch.

"Afternoon, Red." An engaging grin revealed that the Natural was not as pure as he first appeared. He had undergone at least one detectable cosmetic manip: he'd had his teeth pearlized. When he smiled, small rainbows flashed between lingering bits of breakfast.

At least now we have confirmation of the time of day, Ingrid told herself. She smiled back.

"Good afternoon." She tried to go around him. He was having none of it.

"Hey, why such a hurry? I don't think I've seen you around the clinic."

"Been sick recently?"

"Well, no." The wattage of his dentition increased. "I don't get sick."

"Then you wouldn't have much occasion to see me, would you?" She looked back at Whispr, her tone thoroughly professional. "Eric, don't forget to take a double antiseptic shower tonight. I'm afraid some of those local cultures might have gotten on your skin."

The science Meld spoke up uncertainly. "Cultures?"

"Yes." She smiled pleasantly. "We're working with some derivatives of local hederotoxin and the stuff can be hard to handle. You have to wash carefully when you're finished working with the syringes because . . ."

"See you around some time, Red—maybe." Clearly alarmed, the Natural stepped quickly out of her path. He and his friend resumed walking in the other direction—a bit faster than before, she thought.

"You're learning," a pleased Whispr told her softly. They continued on. A pair of women in mechanics' outfits waved as they turned up another corridor. Ingrid smiled pleasantly and waved back.

"I've had a good teacher," she told him.

The seemingly interminable subterranean passage continued to stretch out before them. With no end in sight she hoped as much as felt that they were still heading north. Occasionally a man, woman, or Meld would wave or smile in their direction. While Whispr continued to ignore all such acknowledgments of their presence, Ingrid's confidence grew each time she returned a casual greeting.

Maybe we *can* pull this off, she began to think. Given such crowded and busy surroundings it was starting to seem possible that anyone who managed to penetrate this deep into the complex might pass unchallenged. As they had surmised earlier, external security was so tight at Nerens that it might readily be assumed anyone present truly belonged there.

She had become so relaxed that by the time they paused at another far less crowded pedestrian intersection she failed to react to the curious stare of the young woman who was walking in their direction. At first she thought the woman, who could not have been out of her mid-twenties, was a Natural. Only when the tech came closer did Ingrid notice that each individual strand of the woman's shoulder-length black hair was in fact a prehensile manip. The technician had been melded so that when operating over a work bench, in addition to her hands she would also have the use of hundreds of long, thin tentacles controllable by thought training alone. By themselves feeble, when braided together the Medusa melds would allow the woman to manipulate fine scientific apparatus with the utmost precision.

"Excuse me, miss, but where are you going? You're a long way from the clinic."

As Ingrid hesitated, taken aback for the first time since she and

her companion had exited the lift on this level, Whispr unobtru-
sively began to sidle to the woman's left. If he could get behind her
and get his hands around her neck before she divined his intent . . .

"Research." Ingrid responded to the query with becoming swift-
ness. "We're on our way to do some restricted research."

Strands of her hair writhing like nematodes in Perrier, the
younger woman frowned and gestured in the direction of Ingrid's
left breast. For a wild moment the doctor feared the tech had undergone some kind of bizarre X-ray meld that enabled her to locate
the concealed capsule and the storage thread it held.

"I don't see a clearance tag. Where's your security glowp?"

Glowp . . . glow pin. Ingrid's right hand reflexively reached
toward her chest. Challenged thus a couple of months earlier she
would have dissolved in panic. Time and experience had instructed
as well as hardened her.

"Damn. Must've left it in my room."

This wasn't enough to satisfy her youthful interrogator. "Anyone cleared for Research is supposed to keep their security glowp
fastened to their work apparel at all times . . . doctor."

Queen to knight four, Ingrid thought. What she said was, "I just
had this cleaned. Can't you tell it's just back from the Laundry?"

The young tech leaned forward slightly, studying. There was no
denying the freshness of the older woman's apparel. Still . . .

Before she could pursue the matter further Ingrid added, "I
don't need it because I'm not going *inside* Research. There's a ju-
nior worker who's recovering from a recent bout of non-acid dys-
pepsia and since I'm headed that way anyhow I told him I'd stop by
and see how the medication I prescribed for him is working. He's
supposed to meet me outside Security. But you're right," she concluded apologetically. "I should have switched my glowp over to
my new outfit before getting dressed this morning."

"I understand." To Ingrid's and Whispr's immense relief, the tech smiled. "I'd forget the obvious regularly if I didn't make notes every night. This place is really conducive to daydreaming." Then she did something so blessedly unexpected that Whispr was hard put to restrain himself. She nodded down the branching corridor. "After you're done at Research you'd better go back to your quarters and pick up your tag or somebody else is sure to confront you, Dr. . . . ?"

"MacGregor," Ingrid told her without hesitating.

"Dr. MacGregor. Have a good day." Leaning to one side she peered around Ingrid. "You too, sir." Stepping past both of them she continued briskly on her way.

When speaking of Research, the tech had gestured toward the branching corridor. Inadvertently and unintentionally the guess-work had been removed from Ingrid and Whispr's search. Moving with renewed energy they headed off in the indicated direction. Ingrid tried to hunch over slightly, wrinkling her physician's coat so that the location of the nonexistent security tag would be less prominent. Because of her recent body maniping this proved difficult to do, but she tried nonetheless.

"So we know where we're going." Striding along beside her Whispr kept his voice down. "That still doesn't get us inside."

An increasingly confident Ingrid smiled sweetly at him. "Let's not get ahead of ourselves. One bluff at a time."

"Yeah. You did good back there. Real good. Ever think of working for a living by fronting for a riffler?"

"Like you, maybe?"

He raised both hands in mock alarm. "Hey, no chance! You're too good for me." *In more ways than one*, he thought dejectedly.

Pressure-relieving badinage was set aside and they lapsed into silence as they approached a doorway. It looked exactly like any number of similar portals they had passed on the long walk from the service lift. That is, Whispr mused appraisingly, if one disregarded the subtle gray surface sheen that indicated the barrier was made of military-grade composite and the three reinforced eight-centimeter-thick bolt-hinges that fastened it to the interior wall. Not your average door.

In addition there was a live human guard sitting behind a desk placed off to one side of the passageway. Dressed in the uniform of Nerens Security he wore a holstered sidearm and a look of boredom that bordered on the bucolic. At present he was staring at a box screen. The absence of a projection visible to anyone but himself suggested that he was enjoying entertainment of a private nature. Probably pornography, Ingrid decided as she and Whispr approached the threshold. Good: his thoughts would be elsewhere.

Her companion tapped her on the shoulder and she looked back the way they had come. Conversing animatedly among themselves, three men clad in nearly identical tech garb were coming up fast behind them. Like the guard, two were Naturals. The third sported a reddish beard and a full lab meld right down to his fingers, half of which had been replaced with advanced techrap. From the fabric above the hearts of all three flashed a softly pulsing glowp. Nodding imperceptibly at Whispr, she slowed her pace and feigned conversation.

"Well *I* think you've got it all wrong!" the youngest of the three technicians was insisting loudly. "Interleaved suspension is *not* the best way to manage a volatile blend!"

"Uh-huh." Objecting vociferously the Meld wiggled the fingers of his right hand. Expensive biobond instrumentation gleamed in the light from the illuminating strips painted on surrounding walls and ceiling. "And what would *you* do? Manipulate them manually?"

"Depends on the composition." Ingrid accompanied her unsolicited advice by smiling dazzlingly and inhaling deeply. Six pairs of unmelded eyes immediately shifted in her direction as she al-

lowed herself to be swallowed up and surrounded like a female
humpback suffering the courtship of a trio of smothering suitors.
Had the techs had tails they would have wagged. None of them
paid the slightest attention to Whispr as he fell in quietly behind
the trio that had become a quartet.

"Really?" opined the third tech. "What would you suggest,
Miss . . . uh, doctor . . . ?"

As she improvised cheerfully while managing to say nothing,
the Natural in the lead leaned forward so that a scanner set flush in
the wall beside the door could read his retina pattern. Simultaneously, a second and completely different scanner located below it
read the information on the tech's glowp. From within the wall a
soft buzz was followed by a loud click. Only when the door opened
inward and the technician stepped through was Ingrid able to appreciate its thickness and solidity. Flanked by the other Natural and
the Meld and still talking, she positioned herself carefully between
them. Meanwhile Whispr, striving not to be too obvious about it,
moved up as close behind her as he dared. Absently, the Meld put
his own eye up to the retinal scanner and his glowp close to the
lower reader. Hidden motors continued to hum softly and the
vaultlike door stayed open. Beyond, another corridor loomed invit-
ingly. Ingrid took a step forward.

"Just a moment, please."

Everyone turned. Having risen from his seat and his screen, the
seemingly semisomnolent guard confronted them from behind.
Ignoring the three techs, his attention was focused squarely on the
only woman in their midst.

"Your name, specialty, and purpose, please, miss?"

"Susan MacGregor, general physician. I'm here to check on a
patient." She flashed another award-winning smile. "He's not con-
tagious, if that's what you're concerned about." She turned to go
through the open doorway.

"Your pardon. I must ask you to wait here a moment."

"Look," she began sternly, "I don't know what's going on, but I have work to do and you're holding me up. We can discuss whatever's troubling you when I've seen my patient and I come out."

The guard did not reply. There was a commotion up the corridor. It was caused by the increasingly loud pounding of heavy feet. Half a dozen armed men and women, including two heavyset weapons melds whose left limbs terminated in large-caliber automatic weapons, were hurrying toward the tantalizingly open doorway. Aghast, at least one of the formerly besotted technicians had moved as far away from Ingrid as the enclosing walls would permit. His companions merely looked stunned.

"I am sorry, miss, but in the absence of clarification I must place you under arrest." Leaving her, the guard's glance settled on her companion. "And for security purposes, your assistant as well."

Ingrid launched into a bitter diatribe professing outrage. "I hope you're as bored with your job as you seemed to be when you were sitting behind that desk," she told him angrily, "because when your superiors hear about this you won't have to worry about being bored there any longer! This embarrassment is not going to go unremarked upon if I have to personally contact company headquarters in Cape Town!" Having slowed to a halt, the armed and armored bodies of the quick-response security team now completely blocked the corridor behind her and Whispr.

If he was rattled by her indignation the guard did not show it. "I would recommend that you do that, miss." His gaze dropped floorward. "While you are at it you might also explain why a company doctor and her assistant have chosen to go on duty pairing freshly cleaned clothes with remarkably dirty high-tech desert boots. . . ."

13

There were five of the intruders. Maybe, Kruger thought as he studied the sullen, defiant faces, they thought that would be enough to overpower the security at Nerens long enough to steal whatever it was they had come for.

First the trespassing floater and its crew that had been ambushed by magified meerkats. Now this. It was turning out to be an unusually busy month. Someone else might have found the dual intrusion diverting. Not Kruger. He liked things calm, quiet, and boring.

Two women, two men, and one hermaphro. All Melds. Specialists in killing, infiltration, demolition, penetration — and more killing. They had been picked up several kilometers from the installation. Having been informed of their presence a curious Kruger had observed their approach from the multiple vantage points provided by silent, near invisible drones that flew well above the altitudes utilized by more common commercial searchers.

It had been amusing. Watching them advance in fits and starts, covering their methodical approach with weapons drawn and ready to unleash narcotizing darts on any security personnel who might challenge them. Darts would make no noise and draw no attention. Oh, they had come well prepared, they had. The most likely scenario was that they had been air-dropped by a silent superfast floater.

Keeping them under constant surveillance and curious to see how they would proceed, he had pulled back his people and allowed them to enter the complex. There was often something useful to be learned from monitoring the activities of the unwary. Regrettably, in this instance the intruders had proved disappointingly predictable. Tiring of the game, once they were inside he'd had the section of corridor they had infiltrated closed off and filled with a fast-acting soporific gas. There had been no need to introduce anything fancy or expensive. One minute they were skulking along beside one another; the next they were passing out on top of one another.

Both of the men were quite large and muscular. The bands that bound their arms behind their backs and their legs and ankles together were fastened to the wall. This kept prisoners upright. It was by no means inhumane. If they wished they could relax by leaning against the smooth bare surface behind them. Otherwise their range of motion was circumscribed. One of the power loaders that worked the oceanfront diamond shelves might be capable of breaking such security bands. Mere flesh, blood, and bone, no matter how extensively maniped, could not.

The interrogation room was quite large, with a six-meter-high ceiling and four walls devoid of windows or decoration. Large floating digits marked the day and time. At one end there was a single door and a couple of chairs. Multiple vit pickups embedded in walls, ceiling, and floor recorded every millimeter of the chamber in very high resolution tridee.

Members of Kruger's capable staff had methodically checked the captives for everything from concealed weapons to incendiary clothing to intestinal explosives until they were certain there was nothing left on their various persons capable of shooting, stabbing, cutting, poisoning, or exploding. What was left to answer his queries were four people of different shape and identical demeanor.

The hermaphro had bit down on a suicide capsule before Kruger's people could get to him.

"Hello. My name is Het Kruger. I am the chief of security at this SAEC installation. You made an illegal entry into this facility and were caught. As you surely know, all travel into the Sperrgebeit is forbidden except to those who have been preauthorized by the relevant company department or Sanpark. None of you carry such authorization." Smiling pleasantly, he held up his communicator. Its screen was blank and its projector remained dark. "If you were carrying such authorization, you would have knocked. Who, please, is second in command of your infiltrating group?"

"You'll find out eventually anyway, I suppose." A slender Tibetan woman whose maniped gunhands had been unloaded nodded toward the massive, heavily maniped Dayak occupying the far end of the lineup. "Sulok is in charge if anything happens to me."

Kruger nodded and worked his communicator. From the ceiling a narrow openmouthed cylinder emerged. Emitting a soft pop, it disgorged an opaque yellow bubble the size of a watermelon. As the prisoners looked on, the bubble drifted slowly downward before angling to its right. Though the maniped Dayak fought and struggled with his bonds, he was secured to the wall behind him as effectively as if he had been nailed to it.

Touching the side of his head the bubble hesitated, as if verifying its location. Then, despite the shouted protests of Sulok's comrades and his own violent cursing, it englobed his skull. For a brief moment his furious features, slightly distorted, were visible through the engulfing yellow haze. Then the bubble ignited. This was followed by a great deal more screaming.

By the time the flames had burned themselves out there was nothing left of the man's head. Seared carbon-black, the top of his spine stuck up and out from between his shoulders, smoking like an extinguished match. The fire had burned partway down into the chest cavity. Exhaust systems hummed as the interrogation room's automated climate control worked hard to remove drifting ashes, soot—and the smell.

Kruger stood and waited patiently for the survivors to exhaust their rage. Their insults and threats and unpleasant descriptions of his ancestry affected him like a cold shower: bracing and cleansing. When they had finally run down he approached the diminutive Tibetan woman who had identified herself as their leader and halted a couple of meters away. Though the bindings securing her to the wall were unbreakable by any known organic force irrespective of meld, Kruger always prepared for the unexpected.

"You suckling yak bastard!" Evidently she was not quite finished. He raised one hand to his communicator. She stiffened and went quiet.

"Better," he told her. With a slight nod he indicated the still-smoking corpse hanging limp in its bonds at the far end of the lineup. "A necessary demonstration. To show that I have little patience with intruders. If you are curious, it involves a blend of aerogel and napalm. For the recalcitrant, it can be substituted for a meal. Acutely indigestible." Holding the communicator up to his mouth he noted the fear the movement engendered in their expressions. Purely from a professional standpoint, he enjoyed the reaction.

"They're ready, I think."

Two figures entered the room: a man and a woman. The reaction of the three remaining prisoners to the appearance of the new arrivals was as varied as it was confused. Het Kruger was a type known to them: physically imposing, tough, lethal, completely self-controlled, and dedicated to his work. But this pair . . . the prisoners did not know what to make of them. They could console themselves with the knowledge that neither would anyone else.

They had to be Melds: no Natural human could grow so obese and still move with such apparent ease. What passed for clothing on their enormous bloated bodies consisted of colorful but untailored overshirts that fell almost to their knees. Matching blue or yellow pants accumulated in loose folds around huge feet that were encased in dark, loose-fitting boots of unnatural height and width. The woman had skin the color of burnt chocolate while her companion's complexion suggested that he was suffering from an advanced case of jaundice. Their huge dark eyes were sunk so deeply in their bulging, fat-larded skulls that it was impossible to identify their exact color. Nostrils were wide and mouths reminded a couple of the prisoners of bottom-dwelling fish.

Advancing with a balletic waddle, they halted directly behind the security chief. When they spoke, the unexpectedly faint words seemed to come from somewhere deep within their massive, lumbering bodies.

"Why you try to enter Nerens?" the man asked.

The leader of the infiltration party strained to hear. What accent was that? Tongan, or perhaps Samoan? But there were too many clipped consonants, none of the softness in the brief query that would define Polynesian origins. Melanesian, perhaps, or even something local—meaning anywhere south of the Sahel.

She responded without hesitation. The security chief had not put away his communicator. Not that it mattered whether she replied or not, she knew. She and her associates were dead anyway. It was the manner of dying she was bargaining.

"We were dropped off by floater and asked to perform a general reconnoiter and report back to Guangzhou."

"Report on what?" inquired the corpulent female. Despite her similar size and shape her accent was completely different from that of her male companion.

The bound woman shrugged as definitively as her bonds would permit. "We were told to keep an eye out for unusual materials. Plastics, composites, especially metals."

This response sparked a surprisingly animated conversation between the two blobs. Though the leader of the infiltrators strained to hear, the phrases being enunciated were too low and too garbled for her to glean more than an occasional word or two of the debate. When the overweight pair had concluded their discussion the man addressed the security chief. This time his speech was loud enough to be overheard.

"That is all. We are done here. Dispensation is yours, Mr. Kruger."

The security chief nodded and the pair departed, barely managing to squeeze their respective bulks through the single portal. When the door had closed behind them Kruger turned back to the remaining captives.

"You heard the man. Dispensation is mine. Given your collective incompetence I'm inclined to think you're relatively harmless. From the time your bumbling alerted the facility's outer perimeter to your presence until the moment when you were rendered unconscious you were always under surveillance. You were only finally picked up because we got tired of monitoring you."

To the prisoners' credit a couple of them muttered a few choice sardonic comments.

"I'm not going to waste time haranguing you. I have better things to do and more important demands on my time. You have cooperated, so you're going to be released. After all, you're only low-level contract employees carrying out orders, and you didn't harm anyone while you were inside." He gestured toward the burned-out human wick at the far end of the line. "You've paid a twenty-five percent mortality penalty, chosen at random. We consider that warning enough."

The captives could not have been more startled had Kruger suddenly morphed into a media star and announced that their present circumstances were a cleverly concocted sham and they were actually participants in a live reality vit. As he raised a hand to still their surprised murmuring, the group's leader eyed him coldly.

"We answered a couple of questions and now we're free to go?"

Kruger gave an indifferent bob of his head. "In a manner of speaking. You'll be taken well outside Nerens's security perimeter and set free." His tone hardened slightly. "Without gear or clothing. Not even shoes. I've been security chief at this station for a long time and I have confidence that the Namib will render the final judgment on your illegal intrusion."

The other woman started to protest, only to be silenced by a sharp "Shut up!" from the group's leader. No one knew better than her what a tremendous break they had been given. She was careful not to smile.

"We're very grateful for the compassion. Speaking as a professional I know we don't deserve it. I for one certainly didn't expect it."

"Speaking as a professional," Kruger replied evenly, "you're absolutely right." He raised the communicator. The prisoners tensed, but the commands the security chief uttered were directed to his staff and not at lethal apparatus. Entering the room through the single doorway a couple of security personnel commenced to free the prisoners' limbs while others (too many others to try anything, the leader of the intruders knew) trained short-range riot control weapons on the surviving trio.

As Kruger had promised they were released, sans clothing, in an area of low dunes and gravel plains an indeterminate number of kilometers from the facility they had infiltrated. A light but thankfully warm breeze was blowing, uncertain whether to whoosh toward distant mountains or remain close to the nearby ocean. As their heavily armed escort trooped back into one of the two floaters that had carried them from the facility to this spot, the group's leader put her hands on her naked hips and took stock of their immediate surroundings. She did not speak until both transports had disappeared to the west.

"They think we're going to die here." She spoke with a confidence born of extensive training. "As if we need clothes or modern equipment to survive."

Moving up alongside his commander, the big male Meld joined her in studying the southern horizon. "Maybe they're thinking that even if we do survive they can pick us up whenever they want."

She nodded thoughtfully. "We'll have to keep well under cover. Fools. That Kruger: you could smell the arrogance drifting off him. He thought he had us cowed when he vaped Sulok. Probably he's used to frying poor stray prospectors and wandering animal poachers. He has no idea what we're capable of. We'll get out of this." She spoke through clenched teeth. "And one of these days, in a restaurant or a pub or on a public transport, I'll make his acquaintance again." She regarded her companions. "We're supposed to die out here. Well, the local animals don't, and if there are any Rousseauean natives, they don't either. None of them have our training or our survival skills. Let's get moving." She started southward, marking her heading by the sun. "Keep an eye out for anything that looks useful; as food, weapon, or shelter."

"What about water?" the other female Natural wondered.

"Don't worry—I can smell water. What, you thirsty already?" She jerked a thumb in the direction of now distant Nerens. "If your mouth's feeling dry why don't you head back toward the facility? I'm sure they'll be happy to give you a drink."

The other woman went silent.

By evening they had managed to accumulate an impressive collection of found objects. Some bush berries proved bitter but edible and, more important, moist. Using their fingers and rough-edged rocks the three of them were busy putting points on tough sticks to serve as spears. Clouds on the horizon held the promise of possible rain. Water-carriers could be fashioned from suitable plant material. Oh, they would survive, all right. They would make it all the way south to the Orange River, avoid the town of Orangemund and any company agents waiting there, and work their way inland. All they needed was access to a single communicator and help would be forthcoming. Their employer would be disappointed, but not crushed. While their mission had been far from completely successful, neither was it a total failure. They had information to impart: details on Nerens security, memories of a portion of the internal layout, and a good deal more.

A fire was easily built from scavenged dry sticks and the waxy branches of bushmen's candle. Ancient human hunter-gatherers had utilized the same survival techniques. Seated around the blaze and building it higher let them ward off the chill of the desert night. Yes, it was cold, but being dead was colder. Each of the trio was resourceful, well trained, tough. The Namib at night was chilling but it was not the Arctic. In letting them go, Nerens's overconfident security chief had seriously underestimated them.

The group leader had closed her eyes and was resting her head on a small pile of dead brush when she heard the cough.

At first she thought it was one of her comrades. Only when the deep, rough sound came again did she lift her head to blink into the darkness. Moon- and starlight showed her companions dozing peacefully beside the fading fire.

Rising to her feet, she threw a few more twisted, wind-scoured branches onto the blaze. Flames sprang higher and sought the sky. Embers danced briefly before flaming out. Turning a slow circle she sought the source of the sound that had disturbed her. She was not worried. If there was something out there it was probably only curious as to the nature of the intruders on its turf. If there was something out there that was more than curious, the substantial campfire would keep it at bay.

The big Meld blinked sleepily and found her with his eyes. "What's on, Shu?"

Still studying the darkness beyond the glow from the fire the group leader shook her head. "Not sure. Probably nothing. Thought I heard something." She stopped turning. Staring at her, the Meld started to sit up.

"Shu, what . . . ?"

The eyes looking back at her did not blink. They were large and in the light from the fire yellow. Advancing with great deliberation, regal poise, and in complete silence, the male lion advanced toward her. Black of mane, he was at least three meters long and massed a couple of hundred kilos. Keeping her eyes fastened on the cat she knelt, reached behind her to grab one of the flaming branches from the fire, straightened, and thrust it forcefully in the lion's direction. Exhibiting utter disdain for the crackling flames it continued its measured approach.

This wasn't right, she told herself as she started to back up. Something here was not natural. All cats were at least wary of fire.

The tawny quarter-ton beast in front of her was coming on as if the torch wasn't there, as if she held nothing in her fist more primevally threatening than a sprig of parsley.

By now both of her companions were awake. Taking immediate notice of the nocturnal visitor they had similarly armed themselves with blazing branches. The male Meld began yelling at the lion even as he scrambled to keep the fire between it and himself. Meanwhile the other woman hurried to add the remainder of the wood they had gathered onto the blaze. This caused the flames to shoot several meters high.

Without breaking stride, the lion walked majestically through the center of the conflagration.

A few wisps of smoke trailed from the tips of its mane as it emerged on the other side. At the same time the light from the blaze was strong enough to reveal the small box of tan-colored metal that was mounted on the back of the big cat's skull. Her initial reaction had been more accurate than she knew: this lion was indeed not natural. It had been magified.

At the same time as she threw her makeshift torch at its face and turned to run she caught a glimpse of something else poking out from the depths of the magnificent mane: a tiny black spot sporting a bit of gleam in its center. A vit camera. Grabbing a handful of sand as she ran and ignoring the screams and curses of her comrades she threw the sand in the lion's direction, hoping to hit its eyes, and raced for the ravine they had crossed earlier. In its depths she might find shelter; an overhang, a cave, something. Behind her the cries of panic had turned to shrieks of agony and pain. They were nearly drowned out by the butchering roar of not one but several desert lions.

A regular perimeter patrol, she wondered as she fled, or a special surprise dispatched from Nerens specifically for the purpose of disabusing the freed prisoners of any notion of escape?

The ravine lay just ahead. Ignoring the sharp rocks that cut and tore at her bare feet she plunged over the side. Out of sight was not out of smell, but at least this way the maniped cats could not be put on her trail by controllers monitoring the activity from Nerens. The co-opted carnivores would have to find her on their own. Judging from the awful sounds of rending and tearing and the snapping of bone that filled the night behind her, the lions, magified or not, were likely to settle down to feed. If sufficiently preoccupied with their hominid meal they might well forget about her.

Moving fast along the sandy bottom of the ravine she sought to put as much distance between herself and the continuing carnage as possible. When she finally did stop, utterly out of breath and with leg muscles screaming, she could hear nothing behind her.

She'd done it, she told herself. She was the only one to escape the slaughter. But then, in the final analysis she was the only one who mattered. By the time company security arrived at the scene to clean up after their feline patrol, probably in the morning, they would find only the remnants of bodies that had been dismembered and consumed. Sufficiently masticated and disarticulated, the remains of two might well pass for three, in which case they would not come looking for a single survivor. Living to tomorrow night would tell her if she was safe from the further attention of Het Kruger and his minions. As the seconds and then the minutes ticked away with no hint of leonine attention she was increasingly convinced that was indeed the case.

If only she had not sat on the snake.

14

Kruger was relaxing in his office contemplating his vit wall when the call came. As it did on alternate days the projected depth image had automatically changed. This morning it was showing the boulder-flecked beach of Anse Source d'Argent in the Seychelles, perhaps the most famous if not the most beautiful beach in the world. Wavelets the color of peridot broke on smooth white sand while unseen gulls called softly. A study in feathered obsidian, a black paradise flycatcher sat on a rock preening its extraordinary tail feathers.

Irritated at the interruption, Kruger muttered a curt order. Advanced by verbal command the image refreshed. Now it depicted the verdant depths of the western Amazonian rain forest. The chatter of monkeys replaced the calls of gulls. Being surrounded by sand he was not as enamored of beach scenes, no matter how spectacular, as someone else might have been. As he turned back to the vook he had been reading, his desk communicator sounded a second call. This time he acknowledged it.

He listened to the details, verified receipt of the transmission, and rose. What had gone wrong with the world that he should receive three such notifications in the space of a single week? What was this—intruder season? With a sigh he deactivated the vook, which automatically marked the vit-illustrated page he had been reading, picked up his portable communicator, and headed for the door.

"Back soon, I expect," he told his receptionist. "Another set of infiltrators."

"*Another?*" She eyed him in disbelief. Danae was beautiful, they both were single, and their relationship was strictly one between two professionals. Sex was easy to find, he knew. Competent staff was not.

"Sounds like it, from the description. Only these two somehow got inside—deep inside—without setting off a single alarm. Made it all the way to Research before one of our people, thank Oompaul, spotted an incongruity."

"You don't think they actually could have penetrated Research security, do you, Mr. Kruger?"

"Based on the brief description I just got I don't think they could have penetrated security at the Tusker Bar in Pretoria, much less here. But they did." His expression was grim. "There has been a lapse somewhere. A serious lapse. I will find out where the gap exists, and it will be plugged."

She watched him leave the reception area and returned to her own work. For all Het Kruger's buff construction, gentlemanly politeness, and manicured speech she would never have considered embarking on a relationship with him. The chief of security was solid as a rock, through and through. Emotionally as well as physically.

. . .

THE CONTRAST WITH THE previous quintet of intruders could not have been more striking. Just by looking at the pair Kruger could tell they bore no relationship, professional or otherwise, to the infiltration team that had preceded them. Taking up his usual position in the interrogation room he regarded the two new prisoners thoughtfully. Like their now deceased and dismembered predecessors they were bound arm and leg and had been fastened securely to the back wall. The longer he examined them, the less he thought the bindings necessary.

These were not trained assassins or sinister agents of industrial espionage. One was as thin a man Meld as the security chief had ever seen. Hanging in his bonds the scruffy Meld alternated strings of curses with wracking sobs. His Natural companion was a highly attractive and to Kruger's practiced eye recently maniped redhead who seemed as out of place in the depths of the Namib and the bowels of Nerens as a maniped multilimbed ecdysiast delivering a lecture on Kierkegaard at Oxford.

What the devil were these two doing in Nerens? More important, how had two such obvious amateurs succeeded in penetrating not one but three separate concentric security perimeters without setting off a single alert? Though his employers might feel otherwise, his personal responsibilities demanded that he show more interest in the latter conundrum than the former.

One thing was certain: he would learn nothing by speculating. His right hand did not move toward the communicator resting in his shirt pocket. No ominous apertures appeared in the ceiling in response to a command. Immoderate methods of persuasion would not be necessary with these two. At most, a few selective descriptions of what could happen to them if they refused to cooperate should be sufficient to overcome any hesitancy. Muting the aggra-

vation he felt at this latest interruption in his copacetic daily routine, he sighed and began.

"What are your names, please, and who do you work for?"

He did not even have to threaten. The slender Meld spoke up
without hesitation. "Everybody calls me Whispr, and this is my
friend, Dr. Ingrid Seastrom."

The woman looked shocked. "Whispr! How could you . . . ?"

Kruger cut her off. "Your friend is being sensible as well as perceptive. These walls contain many monitors of diverse ability. As
you hang there they are reading your blood pressure, heart rate,
neurological output, cranial cortex response, and enough additional physiological factors to tell me whether you are lying or not."
He nodded approvingly at Whispr. "I can see that this interview
will go quickly and responsibly."

"And then you'll kill us," Ingrid muttered bitterly.

"Not necessarily. Termination, in every sense of the word, depends on your responses. Now, who are you working for?"

Head down, she stared at the floor. "Go ahead and talk, Whispr.
You're going to anyway."

"I'm sorry, doc. I know people like this. There's nothing to be
gained trying to fool him. It'd only go harder on both of us."

Again Kruger nodded. "Extremely sensible. Continue."

"We work for ourselves."

Kruger pulled his communicator. Not to order incineration of
the speaker, but to check the readouts from the concealed monitoring instrumentation. He was more than a little surprised to see that
the ganglion of sophisticated apparatus insisted that the speaker
was telling the truth. Though he knew they couldn't be wrong, the
security chief was still reluctant to accept the results.

"Yourselves? You don't strike me as the kind of independent
operators I'm used to dealing with. So you say you're working for

yourselves. To what end? Why did you risk your lives to break into a private, secure facility in the Forbidden Zone?"

Ingrid sighed. Whispr was doubtless correct. There was nothing to be gained by trying to withhold information from this man. But if the opportunity presented itself, they could be less than directly forthcoming.

"In my work as a practicing general physician . . . ," she began.

Kruger interrupted again. "You're telling me that you are truly a licensed doctor?"

"Really, yes."

Once more the security chief checked the readouts on his communicator. Once again he found it difficult to credit the information he was being given. If the monitors were to be believed, like her companion the woman was also telling the truth.

In the absence of comment or question from their captor Ingrid decided it would be prudent, or at least acceptable, to continue. "In my work I came across some objects fashioned of what appeared to be metastable metallic hydrogen. A material that should not exist—at least, not on the surface of the Earth." Her head came up. Might as well plead for mercy with her eyes as well as her voice, she thought. "I became obsessed with it, with trying to learn how something like that could be manufactured. I started trying to research it." She nodded to her right. "Through circumstances that we needn't go into I made the acquaintance of this gentleman here. . . ."

Gentleman. Whispr's bonds seemed to slacken a little.

". . . who is far more street-wise than I am." Her gaze returned to their dubious but attentive interrogator. "I employed him to help me negotiate certain strata of society that would eat me alive were I to try to penetrate them by myself." Somehow she managed a smile. "As you can see, we made a pretty decent team. We got this far. We were so careful." She looked down at her booted feet. "In the end we were tripped up by something quite ordinary."

Kruger was understanding. "You would be surprised, Ingrid Seastrom, how often that occurs in my line of work. It's so often the simplest things that undo the best made plans."

As he listened she laid out the details of the journey that had taken her and her companion all the way from the civilized surrounds of Greater Savannah to the barren depths of the Namib. She spoke plainly and straightforwardly. It sounded like someone dictating a will.

These were ordinary people, he told himself. He didn't need expensive concealed instrumentation to tell him so. Perhaps that was how they had made it this far; by relying on their very ordinariness. If *he* didn't think they were anything special it was reasonable to assume that those responsible for a succession of safeguards stretching all the way back to Cape Town might think likewise. For those seeking to accomplish the impossible it is a wonderful thing to be overlooked and underestimated.

He would not commit that sin. They had penetrated Nerens and nearly made it into Research. There must, there *had* to be more to them than was discernible at first sight. Despite his initial impression he did not discount the possibility that they might be the most sophisticated infiltrators he had ever encountered, capable of fooling not only him but the perceptive mechanisms that were designed to flush out even the most accomplished liars.

Bringing his communicator up to his mouth he murmured a command. A fresh set of instructions appeared on the screen. He touched one.

Two pairs of finger-thick metal rods rose from the floor, one set flanking each of the prisoners. Each rod was topped by a fist-sized silvery metal sphere. His fingers hovered over the communicator screen.

"You've been very cooperative, but now I'm going to have to ask you some questions you may not want to answer."

"There are no questions I won't answer." Sensing all too well what was coming Whispr began to twitch fearfully in his bonds.

"Nevertheless . . ." One of Kruger's fingers started to descend.

"Just me, just do me!" The skinny Meld's voice rose for the first time since the security chief had entered the room. "Don't hurt her!"

Startled as much by his outburst as by its subject matter, Ingrid gaped at him.

Kruger paused. "Interesting. Spindly as you are I wouldn't have thought there'd be room enough in that shriveled frame for chivalry. It doesn't matter. Personally I'd be glad to grant your request. Professionally I'm afraid I can't allow any plea, heartfelt or otherwise, to interfere with business."

But it did matter—at least to Ingrid. Lips slightly parted, she continued to stare at her companion as she waited for whatever was to come.

The opening of the sole door behind Kruger beat the descent of his finger to the communicator's responsive surface by a second or so.

Whispr just stared, but Ingrid couldn't help herself. She gasped audibly at the sight of the two grotesquely corpulent figures who shambled into the interrogation chamber. Though they were quite real, they made no sense. Especially to a physician. In an era of readily available cosmetic melds beyond anything people of earlier times had ever dreamed of there was no reason for any human being to look like the newly arrived couple. While every imaginable physical fetish could be readily realized, gross obesity was one she had never encountered either in person or in the medical literature. There was no body type that could not be altered, no genetic idiosyncrasy that could not be realigned. Adjusting hormonal imbalance was as straightforward as mixing a cocktail in a bar.

Given the multiplicity of easily available alternatives, why would anyone *choose* to look like this? She could not keep from staring.

The gobsmacked unswerving gazes of the two prisoners in no way unsettled the waddling pair. No doubt they were used to such appalled stares. Leaning toward the security chief, the woman whispered in his ear. Kruger did not pull away in disgust as another might have. Instead, he replied with equal softness. It was apparent that he knew these two well and they him.

The security chief concluded the brief conversation by murmuring into his communicator. He appeared neither disappointed nor pleased. The deceptively innocent-looking metal standards remained upright where they had emerged from the floor and did nothing. Moments passed while he and his outrageously corpulent visitors engaged in conversation that was inaudible to the two prisoners. This ceased only when the door opened again and they were joined by a fourth figure. At the appearance of this new individual Whispr let out a small moan. For the second time since she had been pinned like a fly to the wall, Ingrid gasped. The newcomer was short, stocky, elderly—and familiar.

Kruger nodded toward the new arrival. "Are these by any chance the two Namericans you thought might show up 'somewhere in the Namib near Nerens'?"

Napun Molé's gaze focused on Whispr before shifting to Ingrid. It was strange seeing his frustratingly elusive quarry here like this, helpless and collared after the long, long chase they had led him on. A part of him expected them to vanish in a puff of smoke, forcing him to resume the trail yet again. But only a very small part of him.

"I anticipated that they would be detected and picked up much farther south. The last thing I expected was to find them within the confines of the facility itself." Affecting a nonexistent innocence, the older man looked up at the much bigger Kruger. "There would appear to have been a breach of security."

Kruger's muscles went taut. If there was anything he loathed it was having his competency questioned—especially when the accuser happened to be right. His reply was just shy of a snarl.

"You're damn lucky you come with the kind of company rating that prevents me from hitting you with more than the occasional bad word."

"Please." Molé waved it away. "Sometimes I am too direct. I mean nothing by it but at the same time I cannot help it. It is my manner." Turning back to face the prisoners he raised his voice slightly. "No doubt you are surprised to see me here. A late young lady who was part of an ill-conceived bunch that broke into the sangoma Thembekile's house in Cape Town succeeded in accessing a small amount of information from the witch doctor's box storage. The young lady could only remember a single word, but because of its repeated use and singular nature it stuck with her. Right to the end, I might add.

"That word was 'Namib.' Now, knowing full well your interest in a certain piece of riffled company property and your self-confessed desire to learn its meaning, the knowledge that you were heading for the Namib could only mean you intended to try furthering your knowledge at the one place in this part of the continent that might offer such information. That would be the Nerens facility." He shook his head, the gesture expressing a mix of admiration and regret. "I confess I never expected you to get this far. I thought you would be picked up on company surveillance and brought in before you could get ten kilometers out of Orangemund." With spread hands he indicated their surroundings.

"Yet here you are. Inside Nerens itself. I am as astonished by your persistence as much as I am charmed by your naïveté." He turned to Kruger. "Excuse me a moment. This has been a very long and tiresome time coming."

Walking up to the two captives, the elderly assassin halted between them. "Who presently has the thread?" Despite his earlier insistence that he would answer any question, Whispr now said nothing. It was neither his place to do so nor his decision to make. As for Ingrid, she saw no point in trying to delay the inevitable.

"I do. It's"—she bit her lower lip—"it's in a safety compartment in my brassiere. Left side."

Molé nodded. "Safe and warm." Reaching into the top of her overgown he felt around briefly until he found the compartment, unsealed it, and removed the storage capsule. Within the small transparent cylinder the thread gleamed, intact and unharmed. He held it up between them. His expression roiled her stomach like month-old milk.

"Did you expect me to linger over the recovery?" He shook his head sadly. "I favor the kind of physical infarctions that involve rather more than casual tactility, Ms. Seastrom. As a doctor, you will have the opportunity to appreciate the diversity I can bring to more in-depth physiological exploration." He smiled unpleasantly. "Very soon now, I hope."

Kruger was growing impatient. Such taunting displeased the professional in him. "I still need to find out how they managed to get inside."

"Certainly, certainly. First things first. I have waited this long; I can wait a little longer."

Stepping back, Molé took one last long look at the capsule and its contents whose recovery had consumed him for more weeks than he cared to count. Except for its silvery sheen the storage thread within looked little different from hundreds of others he had seen and used himself. Its composition and contents were none of his business. Pivoting, and with some ceremony, he placed it in the pudgy palm of the indifferently coiffed overweight man.

"I declare this SICK, Inc. property officially recovered. This concludes the formal part of my assignment. One that I regret took up entirely too much time, at considerable expense both to the company and myself." Turning back to the prisoners he locked eyes with Ingrid. He had begun to perspire ever so slightly.

"There will be no charge for the follow-up interrogation, which I expect to also take a considerable amount of time." He glanced at Kruger. "I will unearth that which you wish to know, as well as satisfying myself as to the processes followed by these two in managing to evade my notice for such an extended period of time. You may of course participate if you wish." The snake smile returned. "Or you may just watch."

"I think I'll give both a pass." Kruger's distaste was evident. "I'll read your formal report."

Molé shrugged indifferently. "It may take several days. I intend to make it so."

"Whenever it's done." Kruger's distaste intensified as he turned to leave.

As Molé turned back to the prisoners and the security chief headed for the door, the fat woman lurched lightly forward. For the first time, her voice rose to the level of audibility. The words that emerged were formal and oddly stilted. Try as he might, Whispr couldn't place the accent, nor could Ingrid.

"We will assume control of the interrogation at this point," the woman announced.

Her companion had lumbered up beside her. At closer range Ingrid saw that despite their weight neither of them appeared to be breathing with much effort. She was surprised that there was no indication of respiratory stress. Dwarfed by the massive pair, Molé nonetheless protested vigorously.

"Pardon me? I have spent many frustrating weeks chasing this pair of thieves across two continents, at considerable risk to my constitution and, in one instance, to my physical person. Oftentimes I was sustained principally by the expectation that I would eventually be able to conclude the matter personally."

The obese man trained enormous dark eyes on Molé. Far too large to be natural, they must have required an extensive optic meld, Ingrid knew. Something about the sheen on the corneas left her puzzled.

"Your individual concerns and preoccupations are of no interest to us, Mr. Molé. You were engaged because you are a professional and were given a job to do. You did not fail, but you did not exactly succeed, either. The individuals in question and the stolen item presented themselves here, for capture and recovery not by you but by the forces of Chief of Security Kruger. Nevertheless, it is taken into consideration that you carried out all that was asked of you, and you will therefore be recompensed accordingly. But this interrogation is now concluded. We will conduct the follow-up."

While Ingrid accepted that the fat man's final pronouncement was less than reassuring, she was enormously relieved that further questioning would not be carried out by Napun Molé.

Like a dog forced to watch as its favorite bone was taken away by its master, the elderly executioner persisted.

"If it's answers you wish from them, no one is more skilled at information extraction than myself. I have the experience and the desire. I plead with you; leave them to my care."

"I fear," declared the vast woman from the depths of her bloat, "that the methods I perceive in your heart would involve extracting more than information. The decision is final."

Molé was left standing and shaking with disappointment. After all he had been through, after all the slights to his skill and experience, now even this small compensation was to be denied him.

"What can you possibly want with these two? They are beneath ordinary. What good can they do you?"

The big man seemed to swell beyond the bounds of his already immense girth. "If she is truly a competent physician then she can possibly be made useful. We always have need of pliant doctors. She is not to be harmed."

Kruger was buoyant as the door to the interrogation chamber shut behind him. Napun Molé might be the most highly thought of hunter-tracker in the company's arsenal, but he was also an arrogant old prick. It had been a quiet delight to watch as the two executive untouchables pulled his expected prey right out from under him. Cut him down a notch. *Arshloch*, he thought as he rounded a corner.

No less than the thwarted Molé, Kruger wondered why the untouchables had decided to spare Ingrid Seastrom. Why did they "always have need of pliant doctors"? Well, it was none of his business. He had a break in security to locate and plug and plenty of paperwork to attend to. It was all out of his hands now in any case. The untouchables did not explain or elaborate upon their decisions. They did not have to. From the time the installation at Nerens had been established it was understood that within the facility's boundaries, the corpulent commanders' words were law. That suited the security chief just fine. It was much easier to follow orders than to propagate them.

Within the interrogation chamber Molé was pointing toward the back wall. "What about *him*?" Fixed in the assassin's glare like a moth under a magnifying glass, Whispr tried to shrink back into the whiteness. Ingrid held her breath.

The paired masses of flesh consulted. "We have no interest in him and he is of no use to us," the man finally burbled. "You may do with him as you wish."

Molé looked satisfied. If he could not play with the striking doctor, he could at least amuse himself with her companion. Small consolation but better than none.

"*Like hell he can!*"

Corpulents and killer alike turned at Ingrid's shout. Having already surprised herself, she plunged onward lest she think too much about what she was doing.

"Unless Whispr is allowed to stay with me and remain unharmed, I won't—help you—with whatever it is you have in mind for me." Looking to her right she mimicked her companion's voice along with his earlier words. "Don't hurt him."

"This is absurd!" Molé protested. "I am entitled to *some* satisfaction!"

The untouchables conferred. As a tense Ingrid and Whispr looked on, the woman spoke to the assassin.

"Your monetary recompense will be doubled. Consider that your satisfaction."

As far as Molé was concerned, it was a dismissal. The woman turned her attention to the prisoners. Perhaps at the same time she gave a hidden signal, or perhaps her male associate conveyed unseen instructions with chunky fingers. However the command was transmitted, it resulted in the bands that secured the prisoners' limbs debonding. Both Whispr and Ingrid promptly collapsed to the floor; two piles of skewed limbs and cramped muscles.

"He lives as long as you cooperate." As he addressed Ingrid, the fat man's voice was perfectly flat and devoid of emotion. He might as well have been warning a child that she could keep her teddy bear so long as she minded her manners at the dinner table.

His companion was gazing unblinkingly at the elderly but ramrod straight hunter-killer. "Is there a problem remaining, Mr. Molé?"

"No," the oldster replied curtly. "No, there's no problem. I will deal with my disappointment." Collecting himself, he mustered a smile. "I am, as you say, a consummate professional. The additional funds you have promised will allow me, among other things, to indulge in the diversion you have blocked here."

"You are comfortable with this?" the woman persisted.

Molé adopted his most avuncular mien. Still smiling, he walked over to where Whispr was now sitting up with his back against the wall trying to rub some feeling back into his legs. At Molé's approach his fingers ceased their ministrations.

Inclining slightly, even elegantly, forward at the waist, the assassin proffered an accommodating hand.

"I have only been doing my job. In a sense, you have bettered me. In my entire experience this has never happened before. Yet still I extend my hand."

Whispr's reply was cold and even. "You tried to kill me. Me and Ingrid. Several times. I watched you kill other people."

Molé's acknowledging nod was barely perceptible, as was the mockery in his voice. "How fortunate you have never had to kill other people." His eyes fastened on Whispr's. "Have you, riffler?"

Whispr stole a quick glance at Ingrid. Then he reached up and took the assassin's hand. Aware that the oversize eyes of both obese executives were on his back, Molé pulled firmly until his former quarry stood standing before him, swaying slightly. He eyed the stick-man appraisingly as the latter cradled his slightly bruised fingers.

"I have always felt height overrated. In my profession, anyway, the last thing one wishes to do is stand out." Turning, he walked over to Ingrid and once again extended a helping hand. Having watched him assist Whispr to his feet without incident, she accepted the reaching fingers.

Yanking on her arm forcefully and with artfully concealed power, he pulled her hard up against him and jammed his aged lips against hers. Those fleshy flaps, at least, remained unmelded.

They tasted of a moral and physical decrepitude no biosurge work could purge. His sallow breath rose from lungs that, no matter how skillfully and repeatedly had been maniped, were still reflective of his age. Before she could pull away he gently but firmly bit her.

She yelped and wrenched free of the noisome embrace. Or rather, he let her go. Had he so desired, he could have held her against him no matter how many kicks or punches she tried to deliver. Ever mindful of the heavy-lensed executive eyes monitoring his every move, he had released her. Stepping away, she put the back of her left hand against her mouth. It came away stained crimson. He smiled one last time.

"All the blood I'm going to get today, it would seem. Goodbye, Dr. Seastrom. Whatever the untouchables decide to do to you, consider yourself fortunate."

With that he turned, strode wordlessly past the pair of hulking decision-makers, and disappeared through the doorway.

Behind him he left a slowly strengthening Whispr and Ingrid facing their podgy, soft-voiced saviors. If savior was indeed the right word. At least whatever happened now they were free of and safe from the perverse and deadly attentions of Napun Molé. Even if they ended up dead it would count as a victory of sorts.

She tried to read the man and his female colleague and failed. Their expressions never varied and it was impossible to tell what their heavily maniped eyes concealed. Judging from their words, not empathy. They had preserved her and Whispr from the attentions of Molé out of a self-interest that had something to do with her being a doctor.

"Please come with us," the woman requested. No explanation, no elaboration. Under the circumstances Ingrid decided that a thank-you for saving them from Molé would have been superfluous. Not that it would necessarily pass unrecognized. She just suspected it would be ignored.

They were not bound prior to exiting the interrogation room. There was no need. They could not possibly escape the complex without being recaptured. Ingrid almost smiled to herself. It had proven easier to break in than it would be to break out. So confident were the overweight escorts of their prisoners' security that they led the way down passages and hallways without once looking back to see if Ingrid and Whispr were still following.

Maintaining an unexpectedly fast pace for such a hefty couple, they forced their prisoners to break into the occasional jog to keep up. Along the way they passed dozens of other employees, Meld and Natural alike. A few glanced in the direction of the two oversized striders and their trailing captives, but no one said anything.

"What do you think they want with us?" Whispr spoke as they all but ran down one corridor after another, making remarkable time through the complex.

"I don't know, I don't know. Whatever it is, it can't be worse than what Molé had in mind for us."

Her companion had reverted to his usual optimistic self. "Sure, you say that *now*, but when we get to wherever it is that we're going . . ."

"Have you noticed, Whispr? I think we've been heading north."

"You think maybe they're taking us to Research?" He considered. "That could be a good thing or a bad thing. Good if they're going to explain what their research here is all about." His voice fell. "Bad if they're intent on making us part of it." He hesitated, swallowed. "I really appreciate what you did for me back there, doc. Ingrid."

She meet his gaze evenly. "Earlier you did the same thing for me, Whispr. Archie."

"No." He shook his head firmly. "I screamed on your behalf out of desperation. You had a choice. You put yourself on the line for me."

She shrugged, suddenly embarrassed. "You're the only piece of useful equipment I paid for that I've got left."

"*Huh*," he grunted. "You'd better check again. I think the warranty's expired."

The entrance to Research before which they finally slowed and stopped was different from the one they had tried to bluff their way through previously. But there was a similar desk set off to one side, and the chair behind it was occupied by a guard clad in a uniform identical to the one worn by the all-too-alert young employee who had called them out. What happened next was instructive.

The guard looked up, then immediately and without comment returned his attention to whatever he had been perusing on his box monitor. He did not ask questions of Ingrid and Whispr's escorts nor did he seek any form of identification. Recalling previously observed security procedures Ingrid expected one of the massive interrogators to run a retina check, or flash a glowp tag. Their escorts did nothing. Despite this, the massive doorway swung silently inward to admit them. Without being bidden, the two mystified Namericans followed.

Two more security barriers had to be passed. Following the third they found themselves in a series of brightly lit corridors and rooms whose functions Ingrid could not divine despite passing rank after rank of glistening equipment. Men and women, Naturals and Melds, and most notably several more of the exceedingly large people labored intently and often silently at tasks whose purpose remained a mystery to her.

As far as Whispr was concerned he might just as well have stepped through the looking glass into Wonderland. Not a bit of the suddenly bewildering surroundings registered on his experience. The most apropos adjective he could think of to describe what he was seeing was "expensive."

Directed into a small room they were instructed to sit. The

walls, ceiling, and floor were a pure, flawless white, as was the single simple table and several chairs that constituted the only furniture. Their new surroundings made the recently vacated interrogation chamber seem dirty. Ingrid felt as if they had been injected into a square eggshell.

Their escorts did not sit. Waddling to the far side of the room the female began dragging sausagelike fingers over the slick plasticky surface of one wall with all the adroitness of a concert pianist essaying a sonata by Schubert. Wherever her blunt fingertips lightly made contact with the wall, strange glowing shapes appeared in their wake. Swathes of pastel color took on depth and shadow as the nebulous rainbows she conjured became solid. Ingrid thought of languid Greek letters entwining in linguistically incestuous relationships. As to whether the writhing, morphing shapes represented language, advanced mathematics, or something else, she could not have said.

"Real pretty." Whispr's comment reflected his characteristic preference for brevity. "If it's show and tell time I'm afraid our hosts are out of luck: I left all my toys at home." Not for the first time Ingrid could only sit back and admire his bluster. Raising his voice, he unflinchingly addressed their captors.

"Mind telling us what this is all about?"

By way of reply the male escort came near. Huge dark eyes peered into Whispr's own. An emboldened Whispr held the stare unblinkingly.

At least, he did until the fat man began to unzip his face.

15

While Whispr uttered a little gargling sound and drew back, Ingrid simply sat and stared. As the man's skin split down the middle she could see that his female companion was likewise shedding her epidermis. The halves of two humans formed wrinkled piles at their owners' ankles.

What stood revealed in their wake was not a pair of butterflies.

"Oh shit," Whispr mumbled. He repeated it over and over. As a defensive mantra it was singularly unhelpful.

The exposé was the more shocking for the fact that it was unpreceded by any hints. Neither their captors' ventral or dorsal sides had revealed the slightest indication of a seal or seam. Now their skin and clothing lay mounded up around their feet. Or where their feet would have been if they'd had any.

Where the fat woman had been standing, a complex of meter-long golden spires unfolded. Each terminated in points save for several that devolved into smaller prehensile spires that replaced sloughed-off hands and fingers. From the center of the architecturally admirable being a pair of glistening lenses protruded on stalks to contemplate the two stunned Namericans. Light shimmered on this confusion of limbs that appeared to be fashioned of pure buttery gold. Could this motile clash of golden spears still be considered a "her"? Ingrid wondered.

Stepping clear of his mound of shed epidermis and now unnecessary clothing, "her" companion had also straightened up. At least he was composed of flesh and bone, Ingrid concluded as she studied the creature. This notwithstanding the fact that the head seated on the flexible neck consisted of a single spherical multilensed yellow eye, or that both arms terminated in single-lensed eyes of a more familiar sort, or that lenses different from the other two shone from the vicinity of his bare hips. Covered in centimeter-long brown fur, the torso was centered on a sturdy square base from whose underside jutted four legs. A gripping tentacle protruded from each knee.

The female had stepped out of a sketch by Wright while her associate would not have been out of place in a Lovecraftian po-pent. As a still stunned and speechless Ingrid and Whispr looked on, the mélange of golden spires ambled stiffly over to the table where they sat. Though no mouth was visible, a voice emerged from the clashing, organo-metallic depths. Not only were the words it uttered comprehensible, the vowels emerged in a surge of syntastic liquidity that was positively soothing.

"You are confused. That is to be expected."

"Are we also expected to be frightened?" Whispr had pushed his chair as far away from the table and the being in front of him as the wall behind him would permit. "Because that's really what I am."

Oblivious to any intended irony, the spire being focused her singular gaze on the slender Meld. "That is to be regretted even as it is understandable."

Ingrid swallowed hard. "What—are you? You're not, you can't be Melds."

"But we are." Though it was impossible to tell where the great compound orb that topped the male's body was looking, his multitude of lesser eyes were inclined in her direction. "Though not as you are thinking of us. In the End there are only Melds."

"I'm not a Meld," she countered reflexively. "I've had a couple of recent manips, but they're only cosmetic and easily reversed."

"Baby steps," observed the female. "For purposes of further dialogue you should know that my name is Sarah."

Sarah. Ingrid found that she had been invaded by a frightening calm. Sarah the perambulating, intelligent sculpture.

"And you may call me Johan." The voice of the spire's companion emerged from somewhere within the thick fur that covered its body.

Ingrid fought to hold on to her sanity. "You said that you're not Melds as we are thinking of you. What does that mean? What did you mean when you said that 'in the end there are only Melds'?"

Through a subtle physical shuffling that might have been used to indicate emotion, Sarah realigned her gleaming golden integuments. "We are Melds, doctor, but we proceed from a different starting point. When I say that we are not Melds as you think of us, that is because we are not human."

Tilting his head back Whispr rolled his eyes at the ceiling. "Sure you're not." Lowering his gaze once again he looked over at Ingrid. "I don't know what's going on here, doc. Maybe this is some elaborate variation on the usual interrogation-of-intruders scenario." He gestured at the two utterly incomprehensible figures standing before them. "But I do know that these are just melds. Or automatons. Probably designed to jar us out of our mental comfort zones so that we'll be scared enough to do whatever they want."

Ingrid was less willing to dismiss the claim out of hand. As a doctor she could not envision how any human body could be pushed, shoved, and crinkled into the quadrupedal eyeful that was

Johan, far less into the structural impossibility that was Sarah. Still, where the eyes could be fooled the mind would follow.

"You're saying that you are—aliens."

"Indeed." Johan spoke in the same flat tone he had employed when he had been encased in the camouflaging fat suit.

Ingrid noted with interest that his crowning compound eye was capable of full rotation, like a hematite sphere suspended in a magnetic field. What must it be like, she wondered, to be able to see in every direction simultaneously? What unimaginably elaborate neuroptic connections were required to process so much visual information? For that matter, where in that furry mass was the controlling brain located?

Sarah was clashing toward the door. "Come with us."

As they followed the two no-longer-disguised shapes, Ingrid found herself trying to make eye contact with several of the other overweight—or perhaps simply oversized—figures they passed in the wide corridor. None glanced in her direction, though several did speak to and exchange gestures with the outré shapes who were leading the way. Did all of the obese shapes contain within them spires or seers? Or were there other forms, other shapes even more extreme than those represented by Sarah and Johan? Were their radically different escorts the purveyors of outrageous lies, nothing more than extreme Melds as a scornful Whispr insisted? Or . . . ?

Aliens? Truly, she thought, what was more alien to human experience than the existence of metastable metallic hydrogen? Except possibly quantum entangled nanoscale cerebral implants. Her head was pounding.

Was Nerens the headquarters for some kind of invasion? Assuming, she told herself as calmly as she could, that more than one kind was possible.

When they reached an oval opening at the end of the corridor, Johan stepped to one side and gestured with an eye-arm.

"Please. . . ."

It took Ingrid a moment to discern the outlines of the vehicle she was being asked—politely, she noted—to enter. Transparent as a soap bubble and to all outward appearances no thicker, it had a single curving bench but no visible instruments, machinery, or means of propulsion. Whispr held back.

"We go in there," he murmured, "and maybe we don't come out again."

She met his concerned gaze. "Like we have a choice. What alternative do you propose, Whispr?" She gestured back the way they had come, down the length of what was only one corridor among many. "That we make a break for it?" Turning away from him she nodded understandingly at the thing that called itself Johan, stepped into the bubble, and nearly lost her balance. Unexpectedly, the floor gave slightly under her weight, like a transparent spring. Devoid of options, as his companion had coolly pointed out, a wary Whispr followed.

Their escorts joined them. Ingrid had to concentrate in order to be able to see the walls of the oval opening close. There was no door. The surrounding material rippled like a pond that had been struck with a stone as it sealed tightly behind them.

A moment later the bubble began to move. It did not accelerate sharply, but once in motion neither did it ever seem to slow down. Other than the occasional appearance of an overhead light, the tunnel down which they were speeding was pitch-black. Within the bubble it was not completely dark, however. Portions of Sarah's golden limbs emitted a pale purple efflorescence of their own.

So absorbed was Ingrid in her own thoughts that she did not notice when they hit the midpoint of their journey. There must have been a midpoint because that was when the remarkable vehicle began to slow. She estimated that they had spent the same amount of time decelerating as they had in speeding up. When it finally stopped moving, the bubble came to a halt opposite a portal exactly like the one through which they had entered.

"How far do you think we've come?" she asked her companion as she exited the transportation device. "Or did we just go in a big circle?"

Whispr's expression was grim. Plainly he was preparing himself for the worst. "Can't say. Tunnel was too dark, no landmarks, impossible to estimate direction or speed. More than a kilometer, less than a hundred, maybe. I think there near the end we were traveling on a downward grade. But I'm just guessing." His smile was crooked. "I expect it's all guessing from here on out."

In the course of the short walk that followed, Ingrid noted other Melds who were recognizably human, but only one or two possible Naturals. Their familiar shapes helped to mitigate the shock of encountering one being after another who made Johan and Sarah look positively normal.

There was the giant who was forced to walk hunched over. Nearly all white, he (for unsupportable reasons she thought of it as a he) managed the feat only because a dozen or more short legs ran the length of his upper torso from where the hips began to where the long, backward dragging arms protruded. The head—she turned away from moonlike eyes and piercing azure pupils that floated freely from one side of the iris to the other.

The giant was the largest of the creatures they passed, but far from the most exotic. A pair of perambulating, big-eyed seashells came toward them. They flanked a very ordinary-looking Natural woman. Workpad in hand, brown hair tied behind her in a bun, she reminded Ingrid of hospital staff she often encountered while having lunch in one of her home tower's restaurants. Striving to catch her attention, Ingrid gazed fixedly in the other woman's direction. When the Natural walked right on past without acknowledging the stare, Ingrid considered calling out. Ultimately she decided to hold her peace. She and Whispr were still prisoners, still considered intruders and trespassers. Untimely vocal outbursts might not be the best way to ingratiate themselves with their escorts.

There was an individual who looked like an emaciated horse crossed with an industrial robot, several walking crystals with rotating faces, and a whole platoon of creatures that might have been meter-tall upright millipedes save for their bright rainbow colors and the dozens of tiny gloves they wore on their multitude of hands. If these were merely Melds, as Whispr stubbornly continued to insist, then they represented manipulations of the human body far beyond anything she had ever heard of, read of, or dreamed of. So extreme was the eclectic panoply of shapes and sizes that they passed in the passageway that they looked to be the product of magic and not science, as if they had been maniped at the hands of a djinn instead of those of a biosurge.

She was looking back at still another biological impossibility when they turned a corner. As her attention shifted forward once again she found herself smacked by a sudden dollop of vertigo. Whispr had to grab and steady her to keep her from falling. For once she welcomed the contact.

Someone had punched a hole in the world in front of them and filled it with sublime.

IN AN IMMENSITY OF darkness floated a black ovoid bleeding chrome. Only its vitreous sheen, reminiscent of polished onyx, enabled her to distinguish it from the surrounding blackness. That, and the ripples of sinuous silver that occasionally materialized from deep within the gigantic object to flow from right to left before being reabsorbed into the specular body from which they had initially emerged. No railing, no barrier separated her and her companions from stepping into gaping infinity.

As she recovered her equilibrium and her brain struggled to make sense of what she was seeing, she picked out in the downward distance some sort of ramp or avenue. Suspended in the dark, it pierced the side of the ovoid like a hypodermic, drawing out not cells but tiny figures. Her pounding heart seemed to have risen into the vicinity of her throat. She grew aware that Sarah was speaking.

"Very few humans, Naturals or Melds, have seen the ship. But you needed to be convinced. We want you to be convinced because we require the assistance of human doctors. Naturals such as yourself are especially valued."

She hardly heard the escort. Staggered by the sight before her, still fighting to maintain her balance, she realized now that the industrial fabrication site she and Whispr had discovered after crawling through one of Nerens's climate control ducts was not Morgan Ouspel's Big Picture. *This* was the Big Picture. "It's real, and it moves," Ouspel had told them. And the Painters of the Big Picture, those who made it move, were . . .

Alien. Not of this world.

And Het Kruger had called *her* an intruder.

Having seen far more of the extreme than his companion, Whispr was better equipped to maintain his mental stability. Concentrating on the prosaic helped.

"How can you get something this big on and off the surface of the planet without being detected coming or going?" He nodded into the abyss. Sounds muted by distance drifted up to them. "You're gonna tell me you've got some kind of cloaking device or something, right?"

"No," Johan corrected him. "The ship does not move from space into this place. Instead, we shift the very small bit of space that contains the ship. Your simple detection devices do not detect the movement of space. You do not yet possess the math necessary to comprehend the relevant field equations."

"That's all right," Whispr murmured. "I don't feel deprived. So it *is* an invasion."

"Not in the sense you are thinking of it," Sarah told him. "An agricultural metaphor would be more apt. We are turning the soil and watering the first seedlings."

The slender Meld's tone darkened. Regarding himself as dead already he saw no point in holding back. If nothing else he could at least express his outrage and thereby gain some final, if not lasting, satisfaction.

"What the hell are you monsters 'watering'?"

Ingrid flinched. Calling their escorts "monsters" was unlikely to help their situation. Johan appeared to take no umbrage, however.

"We are watering those shoots that are having difficulty thriving among your kind. Logic. Reason. Common sense. The realization that the cosmos is vast and sentience rare." Weaving slowly back and forth atop its neck, the great compound eye tilted in the humans' direction. "We do not seek conquest. That is an ancient and self-defeating attitude. We wish only to establish a permanent friendship. New friends are forever welcome."

Whispr was not appeased. "Funny kind of handshake you have."

"Your kind is not ready to receive it in full. Your world is seething with frustration, confusion, uncertainty. You need help. If it was offered openly, you would refuse it. As a species you are close to suicidal. This pains us to an extent you cannot imagine. We cannot stand by and watch you consume yourselves. To do so would be morally indefensible."

The jumble of golden spikes that was Sarah tiptoed closer. Ingrid held her ground. Though still distrustful she discovered that, unexpectedly, she was no longer afraid. While the aliens' intent was still unknown, their tone and manner was anything but threatening. Some of Sarah's earlier words came back to her.

"You said you require the assistance of human doctors. What for?"

Once more the male voice emerged from beneath the eye. "To install the implants, of course."

"Aha!" Whispr's shout was accusing. "If that doesn't signal a hostile invasion I don't know what does!" He whirled on Ingrid. "They're taking control of our youth. You told me yourself that the implants have only been found in teens."

"We are taking control of no one," Sarah explained. "Of what use is a friend devoid of free will?"

Ingrid was torn between Whispr's indignation and the alien's protest. "If not control, then what is the purpose of the implants?"

An analog of a sigh issued from the center of the intertwined gold spires. "Human couriers transport them around the world to those physicians who have engaged with us."

"Traitors to the species," Whispr growled. "The old man Cricket and I riffled in Savannah: he was a courier. Or a co-opted doctor. Or both."

Ingrid was nodding vigorously. "Remember Morgan Ouspel's reaction when we showed him the thread? He called it a 'distributor.'" She looked back at the alien Sarah. "It was full of your implants."

"That is how they are transported," Sarah admitted. "On the thread they exist as a stabilized dichotomy: field circuitry imprint in one part, foiled metal in the other. It is only when they are combined that a functional implant results."

Ingrid recalled her and Whispr's several attempts to divine what was on the thread by probing it with various readers. No wonder all had proven futile.

"When the particular distributor of which you speak disappeared on your continent, steps were taken to ensure that it did not come to the attention of one of your tribal governments or your wide-ranging media. We were only peripherally involved in these prophylactic steps. That is one reason why initial attempts to recover it on a local basis were clumsy and awkward. Such recovery procedures are the responsibility of our human associates, a portion of whom operate within the organization you commonly call SICK, Inc."

"More traitors." Whispr could barely restrain himself. "Their 'clumsiness' got an old mudbud of mine deaded."

"You haven't told us what the implants do," Ingrid reminded their escorts.

Sarah continued. "The implants are tiny—you would say transmitters."

Ingrid remembered the signal-boosting experiment they had performed on the thread in the shop of the tech Meld Nokhot, in underground Orangemund. "What do they transmit?"

"Endocrinal suggestions," Johan told her. "Neurological correctives. Very slight adjustments to the dispersion of endorphins and other substances. Your kind still exists in a state of evolutionary stasis that prizes self-preservation over cooperation. This hinders both the survival and maturation of your species. Confined as it is now to a single habitable system, the cosmos could wipe out your entire population in a single stroke. An exceptional series of solar flares, comet strikes, a high-energy particle storm from a nearby supernova—this has happened before, to others. To survive potential catastrophe on a cosmic instead of a local scale you will need the help of—everyone else."

"But you are not socially or culturally prepared for such intervention," Sarah informed them. "That comes only when the individual members of a species recognize that the survival and well-being of all supersedes and takes precedence over the survival instincts of the one."

Whispr turned bitter. "Some of whom you don't mind killing if they threaten to interfere with your galactic good Samaritans."

"That cannot be denied," she replied calmly. "We regret the need to employ such means. But your people cannot be made aware of our presence until such time as they have matured sufficiently to accept it for what it is: an intervention for the benefit of the entire species." The odd twang in her voice hardened slightly. "The methods employed to preserve the secrecy required for the continued proper functioning of this facility are your own. We did not import them."

"What do these 'correctives' and 'suggestions' you're talking about actually do?" Ingrid continued to be fascinated both by the alien speakers and their explanations.

Subsidiary orbs as well as the big compound eye turned to her. "In summary and taken together they serve to mute the destructive priorities that favor individual self-preservation over that of the species as a whole. The neurological signals are most effective when applied to the mature but not yet fully fossilized cortical structure of humans of a certain age. Given the very limited number of your colleagues who have agreed to cooperate in achieving these ends and who have been trained in the implantation procedure, it was decided to concentrate on those of your young who have suffered poor or inaccurate meldings.

"Eventually the changes necessary to ensure humankind's survival will have been inculcated in enough of your youth so that inducing neurological adjustments by means of the implants will no longer be necessary. It will take some time. But time we have, and we have learned to be patient. We cannot suddenly fix all that is wrong with your present social order. For an indeterminate amount of time, more of you will perish at your own hands than should be necessary. But we can, slowly, fine-tune your future for the betterment of your kind. And one day, when you face a global catastrophe, or when the time is simply right, we will reveal ourselves." All his eyes looked at Whispr. "Then will occur a collective mental handshake that will encompass every sentient being on this world."

Ingrid remembered the potentially deadly intertribal clash that had been broken up in Cape Town by a band of singing, unarmed youths. She struggled to recall the words of the young lemur Meld who had tried to pickpocket her purse. What was it he had said when he had abruptly scurried off to help put a damper on the looming conflict?

"The old ways must go passing by. Tribal feuds must be stopped. Not only here but everywhere. Is for betterment of human species I go."

And when Ingrid had wondered aloud why he had chosen to risk his own welfare on behalf of people he did not even know . . . ?

"Not sure. Must try," he had replied. She understood now. It made sense now. Three bad melds he had undergone, the young Meld had told her and Whispr. Three times under the biosurge's instruments, and still he was not right. Which meant there had been three opportunities for a human doctor to install one of the clandestine "corrective" alien implants. Apparently it took only one such quantum entangled bit of intervention to turn a street thief into an effective mob suppressor.

Was it so bad, then, what the aliens were doing? she thought. Helping the human species to mature? To focus on cooperation in place of conflict? If Sarah and Johan were to be believed, every young person who had been implanted still retained full control of their faculties, still functioned with free will. That wasn't mind control. The fact that the youthful lemur Meld was still practicing riffling when they had encountered him was proof enough of that.

But when the greater good was at stake, when two mobs threatened to engage one another in an orgy of typically human essentially senseless violence, alien "suggestions" kicked in via the transplants to mitigate the aggression.

Realization hit home like a kick in the head. She and Whispr had been rescued from the twisted attentions of Napun Molé, had been brought to this place and shown irrefutable evidence of the alien's existence and presence, for one reason and one reason only. To help safely install the increasing number of implants in meld-damaged young humans the aliens needed human doctors.

They needed *her.*

"I—I understand what you want from me now." She turned away from the black void and the gargantuan craft behind her. "You've explained yourselves clearly and you make a good case. But I—I just don't know. . . ."

"It is a great deal to grasp and comprehend at one time." For the first time, Sarah was openly sympathetic. "When one knows only the insularity that comes from living on a single world and is ignorant of all else, the scale of things on a cosmic basis can be overwhelming."

"Don't do it, doc—Ingrid!" Whispr was slower on the uptake than his more educated companion—but not dead slow. "This could all be nothing but a quick-ass cover story for a real invasion! We don't have any real proof of anything they're saying." He lowered his voice. "The fox is explaining how to fix the henhouse."

Turning to him in a daze, she mustered a response. "Whispr, *look* at all this. The implant technology, the MSMH metallurgy, this facility and this—ship. Even the little underground shuttle that brought us here. All of it examples of technology that are beyond our dreams. Don't you think if they just wanted to 'conquer' us they could do so easily? But what would be the point?"

"You do understand." Johan was plainly pleased. "Planets, astronomical bodies, natural resources—in the galaxy these are as common as dust. Habitable worlds are plentiful. Far more have been discovered than could ever be settled. What is rare, what is precious, what cannot be synthesized, is sentience. That is to be preserved, to be nurtured, to be helped to flourish like the rare flower it is." He paused, the huge multilensed central eye inclined in her direction. "Humankind is one of those rare flowers."

"Yeah, right!" Whispr protested. He was stalking back and forth now, waving his long scarecrow arms for emphasis. "Just like each of your kind is a 'rare flower,' huh? How many of you are there, anyway?" He nodded sharply at the attentive collection of spires, then at the assemblage of eyes. "How many 'helpful' species?"

"We do not know for certain," Sarah told him quietly. "Not anymore."

Her reply caused a suddenly bemused Whispr to halt. "What do you mean you don't 'know for certain'?"

"There was a time when we did," Johan explained. "After a while it was no longer considered important. Save for a few scattered historians the relevant parties ceased to care. We have all become as one."

"Ah." A self-satisfied Whispr looked at Ingrid as if to say "I told you so." "I knew it. There always has to be a boss." He smirked at the two aliens. "There always has to be someone on the top, someone in charge. Someone who's more interested in themselves than in some poofy pie-in-the-sky 'greater good.' Which race is it?" He stared intently at Sarah. "The spine collectives?" His attention shifted to the watching Johan. "Those who can keep an 'eye' on everybody and everything else? Or is it the mammal-bug giant we had to dodge in the corridor, or some species we haven't met yet?"

For a second time something like a sigh issued from the depths of the gleaming golden being that called itself Sarah. "We know the kind to whom you refer, Whispr. They do not dwell in secrecy. They are present everywhere here and in plain sight." The cathedral-like collage of motile gold spires faced him directly.

"They are you."

Ingrid gawked; first at the alien, then at her companion. For once Whispr had nothing to say. At that moment even his innate sarcasm had deserted him.

Sarah broke the stunned silence. "You are a Meld, Whispr. We call such willingly induced transformations by other names, but meld will serve as well as any. What is known as the General Transformation began many thousands of your years ago, when the technology of bodily and biological manipulation on several worlds reached the stage where it is at on your Earth now. You could call it shape freedom.

"As your kind is just beginning to discover, once the techniques of cell alteration and growth, of nonrejecting grafts and aesthetic biodesign and related skills are mastered, it becomes possible for anyone to look like anyone else. Or like anything they wish. Any shape that can be imagined will be. If it can be envisioned, sculpted, drawn, haloed, or described, someone will opt to look like it. The evolution of the immediate individual becomes a matter of personal choice limited only by the imagination of the person and the skill set of his, her, or its attending biosurges, gengineers, and other masters of the meat. Our equivalents of your cosmetic surgeons have mastered techniques of which yours have not yet even fantasized." She turned to Johan and let him continue.

"I myself," the anthology of eyes explained, "have undergone twelve full-body shifts—or melds, if you prefer. My initial self looked nothing like this, nor did several of my intervening physicalities. Twice I chose to look like the original S'than. By all historical accounts a most symmetrical people. But it is almost impossible to find one who looks like that now. They have been shifting and melding for millennia. So the S'than you see today is more likely an honorific meld of an entirely different species who has chosen to become like the S'than."

"You see how it goes," Sarah told them. "An individual may choose to look like an ancestor, another species, or something entirely fanciful that has no precedent in the evolutionary record. It is now simply a matter of moving mind and body, of shuffling organic and inorganic components. As a consequence, the civilized species of the galaxy are all mixed up. No one can say for certain where anyone else comes from. We are all one with the multitude. There is no longer such a thing as shapeism. One is judged on other qualities. As your kind will one day learn to do."

"But only a few of you know this," she finished. "So to prevent panic and forestall defection we move among the majority of you in reassuring disguise, the better not to sow confusion."

"The fat suits," Ingrid thought aloud.

"Yes. With the aid of internal mechanisms and adjustments they are large enough to conceal a multitude of different forms." A tapering spire gestured in her colleague's direction. "Even body types as different as Johan and I. Most who work with us and for us are unaware of our true multiplicity of shapes."

"So then." Multi- and single-lensed, all Johan's eyes focused simultaneously on Ingrid. "You know everything. You know more than most of your kind. Your pursuit of answers in spite of being marked for elimination, in spite of everything, recommends you. Your determination to reach this place of isolation recommends you. Most notably, your lack of panic and your desired skills recommend you."

As an overwhelmed Ingrid vacillated, Sarah added something that hit the beleaguered doctor especially hard.

"If it is knowledge that you seek, if that truly is what brought you to this place and to this moment in time, we can open the universe to you."

Wasn't that what she had wanted all along? Ingrid thought wildly. Answers, scientific explanations, understanding? First they had tried to have her killed and now . . . No, that wasn't quite right, she told herself. Operating semi-independently, it was the aliens' human interface that had sought her termination. Because as far as the aliens were concerned, individuals didn't matter. Not when the maturation and survival of an entire species was at stake. Her species. Didn't she owe it to the rest of her kind to help in accelerating their social and mental growth? Didn't she owe it to herself?

Whispr saw the transformation washing over his companion as clearly as he had seen the churning waters of the desert flash flood threaten to suck her down and drown her. These creatures, these inhuman *things*, were playing with her mind. Persuading, coaxing, cajoling her with lies and falsehoods, alternating threats with promises. And she was falling for it! He could see it as surely as he could see a citizen being scammed on the Savannah waterfront. Interposing himself between her and the aliens he pushed his face close to hers.

"*Ingrid!* Listen to me. It's Whispr. Remember? You brought me along to help you find your way through situations that were alien to you and to your life experience." He gestured at the silently watching creatures. "Well, I can't imagine a situation any more 'alien' than this! It's still an invasion, doc. They still want to take us over and control us—even if only with pretty words!"

"If we wished to take control of you, Whispr," the alien Sarah told him, "we would have done so already. Or allowed the human predator Molé to have you. Instead, we brought you here and fed you freely of the most precious of all nutrients—wisdom." Her mildly mechanical voice fell slightly. "That is the most we can do. We cannot tell you what to do with what we have given you. That is for you and you alone to decide." Light glimmered within eyes on stalks. "Free will."

"Free will? I'll show you free will. I'll show you what it means to be human and 'unimproved.'" Turning away from the honey-voiced spires he tried to will himself through Ingrid's eyes and deep into her being. "Doc, you can't do this. You can't let yourself taken in by these—creatures."

Gazing back at him she said simply, "Why not, Whispr? Why shouldn't I believe them? Why shouldn't I agree to help? For the good of all humankind."

"Because," he choked slightly, "because I—I love you."

"Whispr!" She had thought that nothing could shock her out of her reverie, and he had just proven her wrong.

"Don't do this, doc—Ingrid. Don't listen to them. They spin words the way spiders spin silk. They're 'watering' us, all right. They're watering you with what you want to hear so that you'll buy into their scheme and go to work for them. *Don't do it!*"

She swallowed. "It's too late, Whispr," she told him softly. "I've already 'bought' into it." Looking past him, she locked perception with Sarah. "Are you really female or did you just choose that name to make things comfortable for me and my friend?"

"I was once female," the jumble of mobile spires assured her. "In my present form gender has no meaning."

"I'm not sure I completely buy that." She looked back at her companion. "I'm truly, truly sorry that you love me, Whispr. For a man who's had to deal with so much tragedy in his life I feel bad about having to add to it. But while I've grown—fond of you, I don't love you. Not in the way you want. I do believe these 'people,' and I believe in what they're working toward, and I'm—staying."

He stepped back from her, his expression tortured. "You've been co-opted. I don't get entirely how, but I'm not blind. I don't have to have something thrown in my face to see what's happening."

"Whispr, listen. . . ." She moved to close the physical if not the emotional distance that had opened up between them.

"*No!*" He threw up his hands. What would they do to him now? They had swallowed the doctor. It was Ingrid whose cooperation, whose concession they wanted. He—he was nothing to them. His life was meaningless. As meaningless as that of any individual when measured against the "health" of the species. Hadn't they said as much? He looked around wildly.

"I'll get out of this, Ingrid! Somehow, some way, I'll get out of it. And I'll come back for you, and I'll get you help, I promise!" He was backing away from the three of them now, his hands held out defensively in front of him. "I'll get help!"

"Whispr-man." Sarah Spires was advancing toward him, her golden limbs gleaming and outstretched in his direction, as much machine as mortal. "You are wrong, so very wrong. Let us help you to . . ."

Whirling, his thoughts aflame and his soul burning, he took one step, pushed off, and leaped into the emptiness behind him. As he fell he made no noise and heard no sound save for the swift fading above him of Ingrid Seastrom's scream.

. . .

He MUST HAVE BLACKED OUT, he told himself as he rolled over. He remembered jumping into the void. At the same time as the memory returned he grew aware that he was not dead, not falling, and not in pain. Given his recollections, this conflation of realities made no more sense than did the solid, gritty surface on which he was lying. As he opened his eyes a slight breeze teased his corneas. The air smelled dry and faintly of mint. His view was split horizontally between beige, yellow, and a deep blue.

He was back in the desert.

Bewildered but glad to be alive, he rose slowly to his feet. In place of the medical assistant's attire he had been wearing he found himself back in his desert garb. His backpack lay nearby. A quick check revealed that with the exception of his communicator its contents were intact. Even to, and most important of all, his survival waterpak. How had it come to be here? How had *he* come to be here? Standing, he drew renewal from contact with the clean, natural earth.

He turned a slow circle. There was no indication that he was floating in some alien hallucination or disguised void. Soaring on dark wings, a black and white Namib crow came cawing overhead. He tilted his head back to track its path. No angel ever looked better, no cherubim ever warbled a more welcome aria. Of Nerens there was no sign. He was back in the desert, yes, but it could be anywhere in the desert—and while no Sahara, the Namib was vast enough.

An accident of some sort, he told himself. Something had caught him before he had struck the ebony ship and kicked him out here, like a character in a vit game. He was alive and free. For an experienced riffler like himself that was enough. It was all he needed. He would survive now. He would make it back to civilization. There he would tell his story, somehow hire or inveigle or

persuade others of its veracity, and return here with a whole aveng-
ing army. Let the invaders try to lock him in an examination room
then! It would be he and his allies who would be doing the inter-
rogating.

His one regret, the only thing that gave him pause and kept him
from setting off southward immediately, was that he was leaving
Ingrid Seastrom behind. Brainwashed or otherwise duped, there
was nothing he could do for her now. Not by himself, without outside assistance. Bending, he picked up his pack and slung it across
his narrow back. The weight of it was further assurance that he was
not dreaming.

He didn't need the communicator, he told himself. He was
used to surviving on and with almost nothing. Direction he could
determine by monitoring the sun. Determined and with increasing
confidence, he started southward.

She was waiting for him on the other side of the next dune.

Behind her a flat gravel plain stretched for kilometers off to the
south. Unseen in the distance lay Orangemund and civilization.
Between them lay—a difference of perception.

She had been remelded. Gone was the red hair, the zaftig
shape, the camouflaging adjustments to her cheekbones and ears
and the rest of her face that had been necessary to disguise her from
Molé and the rest of SICK's hunters. She was once again the same
attractive but far more normal woman who had pulled police traktacs out of his back in her office in Savannah. She was, in other
words, more beautiful than ever. Even if her mind had been co-
opted by aliens.

"Ingrid!" He started to rush toward her, then caught himself.
This wasn't right. It couldn't be right. It wasn't a dream, but it was
everything that if given the chance he would have dreamed. "How
did you get here? How did I get here?"

She gave a slight shrug. "The visitors can move space with a starship inside it. Moving a person or two isn't difficult. They prefer not to use the technology here unless they have no choice. There's too much chance of the energies involved being detected and remarked upon. They make exceptions for ships."

"'Ships'?" He remembered the immense black shape. "There's more than one?"

"Many," she told him. "Over time they come and they go. The visitors are patient." She smiled kindly at him. "They moved you. They moved me."

"So you're coming with me, then? You convinced them to let you go?" He tried to restrain his excitement. It was good that he did.

"No," she explained gently. "I convinced them to let you go. I'm still staying. I wanted to say goodbye, Whispr." She smiled anew. "You didn't give me much of a chance. I owe you a great deal. If not for you I wouldn't have been exposed to—everything."

"By everything you mean the invasion and takeover of humanity?" he shot back.

She sighed. "You heard, but you didn't listen. There's no point in arguing and nothing more to be said. I wish you all the best, Whispr. You're a better man than you think you are."

"I'm still coming back for you, Ingrid."

"I won't be here. I'm going back to Savannah to resume my practice. I'll go back to doing what I do best, only now for a greater and more noble cause."

His expression twisted. "I've been around and seen a lot, Ingrid. But I don't think I've ever seen anyone so smart perverted so quickly."

"Converted, not perverted."

"Wait a minute." He stared back at the familiar feminine shape silhouetted against the perfect blue of the Namib sky. "You told me how I got out here, but not why. Why didn't they just let me fall to my death?"

"For the same reason they didn't leave you to Molé's mercies. As you were falling I told them if they didn't help you to live, then once again I would refuse to assist them. They plucked you out of nothingness and put you out here." She shook her head sorrowfully. "More than that I can't do for you, Whispr." She indicated his backpack. "You've got what's left of our supplies. Nerens security won't bother you. I think you can make it out of here. I hope you can." A dark mist began to coalesce around her. She eyed it unperturbed as it continued to thicken, like air made from ink.

"The visitors don't understand long goodbyes. My time is circumscribed."

"I'll make it out of here, all right!" he yelled as he started toward her. "And when I do, I'll tell everyone! About this place, about the invaders and their brainwashing, about everything! I'll come back for you with soldiers and writers and vit correspondents hanging out of a dozen floaters! I'll scatter this whole treacherous implant-invasion plan across both oceans!"

Wreathed in ebon haze, she shook her head sadly. "No you won't, Whispr. Because no one will believe you. To those you'll want to convince you'll be just another crazy-ass street riffler. Just like the one who hung around my office until I had no choice but to acknowledge him and his problems." Her frown turned to a smile. "Kind of a cute one, though. . . ."

The haze became a solid as he covered the last couple of meters between them. He reached out for it; to catch it and hold it and keep it close. Then it was gone. One moment he was running toward a pane of black glass and the next, a puff of vapor that dispersed through his clutching arms to vanish into the desiccated air like dust in a furnace.

He was alone again.

. . .

THE SAN HUNTING PARTY found him out of food and nearly out of water, his waterpak having failed four days earlier. Brought delirious into their temporary hunting encampment, he babbled incessantly. They ignored it all. The poor rail of a Meld was clearly out of his head.

Carried by stretcher and by hand, the half-conscious survivor was transferred from one group to another until he was eventually deposited, still weak but much improved in health, outside the entrance to the national park station at Rosh Pinah. Examining the contents of his backpack and the condition of his shoes led the rangers to believe he was an undocumented hiker who had lost his way in Fish River Canyon. He was quickly airlifted to the hospital at Karasburg. It was while recovering there that he found the rough diamonds that had been secreted in the depths of his backpack.

A gift of the San? he wondered. Or a kindly farewell of sorts from a certain empathetic physician in league with "visitors" for whom diamonds were perhaps nothing more than tainted carbon.

She really must have convinced them that he was harmless.

Converting the rocks to subsist was no problem in Gaborone, a traditional gem-dealing center. From there he fled first-class from the southern quadrant of the continent. But not home to Savannah. Other personages than the doctor might be waiting to see if he did indeed return there. Instead he made his way to India. There he regaled the media with tales of gigantic buried spaceships and the mental manipulation of teenagers supervised by traitorous human doctors who were in league with melded aliens.

His rambling discourses were met with the reception they deserved.

Propelled and supported by the subsist he had realized from his diamond sales he attempted to persuade the Chinese, then the

Japanese, of the truth of his story. One Japanese vit team did pay for a satellite scan of the restricted desert region he had singled out. Detecting nothing, its owners presented the vit team's masters with a bill for costs that they then attempted to pass along to the skinny charlatan who had enticed them with his rousing if outrageous story.

He had no better luck with the media in Oceana or Samerica. Exhausted physically, emotionally, and financially, he finally conceded the unlikelihood of convincing anyone other than the usual conspiracy nuts of the truth of his tale. Taking what remained of his gem money he bought a small house in a northern suburb of Manaus on the bank of the Rio Negro. Though even hotter and more humid than Savannah, the landscape and climate were familiar enough that he felt at home. Freed from the need to riffle to support himself, he settled into a life of subdued comfort; not rich but able to buy what he needed if not always what he wished.

Beyond his porch, pink dolphins cavorted. Maniped *botos* towed water-skiing tourists up and down the great tributary while magified harpy eagles guided unsteady parasailers over the protected canopy forest that still dominated the far shore. Generating turbines moored deep in the river pumped out power as well as accompanying sonorities that were reprogrammed every week lest the tourists grow bored with repetitive water music that was not by Handel.

As the years passed his slender frame shrank in upon itself until age and sun left him resembling a walking stick of beef jerky. Whenever the opportunity arose he would tell his tale to whoever would listen; tourists, children, fellow seniors, workmen—anyone who would tolerate the bizarre ramblings of an old Meld. The hundreds, the thousands of messages he sent to media worldwide were treated with universal disdain. Eventually he published the information himself, putting it on the Box for anyone to peruse. Only fools and swindlers responded; the former to expound their own absurd theories, the latter to try to wrest from the crazy old Meld whatever subsist they could scam.

The few who commented kindly were notably young and oddly sympathetic. From these he recoiled in increasing horror.

Surrounded by the beauty not only of the Brazilian Amazon but Brazilian women, he thought less and less of Dr. Ingrid Seastrom of Greater Savannah. More time fled, more years passed. Decrepitude, even for one who could afford rejuvenating manips, began to press down on him with its inevitable weight. Then one day he had a visitor.

Recalling the presence from previous encounters, he remembered Death as being taller.

Still stocky, still devoid of expression, but moving with a finesse that belied his age, Napun Molé stood on the porch facing the owner of the little house. Whispr's first thought was to slam the door in the assassin's face and make a break for the back room where he kept a small but still functional spray pistol. He had purchased the weapon a number of years ago because of his failing eyesight. It would fire only a few times, but upon discharge the oversized shells would immediately fragment to cover most if not all of a single room. He bought it because it did not have to be aimed.

But he knew he wasn't as fast as he used to be, and judging from his looks the even older Molé would be faster still. Whispr could not have outquicked the hired company killer back in the Little Karoo and doubtless he could not outquick him now. He resigned himself. It was not as if he had died young or lived an uninteresting life. Besides, he was tired of looking over his shoulder every time he left the house to go to the market or stroll the riverfront boardwalk. Tired of always searching faces for signs of mind control, or alien eyes, or hidden purposes.

So he shrugged and stepped back.

"Go on. Get it over with. I'm pretty much finished anyway." He straightened as much as his narrow aged back would allow. "All I ask is that you make it quick."

Molé shook his head. "Can't do that. She has too much she wants to say."

The taller Meld blinked. "'Say'? 'She'?" He came forward until he could lean out the door. Molé did not try to stop him. Instead, the assassin moved aside.

"Bad memories of our previous encounters linger like a wart that refuses to heal. I would very much like to kill you. Instead I was charged with the task of merely locating you again. It was not easy." Molé almost, but not quite, smiled. "You are very efficient at covering your tracks."

"You're not here to kill me?"

"Regrettably, no. Just to find you. I do what I am paid to do. Personal longing never enters into this work. Although just this once . . ." His voice trailed away and he sniffed. "A contract is a contract." Turning to his right, he gestured.

From behind a guava tree a second figure appeared. Whispr sucked in his breath as she mounted the stairs to his porch.

Dr. Ingrid Seastrom did not look as if she had aged at all. She looked, in fact, exactly as she had on the day he had hurried to her office in hopes of getting police traktacs removed from his back.

"You look . . ." Glancing over his shoulder he saw that Molé had turned away from them and was gazing out across the river. "Come inside."

He closed the door firmly behind them and locked it. She smiled and shook her head.

"There's no need for that, Whispr. Molé is as firmly welded to his assignment as an anchor to its ship. He won't bother us."

"So you work with him now?" Though he tried to suppress it he could not quite keep the old cynicism from frothing to the fore.

"No." She frowned. "I don't involve myself with that aspect of the Maturation. If it even exists anymore. My work strictly involves, um, installation."

"Mind control." He slumped down in a chair woven from plantation liana.

She sighed. "It's nothing like that, Whispr, but you should already know that. There's no point in rehashing old arguments."

The fingers of his right hand pressing against the angular side of his face, he stared up at her. "Why are you here—doc? To have a last laugh at my expense? Because you were right. Nobody believes me when I try to tell them about Nerens and what's going on there. I'm just a crazy old man. Living this long is something I never thought I'd do—especially after hooking up with you all those years ago. So why not leave me alone? Why not just let me die in peace?" He could not keep from staring at her. "You look amazing. Advanced alien maniping?" She pursed her lips and nodded. "Huh. Sold your soul for thirty pieces of silver melding."

She rolled her eyes. "I work out of Rome now. I had to leave Savannah years ago before people started noticing that I wasn't aging properly, the usual youth melds notwithstanding. I could keep fooling my patients, but not my professional colleagues. It's all right. I always wanted to live and work someplace like Rome." She moved closer and he unwillingly drank in her perfume. "I'm here to make you an offer."

"Look at me," he muttered dourly. "I'm all aquiver with excitement."

She smiled anew. "Same old Whispr. Listen to me, Archibald Kowalski: you're one of the few humans privileged to have seen the heart of the Maturation. You've seen ship, space, visitors. Friends."

She held up a hand when he started to protest. "You're suffering from advanced melditis and other diseases of aging. Alien biosurge technology can cure you. Make you youthful again. It's not immortality, but it'll do until that comes along. Some aliens die at forty. Others live for hundreds of years. There is only so much even they can do with cell manipulation and prosthetic melds. But if you come back to the Namib with me you'll live far longer than you will here, and in better health. I've persuaded the visitors. There are things you can do to help."

He stared hard at her out of failing eyes. "That's assuming I want to help."

She nodded her understanding. "You're still suspicious. Do you follow the news? Haven't you noticed that over the past years there are fewer riots around the world? Fewer serious confrontations? More cooperation. More hope? The changes are slow and incremental, but they're real, Whispr. The aliens are changing us, and for the better. Each year there are more young people who are a little less afraid of each other. Each year there are more who advance to positions of power, who accept appointments to jobs where they can make a difference. They don't know that they're doing so, of course. They have no notion that their chemical balance has been altered or that their perception of the world around them has shifted a tiny bit more away from the primitive." She stopped to let him digest what she had said.

"Isn't that an improvement? Isn't that something worth striving toward? Even if it needs a little bit of a kick-start from off-world?"

He sat in the chair and brooded. Outside, a flock of scarlet macaws made its screeching way upriver, trending in the general direction of Colombia. Which way was he trending? He had nothing to look forward to except further gradual creaky decline and eventual death. No friends, no family, and he was nearly out of subsist.

He couldn't even riffle anymore. People would laugh at his clumsy efforts if he tried.

On the other hand, if he went with Ingrid and cooperated with what she called the "Maturation," would he be betraying his own species? Or helping to advance it? There was only one way to find out. Reaching out, he extended a hand.

"What the hell, mind-muffin. I might even learn something."

Taking his hand, she helped his frail frame out of the chair and with the same melded strength embraced him tightly. Spindly arms tentatively wrapped themselves around her.

That in itself, he decided on the spot, was worth giving in.

ABOUT THE AUTHOR

ALAN DEAN FOSTER has written in a variety of genres, including hard science fiction, fantasy, horror, detective, Western, historical, and contemporary fiction. He is the author of the *New York Times* bestseller *Star Wars: The Approaching Storm* and the popular Pip & Flinx novels, as well as novelizations of several films including *Transformers*, *Star Wars*, the first three *Alien* films, and *Alien Nation*. His novel *Cyber Way* won the Southwest Book Award for Fiction in 1990, the first science fiction work ever to do so. Foster and his wife, JoAnn Oxley, live in Prescott, Arizona, in a house built of brick that was salvaged from an early-twentieth-century miners' brothel. He is currently at work on several new novels and media projects.

www.alandeanfoster.com